Never Moving On
A Friends to Lovers Romance

C. R. Lee

C. R. Lee Books

Copyright © 2022 by C. R. Lee Books

All rights reserved.

No portion of this book may be reproduced in any form or by any electronic or mechanical means including information storage and retrieval systems without written permission from the publisher or author, except in the case of brief quotations used in book-related articles or reviews or as permitted by U.S. copyright law.

This is a work of fiction. The characters, places and events portrayed in this book are either the products of the author's imagination or used in a fictitious manner. Any resemblance to actual events, locales or persons, living or dead, is purely coincidental.

Cover design by Donovan Valdes

Proofreading by Charity Chimni

Also by C. R. Lee

Never U Series
Love is a Scary S.O.B. (prequel)
Never Moving On
Never Backing Off
Never Letting Go

Contents

1. Twenty Going on Twelve 1
   Stella
2. And That's the Game Folks! 14
   Stella
3. Gotta Love that Lemon Fresh Scent 19
   Jacob
4. Uncomfortable Much? 24
   Stella
5. Because Murder is Wrong 29
   Jacob
6. Am I Still Evil if I Feel Guilty? 33
   Stella
7. Don't Fuck with My Beer 36
   Jacob
8. Boys Don't Want Brains 42
   Stella
9. Well, Whadda'ya Know? 47
   Jacob
10. The Flash Ain't Got Nothin' On Me 51
    Stella

11.	The Power of the Period	56
	Jacob	
12.	Who is This Girl, and Where Has She Been All My life?	59
	Stella	
13.	Commander Stardust and Her Rodent Steed	62
	Jacob	
14.	Getting a Little Help from My Friends	68
	Stella	
15.	Here Comes Mister Neanderthal	74
	Jacob	
16.	Oh, No, He Didn't!	81
	Stella	
17.	Sabotage!	84
	Jacob	
18.	That Took a Turn Toward the Unexpected	88
	Stella	
19.	Hindsight is an Evil Bitch	93
	Stella	
20.	Where's the Rewind Button On This Shit?	99
	Jacob	
21.	Give a Girl a Baseball Bat	108
	Stella	
22.	And Now I Can Breathe	115
	Jacob	
23.	Everything I've Ever Wanted	120
	Stella	
24.	Never Said I Promise	123
	Jacob	

25.	Just When You Think You Know Somebody… Stella	129
26.	Who's Afraid of the PDA? Jacob	134
27.	Haven't I Seen This Horror Flick? Stella	137
28.	Busted! Jacob	143
29.	How Does She Do It? Stella	146
30.	When Things Seem Too Good to be True… Stella	150
31.	And the World Turns Upside Down Jacob	153
32.	What Just Happened? Stella	156
33.	Now What? Jacob	162
34.	Put Some Vodka on That Stella	171
35.	What Goes in the Shed, Stays in the Shed Jacob	183
36.	Are We Having Fun Yet? Stella	188
37.	Surprise! Jacob	197
38.	Should've Seen That Coming Stella	201

39.	Ghosted Jacob	209
40.	Eat, Sleep, Class, Repeat Stella	216
41.	Places to Go. People to See. Jacob	225
42.	Always and Forever Stella	236

Four Months Later... 243
Jacob

43.	Sneak Peek of Never Backing Off There's No Place Like Home	249
44.	Sneak Peek of Never Letting Go Sorry, Not Sorry	255

Also By C. R. Lee 262

Wanna Hang? 263

Acknowledgments 264

About Author 265

One
Twenty Going on Twelve
Stella

"Twenty, really? You look like you're twelve," says the used-to-be hot guy who just approached me at this party. Ah, the five words every college-aged female wants to hear: You look like you're twelve.

Fabulous.

"So, you're a pedophile, then?" I reply because screw him.

That shit-eating smile drops like an anvil and his gray-blue eyes go wide. "What?"

"You said that I looked like I was twelve, yet you're here hitting on me. So that can only mean one of two things: you're either an asshole who never quite got over the *pulling her pigtails* method of courtship, or you're a pedophile. Now, I would hate to be rude and call someone I just met an asshole, hence my original question: Are you a pedophile?"

I raise the red solo cup to my lips and take a small sip of the warm beer I've been nursing all night, nonchalant as can be. While king moron stands there with his mouth hanging open as if he wants to say something but can't find the words.

"You can leave now," I say, as if shooing away a bothersome child.

He mutters, "Bitch," under his breath and storms off.

I sigh. What is it about me that attracts every loser within a twenty-mile radius? Do I give off some special pheromones that only affect assholes and idiots?

A laugh like a dying hyena sounds from behind me and I spin around to see my best friend, and royal pain in the ass, Jacob, doubled over in hysterics.

"So glad my life amuses you, Jake."

He rights himself and presses his lips together as if trying to physically hold back his laughter, and doing a shit job of it, I might add. He lets out a breath and runs a finger under his eye to dry invisible tears. "That was beautiful. Seriously. I wish I'd taken a video."

I fling my arms out in frustration. "Well, what the hell did he expect? Did he think that was a compliment? I mean, how stupid can someone be?"

"Come on." He throws an obscenely muscled arm over my shoulder and gives me a squeeze before heading for the back porch. My whole body lights up at the contact. God, I hate the way I respond to him. It's torture. Not only is he dating my friend, and roommate, Emma, but he treats me like I'm his sister. His very young sister. I, of course, want to rub my face in those beautiful pecks, but I refrain because I am nothing if not a bastion of self-control.

Jacob Gonzales is the epitome of Latin good looks with his chiseled features, golden-brown skin, and dark brown, almost black, hair. Oh, and did I mention he plays wide receiver for Nasser University? Yeah. I caught a glimpse of him in his boxer briefs once and it was enough to haunt me till the end of my days.

"And it's always twelve," I continue. "Always. Since I was fifteen. I keep getting older, but my face stays the same freaking age."

"You don't look twelve."

"Whatever."

"Seriously, that guy's an idiot." Somebody shouts Jacob's name, and he pauses to wave. Turning back to me, he says, "You don't look a day under fourteen."

"Bastard." I slip free of his arm and give him a half-hearted slap on the shoulder. And he's laughing again.

Ignoring him, I scan the yard, looking for my friend Emma. This is my first party at Tri Omega whatever this frat is called. It's not generally my scene. I mean,

I like a good party, but this is seriously bordering on absurd. The huge two-story plantation-looking house is packed to the hilt with people. The night air is crisp and just chilly enough for a light coat or hoodie, but inside it's a furnace. This is why I was standing alone in the unexpectedly tiny backyard instead of hanging out in the house with Emma and Jacob, who brought me. Well, that and the fact that I was getting tired of being the third wheel.

I throw my disgusting beer in an overflowing trash can and follow Jacob back into the house. Immediately, I'm struck by the stifling heat and Billie Eilish playing at a volume no human ear was meant to tolerate. We cross through the kitchen where partygoers are lined up—solo cups in hand—at the keg. I'm fairly certain it isn't going to last very long. Not that I'm planning on drinking more, anyway. As a general rule, I'm not a big fan of beer. I'm more of a mixed drink sort of gal, but that beer is yeasty swill by anyone's standards.

The common area, or what would be the living room in a regular house, is huge—like church cathedral massive—with vaulted ceilings and a mahogany staircase on the far end that curves up to the second floor. And lucky for us, that's where Emma and her troop have set up shop because if they were standing among the mass of bodies milling about, we might never have found them. Jacob's big body cuts a swath through the crowd, and I follow on his heels. Noticing us approach, Emma grins and waves with the eagerness of a rabid Bieber fan.

Quite simply put, Emma Chase is beautiful, almost angelic looking with her wavy blond hair that I swear glows in the sunlight. Add to that a heart-shaped face, pouty lips and truly magnificent breasts and you can understand why a girl like her stops traffic. And why the guy I've been in love with for the past ten years fell for her within the first five minutes of their meeting.

Not that I'm ugly or anything—at least I don't think I am—I'm just cute. Like pinch her cheek, "Isn't she adorable?" cute. I have done everything in my power to combat my cursed cuteness. I wear dark eyeliner to accentuate my amber-brown eyes, and fire engine red lipstick. To give my look a little edginess, I even bleached the tips of my brown hair white. And I'm sorry, but I do not have the body of a twelve-year-old. I may not have Emma's boobs, but I'm sporting a respectable

B-cup with a slim waist and a bubble butt that would have made Sir Mix-A-Lot proud. Yet, I am regularly mistaken for a middle schooler.

Jacob gives Emma a quick peck and goes a couple of steps up to talk to his football buddies, while Emma greets me with a dramatic sweep of her arms and a hug. "Hell-o, gorgeous."

I smile and hug her back, which is a little awkward considering she's wearing a fairly low-cut mini dress and seeing as I'm a step below, that puts me right in line with her only partially-covered boobs. I laugh. "I hope you're not greeting everyone like this, or some guys will think they got lucky."

She pulls back and looks down at her rapidly-escaping breasts. "Shut up." She snickers and attempts to tug the top of her hot pink crop top up a little, but it only immediately goes back to its original cleavage-bursting position. When you've got boobs like Emma's, gravity is not your friend. She continues, "Anyway, Short Stuff," I hate it when she calls me that. "I don't think a difference of five inches is going to put any of the guys here at boob level."

She has a point but... "First of all, Amazonian..." Her eyes squint evilly. She hates it when I call her that. "I am not short; I am compressed awesomeness."

She throws her head back and laughs—I'm thinking she must be a little tipsy because it wasn't that funny.

"And second," I continue, interrupting her chortling, "That's all I've got. Now, can we move somewhere that doesn't give me an unobstructed view of your rack?" In truth, I don't like her drunk and hanging out on the steps, but if I tell her that, she'll spend the entire night up here out of pure stubbornness. "Please."

She rolls her eyes and sighs dramatically. "Fine." Then her face alights into a smile, and she giggles. Yep, definitely tipsy. She doesn't turn around, simply glances over her shoulder and tugs on the back of Jacob's black tee. "We're going upstairs, babe."

Spinning around, he sweeps her into his arms and plants a kiss on her lips. I turn away. After three months, you'd think I'd be used to it. I've seen—and heard—them doing much worse. But nope. Every single touch and kiss is like a knife twisting in my chest. "I'm going to get a beer," he says. "You want one?"

Emma nods and Jacob turns those baby browns on me. To call Jacob's eyes brown, really doesn't do them justice—more like deep mahogany—with streaks of gold that flare from around his pupil like the points of a star. Every time I look into those eyes, I want to melt into the floorboards.

"Stella?" Jacob says and I realize he asked me a question while I've been staring at him like a love-struck idiot.

"Uh, pardon?" I stammer.

"You want a beer?" he asks me, lips pulled into that sexy smirk that does funny things to my lady parts.

Which is probably why I respond with, "Yeah. That'd be great," even though I've already sworn off that shitty beer for the night.

He slaps another kiss on Emma's lips and pushes through the crowd, heading to the kitchen.

Emma loops her arm through mine and, with her snootiest British accent, says, "Shall we mingle, Miss Leone?"

"Indeed, we shall, Miss Chase," I reply in my own mangled version of said accent.

Emma laughs. "Wow, that was so bad. I think you might actually be getting worse," she says as we head up the stairs.

"That's why you're Drama and I'm English—every writer needs her muse, after all, right?"

"At least I'll be somebody's muse." Emma's tone isn't lost on me. One thing I forgot to mention, on top of being a gorgeous football player, Jacob is also a talented artist, and it bugs the ever-living crap out of Emma that he hasn't offered to draw her—not once.

"Emma!" A skinny brunette I've never seen before pushes her way through the throng—arm in the air, beer sloshing from her cup and onto people's heads. A litany of "Heys" and "What the fucks" follow her, but she pays it no mind. She flings her arms around Emma like they're long-lost friends, and I hop to the side, narrowly avoiding a wave of crappy beer.

"Lizzy," Emma replies in a somewhat softer—though equally annoying—shriek. Emma introduces me to her friend who she met in her drama class, of course, and they start jabbering about an upcoming show and auditions, and I can't help but tune them out. I should get an Uber back to the apartment. That way, Emma and Jacob can have their night alone, and I can finish the smutty romance I started earlier today.

"Stella," someone hollers—à la *A Streetcar Named Desire*—and I cringe. It's fascinating how people who have obviously never actually seen the play not only know that line but find it funny enough to warrant a joke. To say it gets old would be an understatement. I turn in the voice's direction and find Trevor, the team's tackle, charging me, and all I can do is brace myself for impact. Two seconds later, I'm hoisted into the air and crushed in a bear hug that is obviously just an excuse for Trevor to press my body against his.

I push away from his chest with one hand and beat it with the other. "Put me down, you Neanderthal." The guy really is a Neanderthal—big and dumb and way too strong for his own good.

Beside me, Emma's pounding on his arm and yelling, but she's about as effective as a mosquito biting an elephant's ass.

"Put her down." Comes a voice from behind, and Trevor whirls us both around to see Jacob holding three solo cups and sporting quite the intimidating glare.

Trevor releases me then, but slowly, so my chest rubs against his the entire way down.

"Jerk," I say, giving him an extra smack for good measure. I hate it when he does that. Moron thinks he's found a clever way of feeling me up—like every single person in the room can't see exactly what he's doing. It's not only violating as hell, but it's humiliating because I can't do anything to stop him, and he knows it.

Emma sidles up next to me, looking a great deal more sober than she did a few minutes ago. "You okay?" she whispers. Boys are constantly pulling this kind of shit on Emma, so she gets how upsetting it is. I nod and she gives my arm a squeeze.

"Trev, man," Jacob says, his voice hard. He sets the cups down on the rail and steps up to Trevor like he means business. "I told you to cut that shit out. She doesn't like it."

"Sure, she does." Trevor tries to lay an arm on my shoulder, but I jerk away.

"No. I don't, and I've told you that a billion times, you delusional prick."

"You. Don't. Touch. Her. Got it?" Jacob says, each word punctuated by his finger jabbing the other guy's chest. It's impressive, and a little scary because Trevor's easily a head taller than Jacob and twice his size. Jacob's a fairly big guy—six-plus feet tall and powerfully built, but Trevor's a monster. He's like an impenetrable wall on the field which, I guess, makes him a good tackle, but also means that he's not so easily intimidated.

"Fuck off, Gonzales." Trevor shoves him by the shoulders.

Shit. This is not good. The last thing Jacob needs is to get suspended for fighting. "It's fine, Jacob. Seriously. Please stop." I try to push the guys apart, but it seems we're in another mosquito vs. elephant situation because they're not budging. Meanwhile, Emma is tugging at Jacob's arm, trying to pull him away.

"W-w-w-woah." Another guy who, by the size of him, I'm guessing is one of their teammates, pushes between the two men and nudges Trevor back a few steps. Gripping his buddy by the nape, he says, "It isn't worth getting benched. Right?"

Trevor hesitates for only a second—holding the other player's gaze. I can see it when Trevor decides to back off. He breaks eye contact with the other guy, his body deflating in a way that rings of defeat more than acquiescence. "Whatever, bro," Trevor says under his breath, but loudly enough for everyone to hear. Then he shoulders past Jacob, bumping him hard enough to make me wince, but Jacob shrugs it off.

"Thanks, man," Jacob says to the other guy, and they do some weirdly complex handshake before Jake settles his eyes back on me. "You alright?"

I wrap my arms around my middle and nod. "Thanks."

The new guy turns to me with a very wide, very white smile. "Stella, I presume?" He's really good-looking, in that all-American, blond hair, blue-eyed, cleft-chinned way that normally isn't my type. But his smile is nice—sincere—and I find myself smiling back.

"Yeah," is all I say. I can't think of anything else, so I just continue to look at him dumbly till he holds out his hand.

"Dean."

My tiny hand is practically swallowed up by his giant paw as we shake. "Thanks for that," I manage to say.

We stop shaking, but he doesn't release my hand, and it's starting to get weird. I glance over at the others who have already moved on. They're all laughing as Emma tells some story, her hands waving animatedly as she talks, but I know, can sense somehow, that Jacob's watching. That feeling is confirmed when I catch his gaze flicking our way. It makes me feel better, safer, knowing he's there. Knowing that he would never let anyone hurt me.

Finally, Dean releases my hand and says, "I'll talk to him. Okay? Make sure he doesn't bother you anymore."

"That would be great. Thank you."

An arm slips around my shoulders and a firm body presses against my side. I don't have to glance over my shoulder to know it's Jacob. Even though I've never actually been intimate with the man, I know the feel of him. Jacob's the most touchy-feely person I've ever known—always touching and hugging and even kissing me. Though the latter is a customary Cuban greeting, and, on my cheek, which is just cruel. I mean, who came up with that shit? I blame his mom for being so ridiculously sweet and loving. I'd hate her, but she's kind of awesome.

This isn't just a friendly hug, though. It's a blatant cock-block. I have half a mind to elbow Jacob in the gut—it wouldn't be the first time—but since he almost got in a fight for me, I settle on just rolling my eyes.

"Thanks again, Dean," Jacob says. Dean's smile fades and his brow pinches. He glances between me and Jacob and Emma, who is now watching us out of the corner of her eye. Yeah, she tries to play it off, but I know Emma gets jealous when Jacob touches me, which is pretty much all the time. It's so ridiculous because—hello—he's dating her, but whatever.

Dean tips his chin at Jacob, which I'm assuming is man code for "I recognize your territory." He gives me a perfunctory smile and a curt, "I'll see you around, Stella," before turning around and striding back the way he came.

Jacob drops his arm and I round on him, arms crossed and giving him my most threatening evil eye. "Why don't you take a piss all over me next time, Jake? I don't think you were quite clear enough."

"That guy's an asshole."

"Every guy's an asshole, according to you." Seriously. For someone who has no romantic interest in me, he sure makes it next to impossible to get a date.

He sips his beer. If I'm expecting an apology, I'm barking up the wrong tree. "They are. Come on." He drags me over to join the others.

The others are in the middle of a conversation, but hell if I know what anyone's saying. All I can think of is how badly that could have gone. Are my hands shaking? I glance down to confirm that, yes, they are shaking and so sweaty I'm shocked Dean could hold on. I rub my palms down the front of my jeans to dry them. Now, I really want to call an Uber.

I'm so wrapped up in my thoughts, I don't even notice Jacob's friend, Malcolm, approach until he speaks. "What's up, my beautiful peeps?" He pats Jacob on the back then zeros in on Emma and waggles his brows. "Emma?"

Emma just smirks and rolls her cornflower-blue eyes.

"Back off my girl, bro," Jacob says, giving his friend a light, backhanded slap to the sternum.

Malcolm laughs. It's an ongoing joke with these two, Malcolm overtly flirting with Emma and Jacob telling him to back off. I sometimes wonder if there might be the tiniest bit of truth behind Malcolm's advances—like he kind of has a thing for Emma but wouldn't actually act on it because he's Jacob's friend.

Emma tried to set Malcolm and me up once, but neither of us was really into it. Malcolm's beyond gorgeous. The problem is, he knows it. He has wavy brown hair, a body that would send any woman's loins into overdrive, full lips that soften his angular features and brown eyes so dark you can hardly make out the pupil. (Sometimes, when he turns those eyes on me, I swear he's looking into my soul).

So, yes, my girly parts were totally on board with the Malcolm-date plan, but my brain jumped ship the moment he opened his mouth. The man is completely full of himself and so smooth, my bullshit alarms were blaring at Defcon one. Not that it would have mattered if I was interested anyway, because considering that the girls he usually dates are tall bombshells with more boobs than brains, I'm thinking I'm probably not his type.

Malcolm finally seems to notice me, and his smile drops. "Why the long face, Stells?" he asks.

I shrug, but Jacob isn't going to let it slide that easily. He rakes a hand through his short hair, disheveling the wavy locks. "Trevor," he says, the gruff tone of his voice making it clear what he thinks of Trevor.

"Again?"

Jacob nods. "Maybe I should talk to Coach," Malcolm says, scratching at the stubble on his chin. "Trev can't keep going around pulling this crap." He looks at me, his expression unusually serious. "You're not the only one. It's like he's got a book, *How to Be a Dick to Women*," Malcolm says, his palm upraised and moving with the words as if reading off a theater marquee.

"No," I almost shout. I pause, take a breath, and continue in a calmer tone. "I don't want him getting benched because of me. I'm fine."

Jacob's eyebrows bunch in consternation. "It wouldn't be because of you; it would be because of him. He thinks he can do whatever he wants because he's a big guy and a football player."

"What he needs," Malcolm chimes in, "is for someone to knock some damn sense into him."

"For real," Jacob agrees.

Emma links her arm through mine. "While we appreciate you guys defending our honor," Jacob whirls a hand and makes a regal bow. Emma attempts a small curtsy, but in her current state of inebriation, it comes out looking more like a squat. "I think Stella's right. Let's just move on. The last thing she needs is people harassing her if he gets kicked off the team."

"That won't happen," Jacob says.

Emma sighs and plants a fist on her hips. "Really? You sure about that? Because it definitely does happen. You want names? I can give you examples."

"No. Nope. We're good," Jacob and Malcolm mutter.

Yeah, they know better than to get Emma started on a tangent. The girl's got a weirdly good memory. Even drunk, she'll be spouting off names, dates and events until their ears bleed.

"Well, then," she continues, "you're just going to need to trust us. Shit like this tends to blow up in a girl's face."

Emma's talking about herself, of course, but the guys don't know that.

Jacob looks back at me for confirmation.

I nod. "Dean said he'd take care of it. Let's give him a chance, okay?"

"Fine," he says finally, "but if this shit keeps happening, I'm going to say something. I won't use your name," he says quickly, throwing his hands up to stop the argument he knows was coming. "But I'm not going to stand by and let him hurt you."

Malcolm presses his lips together and nods in agreement.

I smile. Damn, I have great friends.

"Now," Emma begins, breaking the tension. "We are here to have fun and fun we shall have. Where's my beer?"

Jacob hands us each our cups and smiles, though it doesn't reach his eyes. "Bottom's up," he toasts, then chugs.

The three of us return his toast and each take a long swallow.

Mmm... warm beer. This night just keeps getting better and better.

It's nearly four in the morning when the three of us stumble into the apartment I share with Emma and her sister, Kat. The place is empty, of course. Kat sings in a band at night and goes to school during the day, so she's rarely ever here. I can sum up the condition of our place in two words—a dump. Housing close to campus can be tough to come by, so when this place came up for rent, we jumped on it. In hindsight, it might have behooved us to be a tad more discerning. Now, we're stuck in a one-year lease for a place even the rats steer clear of. The walls look like they got in a fight with a chimney sweep, the carpet is riddled with cigarette burns, and the tiny kitchen—complete with a pink stove, I kid you not—probably hasn't been updated, or for that matter painted, since the seventies.

Any of those reasons would be enough to make anyone want to move, but really, that's all secondary to the bigger issue: the bedrooms. Or more accurately, the paper-thin wall separating mine and Emma's bedrooms. That's right. Not only do I get to enjoy Emma and Jacob's constant PDA during the daytime, but I get it in stereo every night.

Every single fucking night.

Why they can't have sex at his place is beyond my capacity to understand, but they never do. And damn, he must be great in bed because the noises they make are straight out of a porno. Thank god for earbuds, or I would have stabbed a chopstick through my eardrums ages ago.

Almost worse than having a front-row seat to all their kissy-lovey crap is having to deal with their constant fighting, which they're always dragging me into. Sometimes, being around them, it's like I'm living my parents' divorce all over again. At the moment, they're still in the complete silence stage of whatever it is they're fighting about, and the air between them is so tense, it permeates the entire living room.

When they get like this, my only recourse is to move out of the line of fire as quickly as possible, so I throw a "Good night," over my shoulder and make a beeline for my bedroom. The moment my door clicks shut, the fighting starts. I can't understand what they're saying, thank god. The sound just filters through the wall as a bunch of "Wah-wah-woh-wah-wah," like the teacher in a Peanuts cartoon. Hopefully, I'll get lucky and she'll piss Jacob off enough he'll go home. I really don't want to deal with another make-up sex session tonight.

I sigh and cross the half foot of floor space to my dresser. My room is dinky as hell, barely enough for a twin bed and dresser, so the fact that every spare inch is covered with crap shouldn't come as too much of a surprise. What is surprising is that, even so, I know where every item is. At least, I thought I did, but searching for my earbuds in their usual place atop my dresser, all I come up with is an empty charging case.

Everything goes quiet. They've stopped fighting. The door to Emma's room snaps shut, and that's when I know I'm screwed. It starts with a gasp—Emma's—followed by a low moan that could only be Jacob.

Shit.

I'm searching the dresser, the floor, the bed—tossing about every item I own in search of those life-giving earbuds. The more time that passes, the louder they get—Emma's cries of "Harder," and "Yes" sending me into near hysterics. I snatch up my pillow and blanket and rush into the living room. It's quieter here, but just barely. I crash onto the couch, press my head between the cushions and my pillow to block out the noise and curse myself for whatever I did in a past life to deserve this.

Two
And That's the Game Folks!
Stella

"I CAN ALREADY FEEL my arteries hardening," I say, my eyes trained on my basket of nachos and the orangy grease that's oozing out of the cheese to pool in the recesses of the chips—yum.

I'm sandwiched between Emma and our friend Charlie, as we make our way up the bleachers to our seats, which, by the looks of it, will be in another dimension. Emma, the de facto leader of this expedition, huffs out a laugh between labored breaths. "Yeah, but going up and down all these steps totally makes up for it. At least that's what I'm telling myself."

Charlie, who is probably in better shape than Emma and I combined, somehow got stuck taking up the rear of our little caravan, which means she hasn't stopped bitching since we started up the ramp on level one. Charlie Hayes—her actual name is Charlotte, but everyone calls her Charlie—has been my friend since we sat together in Psych 101 my first semester of school and is probably my best friend after Jacob. In some ways, we're actually closer—it's not like I can talk to Jacob about how much I'm in love with Jacob. I love Emma, but when the shit hits the fan, it's Charlie I go to. Charlie presses a hand to my back, urging me forward. "Maybe if you didn't eat that nasty crap, you wouldn't be climbing these steps at the velocity of a sloth."

"I'd stop pushing me if I were you, 'cause if I fall, I'm taking you down with me." I shoot a glare at her over my shoulder, but if anything, Charlie's smile brightens. Everything about Charlie is tiny—tiny nose, tiny ears, tiny rosebud mouth. Even her feet are so small, she actually wears children's shoes. Given that she's five foot nothing and practically a stick figure, I wouldn't be surprised if she shopped the children's section for her clothes as well.

"If only," Charlie begins, her voice thick with sarcasm, "there was a section of the stadium dedicated to students that we could have gotten tickets for."

I'd laugh if I could breathe.

Emma groans. "How was I supposed to know they'd sell out so fast? At least I got us tickets."

"Yeah, in the next state," Charlie chides, though more to get under Emma's skin than because she actually cares.

"Oh, stop it," Emma shoots back. "The seats are fine."

"Emma," I say, my voice thick with derision. "These seats are so high in the nosebleed section we can practically commune with God."

"Well, then we can ask her to support our team." Emma always refers to God as a *her*. It started out as a way to irritate her born-again, mega dickhead uncle. Now, she just does it for funsies.

I glance back at Charlie, who's playfully rolling her sea-foam green eyes at Emma's back. I wouldn't call Charlie gorgeous, but she's definitely got the pretty girl next door thing going on with her shoulder-length, dark-brown hair, fair skin and smattering of freckles across the bridge of her nose. It's really no wonder why she and Emma are dating two hot jocks, and I'm perpetually alone.

Emma finally turns down a row, plops her butt down on the crappy metal bench, then immediately jumps to her feet with a yip.

"Geez, Em." I make a show of looking at her butt and then the seat. "What happened? You sit on a chihuahua?"

Charlie snickers.

Emma purses her lips and gives me the evil eye, and repositions herself on the bench, so the exposed underside of her thighs hangs off the hot metal.

"Seriously," I say, sitting down beside her—damn, these seats are hot. "Aren't the players' girlfriends entitled to some special seating or something?" Charlie's boyfriend, Ryan, is also on the team, though he's a kicker.

"Huh. I wish," Emma blurts.

Charlie laughs and bumps me with her shoulder, her ponytail bobbing about her head. "Be happy they don't, 'cause your ass would be up here alone."

"You know it," Emma says way louder than is necessary, and the girls high-five.

"Uh, rude," I reply, my tone playful, even though the thought of Jacob getting Emma a ticket and not me makes me a little nauseous.

Or maybe that's the nachos.

"So, I heard you got blacklisted from the frat parties," Emma says to Charlie. Charlie got attacked at a frat party over the summer and might have been raped if it weren't for her—now—boyfriend, Ryan, coming to her rescue. That's certainly one way to get a date.

Charlie snorts. "Like I'm ever going to one of those again."

"When did you find this out?" I ask Emma. We spent all day yesterday together and she never mentioned it.

"Last night. One of the sisters from," she pauses, searching for the name. Emma's about as well versed in the Greek life as I am. Which means, not at all. "Alpha Delta Sigma?" She holds up a finger. "Wait. No. Theta? Shit. I don't remember. I'd had so much to drink, I'm sorry. Anyway, she approached me because I guess she knew somehow that we were friends, and she was pissed at her sorority for backing up the frats."

"That's so messed up," I say.

Emma nods. "I guess she wanted you to know that a lot of the girls were on your side but got outvoted."

Charlie shrugs, but I can tell by the way she's rapidly blinking her eyes she's upset. I wrap my hand around hers and squeeze. She gives me a tiny smile that tells me she appreciates the gesture. "I expected as much, to be honest. It's not like the school's doing anything about it. It's easier for everyone to say I'm in the wrong than to face the truth. Anyway, I'm over it." She snatches one of my nachos and stuffs it into her mouth before I can object. Her face goes all scrunched up, like she tasted a sour lemon, and she gasps. "Good god that's disgusting. How can you eat that garbage?"

"You just have no appreciation for quality food," I reply.

Emma laughs. "That's a mighty load of bullshit you're peddling there, Stella." She pops a chip in her mouth. "Mmm, clumpy cheese and grease. My fav."

"Oh, shut up," I say, smacking her hand when she reaches for another chip. "And get your own." Emma starts giving me shit about sharing and what my mama would think if she saw how I treated my friends. We laugh and the tension in my chest eases a little. Charlie hates talking about that night. It might have been what jump-started her and Ryan's relationship, but it was also traumatic as hell.

The team hasn't even taken to the field but Emma, most likely trying to keep Charlie smiling, stands up, and doing a cringeworthy impression of a cheerleader, starts shouting, "Ra-ra-ree. Kick 'em in the knee. Ra-ra-ras. Kick 'em in the ass."

The lady in front of us—an old woman with frizzy gray hair—twists around and glares at the three of us in turn, her eyes wide, as though affronted by our uncouth behavior.

Where does she think she is, the library?

Emma gives her a wide grin and waves, and the old lady turns back around with a huff.

Smile gritted firmly in place, Emma shrugs at Charlie and me, and we all burst out laughing.

It's only an hour into the game and our team is kicking some serious ass. Our competitor, Sanford U, isn't a high-ranking team or anything, but they've got a new red-shirt freshman quarterback that's showing a lot of potential and their defense is no joke. We may be up by ten points, but they were hard-earned.

"Oh, oh..." Emma bounces in her seat and pats my arm excitedly. "Jake's coming in."

I squint my eyes and search the field. Sure enough, I spot Jacob's number eighty-two jersey jogging over to take his position on the field.

"Jacob!" We all scream in unison, then hoot as we pump our fists in the air.

No one can accuse us of not being supportive, that's for sure. Though it's doubtful, our cries will have the power to penetrate the stratosphere and make it all the way to the field where the guys could actually hear us, but I digress.

Malcolm's head swivels back and forth, calling out all that "Hut 1, Hut 2" stuff that never really made any sense to me, and the ball is snapped. Jacob bolts and hangs right before turning back, his hands up and ready to catch the ball. But the offensive line doesn't hold and now Malcolm's dodging for his life. A Sanford linebacker the size of a Mack truck is plowing toward him and a split second before he gets nailed, Malcolm lets the ball fly. It's a beautiful throw, even more stunning because he did it under pressure. It beams Jacob right in the chest. He spins for the end-zone but doesn't make it around before two guys crash into him and tackle him to the ground.

The crowd goes wild.

Malcolm rolls onto his knees, looking a bit shell-shocked, before pushing up to his feet.

And everyone's chanting, "Let's go Eagles," and stomping their feet. Then, just as suddenly as it began, the cheering dies, and all eyes fall on Jacob's body lying motionless on the field.

Three
Gotta Love that Lemon Fresh Scent
Jacob

Everything is hazy. Whether that's a result of the concussion or drugs or both, I have no idea. All I know is, one minute I'm running down the field, the next I'm laid out and my head hurt so bad I thought for sure I'd cracked my damn skull open. That wasn't the scary part, though. No. The scariest part was when I tried to turn my head, but couldn't. I'll admit it. I cried like a fucking baby. It wasn't until one of the paramedics, or whoever they were—my vision was so blurry I couldn't see shit, asked me to wiggle my fingers and toes that I realized I wasn't paralyzed. They'd just put a brace around my neck. It probably only took me thirty seconds to sort out, but those were the most terrifying seconds of my life. Even the worst of my dad's rages couldn't compete.

My eyes are crusty and dry—like I've stepped out of a dust storm. When I finally manage to pry them open, I'm greeted by mint-green walls, fluorescent lights that burn my eyes and make them water, and the cloying scent of lemon cleaner. My head's too heavy, and sort of swollen, like my skull's full of lead. Though the pain isn't so bad anymore, thank god, just a dull ache.

I hear the snick of a door opening, but the bathroom wall is blocking my view. I stiffen. It's most likely Emma and Stella, as the guys are still at the game and Mom couldn't have driven here from Orlando that quickly. I could definitely use the mental support right now. Though I hate the idea of Emma seeing me all laid up like this.

Before I can contemplate further, a nurse enters the room. She's a middle-aged, motherly type, portly and dressed in purple scrubs. When she notices me watching her, she gives a warm smile and says, "Glad to see you're awake. I'm Jackie. I'll be taking care of you tonight. How are you feeling?"

"Not too hot," I reply, but my throat is dry and scratchy, and I start coughing, which turns what was a throbbing discomfort into a fucking pounding, like someone's playing whack-a-mole with my head. I groan.

"Oh no. I'm so sorry." The nurse races up beside me, picks a paper medicine cup off the table, and dumps two white pills into my palm. The bed groans like a pissed-off old man as she raises the back to sit me up.

"What is this?" I ask, eying what looks to be an underwhelming amount of medication.

"Tylenol," she says as she grabs a cup off the table and holds it to my lips, obviously waiting for me to take the pills.

"Seriously?"

She nods.

"Couldn't even splurge for the ibuprofen, huh?"

She laughs. "Sure. I could give you ibuprofen if you want to start a brain bleed and die." She cocks her head to the side, brows raised as if to say, "Now take the medicine, dumbass."

"Uh, I don't think that will be necessary," I say, both chastised and slightly terrified that my nurse could be a sociopath. I pop the pills into my mouth and take a pull off the straw. The water's cold and soothing against my raw throat.

"Sip it," she says. "The last thing we need is you throwing up."

I take a few more glorious sips then let my head fall back onto the pillow.

"Keep taking sips of this. Too much at a time could make you sick. We've got you on meds for nausea, but you don't want to push it." My nurse—Shit. What was her name again?—rests the cup on the raised table before rolling it closer to the bed. "Do you think you're up for visitors? There's a pretty young lady who's been sitting in the waiting room for a while. I'm sure she'd like to see you."

That brings an almost smile to my lips. It's stupid, but it's nice to know somebody gives a shit—other than my mom, that is. "Yeah. Please."

"Excellent. I'll send her right in." She exits the room and a few minutes later, I hear the door opening again.

"Jacob?" a familiar voice calls.

"Stella?"

She smiles sheepishly as she steps into the room, a brown teddy bear clutched in her hands. "Hey." Her voice cracks on the word and that's when I realize, Emma's not coming.

"Hey, Stells." I try to make my tone upbeat, but I feel too shitty to pull it off, and it's obvious from the frown on her face that Stella knows I'm disappointed. Which, of course, makes me feel like shit because I love Stella. I'm glad she's here. She's my best friend in the world. But Emma's my girlfriend. She should want to be here with me too. To give a shit enough to come to make sure I'm alright.

Stella's steps are tentative as she draws closer, as if I'm a wild animal that might lash out at any moment. "Emma wanted to come but—"

I cut her off, "It's fine." I'm being rude, but the last thing I want to hear right now is some bullshit excuse about why my girlfriend didn't come to see me in the hospital.

"She sent this." Stella holds the teddy bear in front of her face and pitches her voice higher, wiggling the stupid bear around like a puppet, "We're very sorry you got hurt, Mr. Jacob. If the doc isn't giving you the good stuff, you let us know; we've got connections."

I can't help the laugh that bursts out of me, then grit my teeth and moan at the pounding in my head.

"Oh, shoot. I'm sorry," Stella says, her face panic-stricken.

"Not your fault," I say, or more accurately grunt. "I just wasn't expecting a drug-pushing teddy bear is all."

Stella looks at me with that "poor pitiful, Jacob," expression that makes me want to punch something. "Emma really did want to come," she starts again.

"Stella—"

"No, really. It's just hard for her to be in hospitals—you know since her dad died."

I'm momentarily hit by a twinge of guilt, Emma's dad died of cancer when she was little and because of that, she hates hospitals. I get that, but still, she's my girlfriend and I need her right now. And maybe that's selfish, but I'm hurting and freaked out, so I think I'm entitled to a little selfishness. Right?

"Did she try?" I ask.

"She made it to the parking lot."

I nod. I get it. It fucking hurts, but I get it. "It's fine." I reach for the teddy and Stella hands it over. "Cute bear. Thanks." I set it on the bedside table. It's a clear dismissal, which is a dick move, I realize, but right now I just want to be left alone so I can wallow in self-pity.

Either Stella doesn't get the hint or she's ignoring it—most likely the latter—because she follows up by saying, "Is there anything I can do for you? You hungry? I could grab something from the cafeteria."

In a last-ditch attempt to get her to leave, I say, "Nah, I'm good. Really, you don't have to hang around, Stella."

Her smile drops and her whole body seems to sag a bit. "You don't want me here?" she asks and dammit if she doesn't look like I ran over her kitten.

"No. It's not that. I'm just not a lot of fun to be around right now, you know?"

She rolls her eyes. "That's a load of crap and you know it." I'm about to argue when she waves me off. "You're just upset about getting hurt and Emma not being here, and you want me to leave you to your little pity party."

Sometimes the way she can read my mind is really annoying.

Leaning over the bed, Stella wraps her arms around my shoulders and rests her head on the pillow beside mine. She's so tiny—delicate—but the way she holds me, her vanilla scent filling my nostrils, it's like a blanket wrapping around my whole body. "Sorry, bro," she says, her warm breath tickling my neck, "but you're not getting rid of me that easily."

And maybe it's all the trauma or that I'm a big frigging sap, but my eyes start to sting with tears. I blink them back and rub a hand along her arm and shoulder. "The nurse said I have to be careful not to get sick; can you ask her what's okay for me to eat?"

She pulls away, her entire face lit up in that way that always hits me in the gut. People say Stella looks a lot younger than she is, but I don't think it's so much that she has a young face as it is that she has this way about her. Not innocence—lord knows the girl isn't innocent—but a sort of sweetness that no amount of eyeliner and red lipstick is going to hide.

I reach up and tuck an errant strand of white-tipped hair behind her ear. I'm so used to her always being there, I think I sometimes forget to really look at her. She really is beautiful, not model gorgeous like Emma but something real and warm.

I must have made her a little uncomfortable because her cheeks go all pink and she backs up, stumbling when her thighs bump the chair. "I'm on it," she says and turns for the door, stopping once to glance my way and smile before stepping out of sight.

Four
Uncomfortable Much?
Stella

JACOB'S NOT SUPPOSED TO watch TV, so we've spent the past couple of hours munching on crackers while I read to him from my latest smutty book. Of course, when I come to a sex scene, I try to skip over it because—uncomfortable much—but he's not having it. He snatches up my hand, engulfing it with his big mitt, and tugs me closer. His hand is warm and callused and touching it sets my stupid heart all aflutter. He doesn't realize that, though. He's just playing around.

"Oh, no you don't," he chastises. "You make me sit through an hour of angsty bull shit and want to skip the good stuff. I don't think so. I earned this." He waves an arm like a king to his vassals. "Read on."

I can't help the silly giggle that escapes my lips. "Yes, my liege," I say, making an exaggerated bow in my chair, still holding onto his hand because a forklift couldn't pry me away. This is the first time in ages that I've hung out with Jacob without Emma around, and I've really missed this. I also feel horribly guilty for being so happy about it because, not only is Jacob really hurt, but he's really upset that Emma didn't show.

She sent a text about an hour ago to see how he was doing, and she asked me to tell him she was thinking about him, but she still hasn't called. If Jacob noticed her lack of a phone call, and I suspect he has, he hasn't mentioned it. I really tried to convince her to come in, I swear. The minute Jacob was injured, Emma and I ran down to the locker room, leaving Charlie to finish the game alone, and stopped one of the assistant coaches to see how he was doing. When he told us they were waiting on an ambulance, we rushed out to the car and headed straight to the hospital. I was driving and so focused on getting to Jacob, I didn't notice how quiet Emma was. It wasn't until I'd already parked and was getting my stuff together to go inside that I looked at her. She was white as a sheet and visibly trembling.

"Are you okay?" I asked.

She shook her head. "I don't think I can do this, Stella." Emma's voice was so small it made my heart hurt. I knew she hated hospitals, but I didn't realize it was that serious an issue.

"Are you sure? You don't even want to try?"

Her hands clutched the fabric of her shorts so hard her knuckles turned white. "I can't," she said, turning to look at the Emergency Room doors. "I can't go into that hospital, Stella, never again."

I sagged into my chair. "He's going to be so upset."

"You just need to explain it to him. Make him understand." She turned to face me, her eyes pleading. "Please. You go see him. Let me know how he's doing, huh? And get him a gift for me." She shuffled through her purse, searching for money and handed me a wad of one-dollar bills. "Some flowers or something. Tell him how sorry I am."

"Alright," I said and stuffed the cash into my pocket. What else could I say? Of course, I was going to do it. If not for her sake, then for Jacob's.

"Thank you," Emma said, wrapping her arms around me.

The door to Jacob's room clicks open, breaking me from my thoughts.

Jacob's mom, Gloria, sweeps in like a tidal wave. Noticing her panic-stricken expression, I hop up, leaving the little lounge chair to rock in my wake, and get out of her way. Eyes wild, Gloria rushes across the space, speaking in rapid-fire Spanish, and crushes poor Jacob in a bear hug. She's got to be in her forties, but you wouldn't know it by looking at her. In a word, Jacob's mom is gorgeous.

She's tiny but curvy as hell with wavy raven-black hair that goes all the way to the middle of her back, olive skin and big brown eyes. I freaking love Gloria. She's the most caring woman you'll ever meet and has been like a second mom to me. What's even cooler is that, through Jacob and me, she and my mom became good friends. Both single moms, they took the "it takes a village to raise a child" adage to heart.

Following behind Gloria is Adriana, who is basically a younger, and at the moment calmer, version of her mother. Ana greets her brother, then leaving him to their mom, comes over and gives me a hug. Adriana was a colossal pain in the butt when we were kids—as is the way of younger siblings—but being an only child, I secretly loved playing the big sister to her. She's two years younger but has at least three inches on me, even more on her mom. I always assumed the height came from their father's side, but considering I've never met the man, or even know his name for that matter, I can't say for sure. Talk of Jacob and Ana's father is taboo in the Gonzales household.

I pull back to hold Ana out at arm's length. "Damn, you look good, girl." Ana's shy about her looks, so it's no surprise when she gets all red and won't meet my eyes. The corners of her lips tip up into a tiny smile, though. "How have you been? How's school?"

She lets out a relieved breath and resumes eye contact. School is a much easier subject for her to discuss. "Good," she says. "Busy. I'm working on my college applications and looking for scholarships on top of classes, so I'm going a little nuts right now. You?"

I shrug but don't get a chance to reply before I'm clobbered by Gloria. "I'm so happy to see you, baby," she says, smushing my cheeks together. "You doing alright?"

"Yeah," I begin, but have to stop when my air supply is suddenly cut off by a bone-crushing hug.

"Thank you so much for staying with him. It means so much to know you're here for him when we can't be."

Finally, Gloria eases up enough to save my bowing ribcage and allow me to speak. "Always," I say and mean it.

She pats my back and returns to Jacob's bedside. I move to the foot of the bed to give his family room. Should I go now that they're here? I do need to call my mom and give her an update on how he's doing. She was watching the game, so she was blowing up my phone the second he got hit.

Jacob gestures to my now-vacated chair. "Sit down, Mama."

"Gracias, Mi Cielo." She slumps into the chair. "So, tell me what the doctors said."

Jacob starts back into the same spiel he gave me, his coach and some of his teammates who've called: Yes, he has a concussion. No, he hasn't seen a doctor and doesn't know how extensive the damage is. Poor guy. It's clear, by his bland expression, that he's already tired of repeating himself.

Adriana props her butt against the side of the bed and scans the room as if searching for something. It isn't until she speaks that I realize what that thing is. "So, where's this girlfriend you've been telling us about?"

Jacob's face goes cold, and he looks away.

Shit. Shit. Shit. I should have warned them.

When Jacob doesn't answer, the two women turn to me, brows raised. Their expressions are almost identical, which would be hilarious in any other situation, but I don't think any of us are feeling particularly jovial at the moment.

I shake my head as if to say, "Don't even go there." They both nod in understanding, and Ana deftly changes the subject to ragging on the bruisers who tackled him.

I take this as my cue to leave. "Well, it's getting a tad claustrophobic in here, so I'll go ahead and free up some space." I hug Gloria, Adriana and Jacob in turn—damn, he's warm. "If you need anything or talk to the doctor, call me, okay?" I say to Jacob, and turn for the door, but I don't make it far.

Jacob tightens his grip on my hand, stopping me mid-stride. He rests his head back on the pillow and smiles up at me and it's so beautiful my chest aches. "Come see me tomorrow?" he asks.

"Of course," I reply, and because I'm a glutton for punishment, I brush a kiss across his stubbled cheek. And though it lasts for the briefest of moments, I feel the memory of that kiss on my lips the entire way home.

Five
Because Murder is Wrong
Jacob

One night at the hospital, that was all I got. Not even a full twenty-four hours and they're sending me home like it wasn't that big of a deal. The hammer that's taken up permanent residence pounding in my head would argue differently—but whatever. Mom and Ana stayed with me all night but had to head back to Orlando today because Mom couldn't take the time off of work. It's been—maybe—two hours since they left, and I'm so bored, I want to pull my hair out. I'm glad to be out of the hospital—and to have my ass in actual pants—but this concussion makes even the simplest things so damn difficult. I can't sketch, paint, read or do anything else that might cause eye strain because my head hurts whenever I focus too long. The same goes for pretty much everything with a screen. Which is why I'm currently laid out on the couch in my living room, listening to some stupid daytime talk show on TV with my eyes closed. I should probably be sleeping or something, but then I'm stuck with my thoughts and that's the last thing I need right now.

I still haven't heard from Emma, which isn't a surprise but pisses me off, nonetheless. It's not like I expected us to go long-term or anything. Emma's fun and sexy, but we fight like crazy and have almost nothing in common. My favorite band is Led Zeppelin. She listens to Taylor Swift. I'm into art and Manga. She thought *Full Metal Alchemist* was a rock band. And don't even get me started on all the dumb-ass romantic comedies she's forced me to sit through. But I never would have expected her to ghost me like this.

As if replying to my thoughts, the universe sends me one more big f-you in the form of a tentative knock on my front door. I don't have to answer it to know it's Emma. I try to ignore it because I really don't want to deal with this right now. Then comes another knock, this one more insistent, Stella I'm guessing, which is confirmed when I hear her voice shout, "Jacob, open up" from out front.

"Come in," I say, hoping she can hear me because I shouldn't yell. I sit up and wait for them, thankful I gave Stella my key because there is no way I'm getting up off of this couch right now. I hear the jangle of keys and the door clicks open.

When I went over this scenario in my mind at the hospital, I'll admit, I expected tears, maybe a little groveling. I did not expect Emma to stride into my living room, smiling as if nothing had happened, wrap her hands around my face and just start kissing me. And not a little peck, full-on fucking my mouth with her tongue, kissing, and I'm so shocked, I kiss her back. At least until the brain in my head catches up with the one in my dick, and I finally push her away. "What the fuck, Emma," I say, wiping my mouth on my forearm.

She doesn't even have the damn sense to look repentant. She clasps her hands together and sways side to side like a five-year-old asking for candy. "I'm just happy to see you."

"Well, you know when I would have been happy to see you?" I ask and she opens her mouth as if it wasn't a rhetorical question. "Yesterday." I glance at Stella, because what the hell is wrong with this chick, but she's off in the corner pretending to be doing something on her phone. Not that I blame her. I wouldn't want to be witness to this shit show either. "Hey, Stells."

Her head snaps up. "Hey," she says with a tight smile.

"Can you give us a minute?"

She glances from me to Emma, then to me again, her eyes wide and cautious, like she's afraid that if she leaves, we might kill each other.

If only murder were legal, Stells.

"Yeah," she says finally. "I'll just go read my book out front."

Emma's eyes follow her friend across the room, panic etching her features. Stella gives her a piteous look and opens the door.

The minute the door clicks shut, Emma tries to deflect. "So... You look good. How are you feeling?"

"Great," I reply, my voice overly chipper. "I was unconscious for almost two minutes. I can barely stand without getting dizzy, and my head feels like someone beat it repeatedly with a sledgehammer. I can't play football until the doctors clear me and who knows when that'll be? And even if I am cleared, I could still lose my spot if they decide they like my replacement better. So yeah. Everything's hunky-fucking-dory."

She huffs out a breath like all this talk is putting her out, and all the blood must have rushed to my head because the pressure in my skull has doubled in the span of a couple of seconds. *Of all the selfish—*

"Look, I'm sorry," she admits, interrupting my inner tirade. Eyes downcast, she toes the carpet—drawing sweeping lines in the matted-down shag. "You know how I feel about hospitals. My dad—"

"And phones?" I ask, cutting her off. Her head snaps up like she's surprised that I stated the obvious. "What exactly is your issue with phones, Emma?" I continue, blood thrumming through my veins like my heart is pumping double-time. "Because you certainly didn't use one to call me."

She turns her attention back to the floor. "I was afraid if I spoke to you, you'd try to talk me into going back to the hospital."

"So, you'd rather ignore me than have an awkward conversation?"

She doesn't reply, doesn't look at me, and I can feel my resolve cracking a little as I watch a tear meander down her cheek.

I sigh. "Emma—"

"I was worried about you," she interrupts, her voice breaking a bit on the words. "I asked Stella to check on you and tell me how you were doing. I just couldn't go into that damn hospital."

"Then you should have called."

"I know."

I rub a hand over my face and sag back into the couch. There really isn't anything else to say. I'm angry; she's sorry. We fall into an awkward silence, neither one of us wanting to voice the two words rattling around our heads: What now?

Emma's eyes roam the room, most likely searching for something to talk about, and settle on the stuffed bear I'd deposited on the coffee table when I got home.

She picks it up, another excuse not to look at me while she examines it. "This is cute," she says.

I don't know whether I want to laugh, cry, scream or put my fist through the wall because it's obvious she's never seen that bear before, has no idea it's supposed to be from her. And for some reason, that cuts the deepest. That she couldn't even be troubled to pick up her own damn gift. God, I'm such an idiot. I was actually starting to fall for her bullshit. I snatch the bear out of her hands and toss it back onto the table. "I think you need to go," I say, my voice cold even to my own ears.

She jerks to attention. "What? Why?" she asks, though the tears welling in her eyes tell me she already knows the answer.

"Because I don't think we should see each other anymore."

Six
Am I Still Evil if I Feel Guilty?
Stella

I knew Jacob was pissed, but I didn't think he'd dump her. When Emma stormed out of that apartment, tears streaming down her face, though, I knew exactly what happened. Am I a horrible person for maybe being a teensy-weensy bit happy about that?

Yes. Yes, I am.

I do feel bad for Emma because she's upset, and I don't want her hurt, but knowing I don't have to deal with the two of them sexing it up anymore, it's like fucking Christmas. I shove that elation deep, deep down because I refuse to be that big of a bitch and follow her down the two flights of steps to where her car sits in the parking lot.

Emma jumps in the driver's seat and frantically attempts to stick the key in the ignition, but her hands are shaking and she's crying too hard to see properly.

"Whoa, whoa, whoa." I swing the door open, grab the hand still holding her keys and push it away from the ignition. "Stop. Emma. You're in no condition to drive."

She looks up, meeting my eyes, and her expression is so pitiful, so devastated, my chest constricts with guilt. Just a few seconds ago, I was happy about this. "He broke up with me," she says.

"I know. I'm sorry," and I am sorry for her, I think. "But you shouldn't be driving right now. Get into the passenger seat, okay? I'll drive us home and we can spend the entire night getting drunk and eating brownies or whatever other boxed goodness I can find in the pantry."

She gives me a pained smile. "You'll call Charlie too?"

"Of course. If I know Charlie, she's already telepathically sensed that you're upset and will be waiting on our doorstep with a bottle of vodka at the ready."

That gets a laugh out of her. "I'd rather Bailey's."

"Will do, chicky-boo. Now get the hell out of my seat."

She nods and plops the keys down in my hand before climbing out of the car. I glance up at the second-story window to Jacob's apartment. I don't want to leave him like this, but Emma needs me too. Shit, this is hard. "Hey, Em. Give me two seconds to tell Jacob I'm taking you home, okay?"

She slides into the passenger seat with a huff. "I think he'll figure it out, Stella."

What I want to say is, "Yes, but he's my best friend who you screwed over, so forgive me for giving a crap." What I actually say is, "I know, but he's my friend, and I want to make sure he's okay before I go. Give me two minutes."

She doesn't respond, just crosses her arms and sinks into her seat like a toddler denied a cookie.

I take that as permission and charge up the stairs. The door to his apartment is still cracked open, but I knock on it anyway before going in. Jacob's still on the couch but lying down now. He peeks at me out of one eye, the corner of his lips lifting into a half-smile that sends a jolt through my belly.

"I figured you'd left with Emma," he says.

"Yeah. She's waiting in the car. I can't let her drive. She's too upset."

Closing his eyes again, he says, "I figured. Can you come by later?"

I grimace. No matter what I do here, someone's going to be mad. "I'm so sorry. I promised to get her drunk."

He nods. "It's alright. Malcolm and Ryan will be here soon."

"I'll text you later."

"Yeah."

He's trying to act all cool and unaffected, but I know every one of his tells: the way his shoulder's tense and jaw pops, the slight press of his lips. He's upset. I pad the rest of the way into the room and kneel beside the sofa. He opens his eyes and turns his head to look at me. God, he's beautiful. I realize that's a weird thing to call a guy—especially one as masculine as Jacob—but it's true. I could spend days tracing the shape of his jaw, and brow and lips. Even more, looking into those eyes that make me want to melt into the crappy carpet. I brush an errant strand of hair from his forehead. "You going to be alright?"

He smiles, but that light in his eyes isn't there. He's just faking it. "Yeah. I'm good."

I lean over and grab his shoulders into the best semblance of a hug I can give when he's lying down like this. He wraps his arm around me, pulling me in closer, and god, he feels so good. I press the bridge of my nose into the crook of his neck, taking in his scent, a mixture of clean soap and a dark spiciness that is all Jacob. My whole body vibrates with the need to kiss that warm bit of skin where his neck and shoulder meet, just centimeters from my lips, but I don't. Calling on every ounce of willpower I possess, I pull away and head out the door.

Seven
Don't Fuck with My Beer
Jacob

"Oh man, I'm bummed I missed it," I say to Ryan, whose brown eyes are lit up like the Fourth of July; he's so excited. Ryan is a kicker on the team and a junior like Malcolm, but he doesn't get a lot of game time because our first-string kicker is a senior and really good. Ryan has been itching to show everyone what he could do, so when he got put into the game yesterday, after they took me to the hospital, and kicked a thirty-yard field goal, it had to be pretty damn awesome. I just wish I'd been there to see it.

"Yeah, it was pretty epic," he replies, his face split into a grin the size of Kentucky, showing off dimples I didn't even realize he had. Ryan Morgan is about my height but leaner and honestly looks more like a rocker than a jock. His ash-brown hair goes to just past his shoulders—Jimmy Page style—his eyebrow is pierced, and he's got a boatload of tattoos all over his body. It's funny that he somehow ended up with Charlie, who's so clean-cut, but they seem to work. "Coach's got to give me more field time after that, right?" he asks.

"I'd hope so," I say, because you never can tell what Coach is going to do.

My roommate, Malcolm, steps out of the kitchen, taking a long swig of his beer as he approaches. I know I shouldn't, but damn, I'd like a beer right now. Shit, I'd happily drink tequila, which I hate, if it meant taking a break from my head for a little while. Probably not the healthiest coping method, but I can't have any, so it's a moot point, anyway.

I don't know if I've got some longing expression on my face or if Ryan is a mind reader or what, but he takes one look at Malcolm and says, "You really gonna drink that shit in front of him? Poor guy just got dumped—"

"Uh, no. I broke up with her."

Ryan waves me off like those sorts of details are inconsequential. "And you know he can't drink."

I'm about to say that it's cool when I see the corner of Malcolm's lip twitch up, which means he's going to be a total dickweed in about three... two... one...

"Not my fault he can't take a hit," Malcolm says with a smirk and lifts the bottle for another drink.

"Asshole," I say, but there's no heat in it. He's full of shit and we both know it.

Ryan, on the other hand, jabs a finger at his friend. "Not cool man," and swats the bottle out of his hand. Beer sprays all over the coffee table before landing with a thump on the floor and gurgling out into the carpet.

"Hey," Malcolm protests, standing the bottle up and sopping up the mess with a couple of half-used napkins he found crumpled up on the table. Meanwhile, Ryan just sits back and watches him with a grin on his face like this was his day's entertainment.

"Whatever happened to solidarity among friends, bro?" Ryan asks Malcolm, who's still cursing him under his breath.

"Whatever happened to don't fuck with my beer, bro."

I sigh and pick up the now-mostly-empty bottle and set it on the table. "All right children. Let's settle down," I say, to which both of them turn to glare at me, and I can't help it. I start laughing.

Ryan is laughing too, but Malcolm looks murderous. I'd be worried, except they've been pulling this kind of crap on each other for as long as I've known them. From what they told me, they met freshman year, but they seem like the kind of friends who've known each other forever—like Stella and me.

"Just get a damn coke," Ryan demands and Malcolm grumbles but stands up and starts toward the fridge. "And get Jake and me one while you're at it," he calls after him. Malcolm flicks him a bird and Ryan snickers. "Sorry man, I've got a girlfriend." Ryan is still chuckling to himself when he turns his attention back to me. "So, I don't get it. If you dumped her, why do you look so dejected?"

"She didn't get him the teddy bear," Malcolm says as he strides back into the living room. He doles out our drinks and plops down on the couch beside me.

"It wasn't about the bear," I say. "It was just the last straw, you know? She doesn't show up at the hospital or call—and I get that shit with her dad was messed up, but she couldn't even be bothered to pick up her own damn gift before she sent Stella in her place. I'm not trying to be needy here, but Jesus, could she have given even the tiniest of shits?" I sigh and lean my head back against the couch cushion. "Honestly, I'd been sort of considering it, anyway. We fought constantly."

"Over Stella," Ryan says. It's not a question, but I nod anyway.

Popping the top, Malcolm downs half the can of Coke in one go, then wipes his mouth on his shirt sleeve in a move that would have sent my mama into hysterics. "Can you really blame her, though?" he says. "For being jealous."

I roll my eyes. Christ. Not him too. "Stella's my friend. She's been my best friend since—"

"Fourth grade, yes, we know," Malcolm cuts in. "But I'm sorry to have to break this to you, man. You don't treat her like just a friend."

Ryan is nodding his head in agreement and I'm a little shell-shocked.

"What the fuck are you talking about?" I say, agitation leaking into my voice.

Malcolm raises his palms, one still holding a Coke, as if in surrender. "I'm not trying to be a dick. It's just... It's kind of obvious. You're always hugging her or touching her."

"And if it was only that," Ryan interrupts. "We may have just written you off as touchy-feely but, come on," he splays his hands apart, "if a guy so much as looks at her, you go ballistic."

I cross my arms and turn my head to look away. There isn't much I can say about that. I hate it when guys hit on Stella.

"What I don't get," Malcolm says, and now I'm starting to feel like they're tag-teaming me, "is why you don't just ask her out. I mean, she's hot, in her own little pixie sort of way." He wiggles his fingers when he says this, like pixies are wiggly or something. "And she gets you. I would have jumped on that ages ago."

I glance from him to Ryan, who's nodding like a bobblehead doll.

"We don't think of each other that way," I say. "She's like my sister."

Ryan chuckles. "You can't be that dense. Seriously?"

He and Malcolm glance at each other like they're in on some big fucking joke, and I'm the punchline. "What?" I rub my temples in a vain attempt to ward off the headache creeping up the back of my skull.

"Look," Ryan says. "If you see her as a sister—fine, cool. I don't believe you, but whatever. But I promise you, that girl does *not* see you as a brother."

"And you know this because?" I pose the question to Ryan, but it's Malcolm who replies.

"Because we have eyes. You'd have to be blind not to see it. That girl looks at you like the sun shines out your ass."

Ryan lifts the can to his lips and pauses. "Thinking about it..." He sets the can back down, eyebrows scrunched like he is, in fact, thinking, and it might be slightly painful. "I'm honestly shocked she's still coming around. It had to be torture, standing by while you screwed her friend. I would have ditched both your asses a while ago if I were her. No way I could just sit around while some guy did Charlie."

"First of all, she's your girlfriend. It's different," I protest. Ryan purses his lips and tips his head from side to side as if to say, "maybe-yes, maybe-no." "And second, you're wrong."

An image pops into my head of Stella the other morning when I left early for practice. She was sleeping on the couch, mascara smeared across her cheeks. I'd assumed it was the aftermath of a crazy night out, but what if it wasn't? What if she was crying because of me? Jesus, could she hear us? What kind of asshole am I to not have even considered that? I rake my hands through my hair. No. I would have known if she had feelings for me. She couldn't hide something that big; I know her too well. I shake my head, but oh yeah, I have a concussion and my head starts pounding at the slightest frigging movement. I have to pause a moment to wait for the pain to dull, then I say, "She doesn't think... want..." I wave a hand as if the word I'm looking for can be plucked from the air. "She doesn't have feelings like that for me."

"She's in love with you," Malcolm says like it's common fucking knowledge.

"No. She isn't."

"Yes, she is," the guys say in unison, which is just goddamned creepy. Of course, they think it's funny as hell and start cracking up and fist-bumping across the table.

Idiots.

I'm struck by a wave of dizziness, and everything goes a little blurry. I rest my head in my hands for a moment while it passes. When I raise my head again, Malcolm and Ryan have gone silent, all brevity evaporated from their expressions.

"You alright, man?" Ryan asks.

"Yeah. I just... need to lay down," I say, my head pounding in earnest now.

I stand up—too fast—and wobble a bit as the room spins. Malcolm shoots up and grabs my arm to steady me. "Careful."

"Thanks, man," I say.

He simply nods.

"When's the last time you took your meds?" Ryan asks.

"You mean the Tylenol," I reply with more venom than his question deserves. "Does it really matter?" I say more softly.

"Better than nothing," he replies. "Malcolm, you help him to his room. I'll get his pills."

Malcolm keeps hold of my arm as he leads me to my room, and Ryan runs into the kitchen. "You should write down the times you take your medicine, or you'll get it all mixed up," Ryan yells over his shoulder.

"Yes, mom," I say too softly for him to hear but elicit a chuckle from Malcolm.

Lucky for me, my room is the first door on the left. Malcolm doesn't bother turning on the lights, for which, I'm grateful. I practically collapse into bed with a loud and extended groan. Damn, that feels good.

Malcolm squeezes my shoulder. "Get some rest." He lays my phone on the nightstand. "Text if you need me, alright?" He turns to leave but pauses and turns back around when I say his name. "Yeah."

My eyelids are so heavy, it's a struggle to keep them open, but I have to ask. "Were you serious… about Stella?"

"I wouldn't mess with you about something like that."

"Why didn't you mention it before?"

In the minute it takes for him to answer, I realize that I've closed my eyes and pop them open again to find Malcolm scratching his day-old stubble, deep in thought. Finally, he lets out a sigh and says, "I guess I just assumed you knew."

Eight
Boys Don't Want Brains
Stella

"What happened and do I need to cut a bitch?" Emma's sister, Kat, says when she sees her sister's tear-stained face. Kat's a year younger, but they could probably pass for twins if it weren't for Kat's pink hair, lip ring and penchant for pleated skirts, combat boots and graphic tees that always say something snarky. Today's reads "I like the sound you make when you shut up."

I'd just finished pouring three obnoxiously full glasses of the cheap chardonnay Charlie brought over when Kat walked in on our little party in the kitchen. Kat occupies our third bedroom, but between school, and her band, she's hardly ever around. I don't need to ask if she wants wine—Kat always wants wine—so I set a fourth glass on the counter and fill it to the rim before handing them out to the girls.

Emma rolls her eyes but gives her sister a tiny smile and a hug. "What have I told you about violence?"

Kat smirks. "Hit them where the bruises won't show?"

I guess Charlie wasn't prepared for that little nugget because she chokes on her wine and slaps a hand over her mouth to hold the liquid in while she lunges for the sink. Kat pats our friend on the back as she coughs and gasps. It's always like this with Kat. She's like a human tornado, always moving, always creating havoc wherever she goes. It's kind of awesome and, if I'm being honest, a little intimidating. Emma's a year older, almost to the day, but if I had to guess, after their dad died, it was Kat who took care of her sister and not the other way around.

I decide to save Emma the torment and spill the beans. "Her and Jacob broke up."

Emma takes an impressive gulp of the wine. "Don't sugarcoat it, Stella," she says, then turns to her sister. "He dumped me."

"What? That asshole—" Kat begins, but Emma cuts her off.

"I deserved it."

Finally recovered from her ordeal, Charlie comes to lean on the counter beside me. "No, you didn't. Don't say that."

I keep my mouth firmly shut. No way am I getting caught up in the middle of her and Jacob's drama. I am Switzerland.

"No. It's true," Emma argues. "Tell them, Stella."

Well, it didn't take long for that plan to go to shit.

All eyes turn to me. "Uh..." I begin. I'm certain she already has something in mind that she expects me to say—whether she wants me to deny or corroborate her claim is anybody's guess. And perhaps I'm a traitor to my gender for saying this, but I hate it when girls do that—expect you to read their minds—because I really suck at it. Say what you will about guys, but at least you know where you stand with them. "Yeah, kind of?" I finally say though it comes out as more of a question.

Everyone goes still for a moment, then Emma lets out a wail and buries her face in her sister's shoulder to cry.

So, I'm thinking that was probably the wrong answer.

Kat glares at me and I shrug. What the hell does she want me to do? Lie. Truth be told, I probably would have broken up with her too. I'm not going to say that because that would be like pouring lemon juice on an open wound, but she messed up. Big time.

Charlie rubs a sympathetic hand on my back. At least someone understands.

"Come on," Kat says, steering Emma toward the couch. I snatch a half-eaten box of chocolate chip cookies out of the pantry and follow behind Charlie. Setting the cookies down on the coffee table, I take a seat on the floor beside Charlie and across from where the sisters have huddled together.

Kat wraps her hands around Emma's. "Look. I know this is hard, but I really think it's for the best. He wasn't right for you."

"Why do you say that?" I ask, honestly curious.

"Because he was only really interested in her for her looks. She needs someone who's going to be interested in her." She taps a finger to her temple. "Someone who wants to be with her because they genuinely enjoy spending time with her, not only for sex."

Emma huffs. "Have we met?" She chugs the rest of her wine. Silent as a wraith, Charlie gets up and heads back to the kitchen. "Boys don't give a shit about my brain."

"That's because they're stupid," I say, my blood boiling not only at the truth of Emma's words but because of what they imply. Jacob is interested in me for my mind; he just doesn't find me attractive. Damn, but that hurts. I fight the tears stinging my eyes because this isn't supposed to be about me. "You're an awesome person, Em. Guys are just idiots led around by their dicks. At least you have that pretty face, so when you find the guy that does see beyond it, he'll actually want you." My voice breaks on that last part and I take a breath, trying to get a handle on my emotions before I break down in front of everyone. Once I feel like can speak again without sounding like a young velociraptor, I excuse myself to the bathroom.

Dammit, dammit, dammit. Closing the bathroom door behind me, I sit on the floor, my back against the cool porcelain tub. I breathe in and out and focus on the bite of my fingernails against my palms. I hate these emotions. It's stupid. I already knew he wasn't attracted to me. I don't even think it occurs to him that I'm a girl. To Jacob, I'm just this a-sexual person he enjoys hanging out with.

There's a knock on the door and I don't have to open it to know it's Charlie.

"I'm okay," I tell her. "Just go back with Emma."

Charlie's voice sounds strangely muffled and echo-y through the door. "No, you're not. Emma's fine, Stella. Please let me in."

Part of me really wants her to go away but the other—pushier—part of me really wants my friend. "It isn't locked," I say.

The door creaks open and Charlie steps into the bathroom, closing it behind her. She sits down beside me and rests her back against the side of the tub. "This must be weird for you, huh?" she asks.

"I feel so guilty. I don't want Emma to be sad—"

"But you don't want her to be with him either," she finishes.

I nod. "Which isn't fair because he doesn't want me. He's not attracted to me." I sniff and it sounds like a waterfall rumbling in my nose. Charlie unrolls a bit of toilet paper and hands it to me.

"I don't think attraction has anything to do with it, Stells." She pauses while I blow my nose and throw the used tissue into the garbage. "I just don't think he sees you. Not that way, at least."

Unable to stomach that pitying look on Charlie's face, I shift my gaze to where my fingers twist and roll the hem of my shirt in my lap. I ask, "Am I really that ugly?" It's a ridiculous, unfair question because even if I was, she would never say it. Charlie's way too nice to do that.

"No. Of course not," she says. Then perhaps sensing my train of thought, she ducks her head and lifts my chin so we're eye-to-eye. "Seriously, Stella. You're very pretty, and plenty of guys notice it. But I don't know; he just has blinders on when it comes to you or something."

I nod. Maybe she's right. I do get hit on some, by good-looking guys even, but I'm always shooting them down because they're not Jacob. For all the billion girlfriends he's had over the years, I've had two boyfriends—neither lasting more than a couple of months. And those were boys back in high school I dated mostly hoping it would get Jacob's attention. It didn't work. Even when I told him I'd lost my virginity, all Jacob did was pat me on the back and say "Congratulations." So, I gave up because what was the point. The sex wasn't terrible, but not really worth giving up my vibrator for either.

"You ready to go back?" Charlie asks because she's an awesome friend who would sit here with me all day if I needed her to. "Kat just pulled out the pot brownies."

Now, that sounds like a plan.

Nine
Well, Whadda'ya Know?
Jacob

"Coming," I holler at the door. I grab a sort-of clean pair of jeans off the floor of my room and hop across the living room as I try to wrangle them on. I'd spent most of the day in bed which seems to have helped a little. My headache's better, and I'm not so dizzy anymore. I finish zipping up my pants as I reach the door and swing it open without checking the peephole. Stella's standing in the walkway frozen and wide-eyed as a deer in headlights. I'm pretty sure she's not breathing. Her eyes rake over my chest and the hunger in her gaze sets off about a billion butterflies in my chest. The guys were right. It's so obvious. How could I have missed it before? I admit, I was totally in love with her when we were kids—as much as a preteen can be in love—but after a while, she sort of became like a sister. *But she's not your sister*, the voice in my head says. I push the thought away. This is not something I have the mental capacity to deal with right now, or ever, really.

"Hey." I open the door wider, inviting her in but don't give her our compulsory hug, because I'm kind of uncomfortable now. Dammit, I wish the guys hadn't told me. This is going to fuck everything up.

Stella steps into the apartment without a word, her manner strained. Can she tell I'm nervous?

"Give me a second," I say and run into my bedroom before she even has a chance to respond. I'm acting like a complete psycho, throwing shit all over my room, searching for a clean shirt. Finally, I settle on a white undershirt hanging half out of the laundry bin and throw it on. I spin back around and find Stella standing in the doorway, watching me. She's clasped her hands together at the waist, a stance that means she's uncomfortable.

"Are you alright?" she asks, brows furrowed.

"Yeah. Of course," I stammer. "I'm great—fine. I'm fine. Why wouldn't I be?" I lean a hand up against the wall in a pose I hope will be natural only to immediately realize it's not and drop my arm back to my side.

She's really giving me the once over now, her eyes all squinty as though if she could only study me a little harder, she'd be able to see what deep end I've fallen off of. "What's going on?"

"Nothing. What's going on with you?" I throw back at her and to my relief she turns her focus to telling me about her night with Emma, and how she tried to call me to check on me, but I didn't answer.

"Sorry," I say, rubbing the back of my neck. It's one of my tells and Stella knows it; I immediately stop but it's too late, I can see the question in her eyes. "I think the guys turned my ringer off so I could sleep. I honestly just woke up."

She seems to accept this, even though the truth is I saw her texts and didn't respond because I'm a chicken-shit asshole. "You're looking better." She gestures to me, and her eyes drop briefly to my, now-covered, chest.

"I'm feeling better," I say.

Her face lights up at that—sending a little bolt of electricity through my chest and straight into my balls. What the fuck? I'm getting hard. She's your best friend you horny bastard. I rush past her and into the kitchen before she sees the ever-growing bulge in my pants. "You want some coffee?" I call over my shoulder, my voice squeaking like a pubescent thirteen-year-old.

"Sure." Stella takes a seat on the couch. She's picking at her nails—another tell. Is she nervous because she can tell I'm nervous or is it something else? I scrub my hands through my hair. I've got to calm down or I'll give myself another headache.

While making the coffee, I recite play calls in my head, so by the time I start for the couch, I've managed to get at least somewhat of a handle on myself.

I hand over her coffee and Stella gives me another one of those beaming smiles and I swear I can feel the warmth radiating from it. She takes a sip, closing her eyes and humming with pleasure, and fuck, that's an image I am not going to get out of my head. She's pushed her hair over her shoulder, so it hangs in natural waves down her back, exposing a long, graceful neck. Everything about her is delicate from her long, thin fingers gripping the mug to her pert nose and full lips—the bottom lip slightly fuller, giving her a perpetual pout. The light catches her eyes turning them from brown to glowing amber. She's fucking beautiful.

"Jacob," Stella says, and I realize belatedly that she was saying something.

"I'm sorry. What?"

"Will you be able to go to class tomorrow?" she asks, but concern is seeping into her voice again. She probably thinks it's my concussion making me crazy. I guess that could have something to do with it, but really, I just don't know what to do with myself—with her. It's like some light has flipped on in my head, and I can't turn that shit back off.

"Yeah. I think so," I manage to answer.

"You need a ride?"

"Oh yeah." I rake my hand through my hair and chuckle. "I hadn't actually considered that. Yeah. A ride would be great."

And now we're sitting in uncomfortable silence. Another thing I've never felt with Stella. "You want to watch something?" I say, picking up the remote. She agrees and I pull up Netflix, stopping on the first thing I see. "How about this?" I turn to her and Stella is staring at me like I've grown two heads.

"Jacob?"

"Yes."

"That's a rom-com."

"Okay."

"Jacob?"

"Yes."

"You hate rom coms."

"Yeah, but you like them, right?"

She shrugs. "I'd rather watch a horror flick."

I can't help the grin that spreads across my face. "Horror it is."

Ten

The Flash Ain't Got Nothin' On Me

Stella

WE'RE AN HOUR INTO the *Texas Chainsaw Massacre* remake, which is just as bad as I'd expected—you can't outdo a classic people—and Jacob's out. Not that it's unusual for him to fall asleep in front of the TV, it's kind of his modus operandi, but the sun hasn't even set yet and people getting slaughtered can usually hold his attention. I realize, I'm a worrier by nature, but his behavior today has been really strange. And now he's falling asleep in the middle of the carnage, and it has me wondering if the concussion might have done some actual damage.

His head lolls to the side, and I brush away a lock of hair that's fallen across his forehead. I love watching him sleep. It's total creeper behavior, I know, I'm owning to it, but it's the only time I feel like I can really look at him—without him thinking I'm some love-crazed weirdo. I am, but I certainly don't want him to know that.

His arm is still stretched along the back of the sofa where it was when he fell asleep, and I want so badly to snuggle into his side; it's like a physical ache. When he answered the door today with his shirt off, my body went off like a live wire. It was all I could do not to grab hold of those beautiful biceps and lick him from stomach to sternum. I've seen him without a shirt before. You'd think I'd be used to it, but it knocks me for a loop every single time. I couldn't stop staring, and I'm pretty sure he noticed, which is so embarrassing.

Screw it. If he wakes up, I'll just pretend I fell asleep too. It works in the movies, right? I scoot closer to him until my thigh is barely brushing his and lower my head to rest on his shoulder. Just this tiny bit of contact sends my stomach into somersaults. He's warm and smells so good—dark and a little spicy. I want so badly to climb on top of him, press my breasts into his hard chest, wrap my legs around his waist and grind against his cock until he wakes up so aroused, he doesn't even take the time to undress. Instead, he lowers his zipper to free his cock and pulls my panties aside, exposing my soaking wet sex to the cold air only a moment before he plunges into me, pounding into me until I come, screaming his name. Then he does the same, shouting my name as he comes inside of me because, in my fantasies, I don't use condoms.

I've gotten myself so amped up, I'm physically vibrating with need. So, when a hand softly runs down my spine, I gasp and jerk my head back to find a very awake Jacob looking at me. Oh god, can he tell? I was snuggled against his chest, fantasy fucking the hell out of him, and he was awake. A hot blush spreads across my cheeks, and that must have been the confirmation he needed because his eyes widen like he's looked into my mind and seen all the dirty things I want to do to him. Shoving out of his arms, I whirl around, snatch my keys off the table and throw the strap of my book bag over one shoulder.

"I've got to go. Sorry," I say as I race for the door.

"Wait, Stella." I hear him getting up but don't stop as I flee out the door and down the stairs. "Stella." He's in his doorway now, watching me make a fool of myself.

"I'm late for study group," I call back to him, my voice surprisingly steady considering I feel like my chest's been placed in a vise. The tears welling in my eyes have turned my car into a red smudge. By some miracle, I manage to not only locate my car but get the door open.

I don't know if Jacob followed me down the stairs. I'm too afraid to check. All of my mental energy is focused on inserting my key into the ignition and getting the fuck out of dodge. I peel out of the parking lot, make a sharp right onto the main road and don't stop until I'm pulling into Charlie's driveway.

Even I don't know how Charlie understands what I'm saying when I show up at her front door crying my eyes out and blubbering like a soap star.

"Let's go into my room," she says, giving the side-eye to her 12-year-old sister, Claudia, who's hovering in the hall and doing a shit job of acting like she's not eavesdropping. Charlie takes my hand and leads me down the hallway, pausing only to shove Claudia's face into the photo she was pretending to examine.

"Oww," Claudia shouts louder than the push called for.

"I better not catch you listening at my door, shit head, or next time it'll really hurt," Charlie says.

Claudia's face scrunches up in anger. She spins around and sprints from the hall and into the living area screaming, "Mom."

Charlie rolls her eyes. "Be happy you don't have siblings."

I smile, though I'm sure it looks pained. I'd always considered Ana to be like my little sister, and she was annoying at times, but I wouldn't have traded her for anyone. I'm not going to tell Charlie that, of course, and in all honesty, I don't remember Ana being anywhere near Claudia-level annoying. Though we are closer in age, so perhaps that had something to do with it.

I follow Charlie into her bedroom, and she shuts the door behind us.

Every time I enter Charlie's room, it's like I'm stepping into the past. It's hard to pinpoint the exact cause, whether it's the white furniture, hot-pink bedspread heaped with stuffed animals, or the pink and purple polka-dot curtains, but Charlie's bedroom is like the room that time forgot. It's as if ten-year-old Charlie decorated the hell out of it, and never touched it again. She crosses to where the twin bed is pushed up against the wall and sweeps probably a third of her animal hoard onto the floor, then scooches across the bed until her back rests against the wall. Charlie pats the now-cleared spot beside her. "Sit."

I crawl across the bed to sit next to her and rest my head on her shoulder. "He knows," I say.

She pats my head. "Context, honey."

I'm finding it hard to formulate words. My skull feels like an overfilled water balloon stretched and ready to burst, and my throat is so swollen and achy from crying, I'm struggling to draw breath, much less speak. Charlie seems to understand this because she waits patiently and strokes my hair until I've calmed enough to get the words out. "Jacob knows how I feel." I plant my face in my palms because I'm so embarrassed, I can't even meet Charlie's eyes when I say, "He caught me having a sexual fantasy about him."

Charlie rubs slow circles on my back. "How did he catch you having a fantasy?" She pauses, then gasps. "Oh shit. Did he catch you masturbating or something?"

My head pops up at that. "No," I practically screech. "Good god, Charlie. If that were the case, I'd be out searching for the nearest bridge to jump from."

She laughs. "Well, at least you know it could always be worse."

"Seriously."

She clears her throat like she's ready to get serious, and says, "Alright then, tell me how he caught you having a fantasy."

I take a breath to steady myself and tell her all of it from me snuggling into him while he slept, to his reaction when he caught me mid—sexy daydream. "It was like he saw all the dirty shit going on in my head." I sweep a finger back and forth in front of my forehead for emphasis. "And I panicked and ran. I ran, Charlie, like my ass was on fire."

"Like ran, ran?" she asks.

"I could have given Usain Bolt a run for his money."

The grimace on Charlie's face tells me all I need to know. I am so screwed. "Jesus, Stella. You might have been able to play it off if you hadn't run off like that but—"

"I know." I flop face-first into the mattress and scream my frustrations into the muffling fabric. Feeling a little better, I roll over onto my back. "I panicked," I say to the ceiling like someone up there gives a shit, then turn my head to Charlie. "What am I going to do? I'll never be able to look Jacob in the eyes again." I groan and start to roll back over.

"Wait." Charlie stops me mid-roll then starts to bounce, shaking the entire bed like something out of a bad porno, and giggling like an idiot.

I fling out my arms in a half-assed attempt to keep her from kneeing me in the face. Even so, her excitement is contagious, and I'm laughing along with her when I ask, "What?"

"I've got an idea."

My head snaps up and our eyes lock. "I'm listening."

Eleven
The Power of the Period
Jacob

I RUB MY EYES, watching the colorful dots dance in my vision. I'm not so dizzy anymore, but a headache is niggling at the back of my head like an awaiting thundercloud. It's been three days, so I can technically start taking Advil, but I'm afraid to. I don't know why. The Tylenol isn't really helping though. I should probably call off my ride with Stella and go back to bed. It would actually be a really good excuse since, after the fiasco that was yesterday, I'm not super keen on talking to Stella right now. I have no idea what she was thinking, though I could guess, but the look in her eyes was fucking carnal. I'd never seen anything so hot in my life. Then that blush, and I went molten. How a woman could switch from sex goddess to blushing virgin in a matter of seconds, is beyond my ability to comprehend, but Stella managed it. If she hadn't run off when she did, I might have made a gigantic mistake.

At least, I think it would have been a mistake.

To make matters worse, I had an explosive—and I mean that word literally—wet dream about her last night. And yes, I admit it, I've had wet dreams about Stella before. She's a pretty girl, and I'm a guy, so I just chalked it up to being a normal reaction to hanging out with her all the time. I never allowed myself to dwell on it because she's my best friend and off—fucking—limits. But now, after what the guys said, and that look she gave me yesterday, it's seriously screwing with my head. I can't stop thinking about it—her kneeling at my feet, lips wrapped around my cock. Her big brown eyes on mine, tears leaking down either side of her face, as I ram it down her throat and she moans in pleasure.

Fuck. I rearrange myself, hoping she doesn't notice the growing bulge in my pants. I need to tamp this shit down now, or I'm going to have a raging hard-on by the time she picks me up. As if things weren't already going to be awkward enough.

As if riding on my thoughts, Stella's faded-red Honda turns into the lot. No use turning back now.

Stella stops at the bottom of the steps and leans over the passenger seat to greet me. "Check it out, front door service," she says with a wide smile. Someone else wouldn't have noticed the way her eyes don't light up or hear the subtle tremor beneath her words, but I know her too well. She's nervous and trying to hide it.

I slide into the passenger seat with a clipped, "Thanks." Stella's wearing a little blue sun dress today that isn't at all revealing but hugs her breasts and dips in to show off her tiny waist. I have this sudden and disconcerting urge to run my fingers down her sides, skimming her breasts, and tracing the line of her waist to that perfect curve where her waist and hips meet. My fingers inch for a pencil so I can draw her.

She gives me another strained smile and starts out of the lot. It's quiet for a while, neither of us knowing how to break the mounting tension. I rack my brain for something—anything—to talk about. It shouldn't be this hard. I always have stuff to talk about with Stella, but it's like my cock has taken over my brain, and I can't think of anything else.

Finally, Stella breaks the silence. "So about yesterday."

And now I'm wishing we could go back to silence. "You really don't need to explain," I say, even though I'm curious what excuse she's conjured up because no way is she going to tell me the truth.

"No. It's fine. It's stupid. I had just realized that I started my period early."

Fuuuucckkk! I let my head fall back against the headrest. This is my punishment. God is punishing me for looking at my best friend's boobs.

"I didn't have anything with me," she continues, seemingly oblivious to my torment, "and things were getting kind of mushy."

Lord, if you could just send a lightning bolt my way, that'd be great.

"And," she keeps going, because why the hell not? "Things were starting to leak and—"

I bolt upright. "I get it, Stella. Alright. Please, for the love of all that is holy, please stop talking about your freaking period." I pinch the bridge of my nose. This is not helping my headache. A few seconds of silence pass, and I sneak a peek at Stella.

She's smirking like a kid who'd set a tack in the teacher's chair. "You sure? Cause you don't even want to know what happened when I got into the car."

"I swear to god, Stella, I will jump out of this car—"

"Okay, okay. You don't have to be such a man-baby about it. Periods are a perfectly natural—"

I reach for the door handle.

"Alright," she yells, slapping my shoulder and laughing her ass off. "I'll stop."

Lightly smacking her back, I holler, "Get off me, woman!" She does some sort of samurai maneuver and whacks me one last time before setting her hand back on the steering wheel.

I relax into my seat—tension abated, if not completely dissolved, and when I glance back at my friend, this time, the smile she's wearing is real.

Huh. I never thought I'd be so happy to talk about a woman's period.

Twelve

Who is This Girl, and Where Has She Been All My life?

Stella

Charlie's a freaking genius. Not only did her little plan work like a charm, but it broke some of the tension between Jacob and me. We're actually having a normal conversation by the time we arrive at the only class we share: Graphic fiction. It's a class where you learn how to create a graphic novel, or at least that's the goal. We've yet to do much of anything, but the semester's only just begun, so I'm hoping to start soon. Of course, Jacob and I took the class expecting to pair up—my writing, his art. In hindsight, that may not have been the best decision.

The English department is essentially a giant square building surrounding a courtyard. It's a nicely laid out area with potted flowers and picnic tables. It's usually fairly quiet, as we English majors prefer to spend more time writing and reading than talking, but today a small, yet noisy, group of guys has commandeered one of the nearby picnic tables. I recognize a few of them from the party last weekend, but one pair of pretty blue eyes, in particular, catch my attention. For a moment, we just hold each other's gaze, then Dean excuses himself from the group and struts my way. When he smiles, it's warm and open, yet I can also see a bit of mischief in the glint of his eyes. My heart is pumping like I just ran a 5K.

Did it suddenly get hot? I tug at the front of my dress and Dean's eyes follow, studying my chest, then roaming down my figure with undisguised interest. I should probably be offended by his unabashed perusal of my body, but instead, it makes me feel pretty.

Jacob tugs at my elbow. "Come on, Stells. We're going to be late."

I shoot Jacob a glare that says "back off," and he drops my arm. We are going to be late, but hell if I care. Dean Taylor is coming over to talk to me.

"Hi," Dean says.

"Hi," I reply, stupidly. Come on, Stells, where's that brain when you need it? *Probably hiding out in my vagina.*

Dean hoists his backpack a little higher onto his shoulder, making the muscle in his biceps bunch. Damn. When the hell did veins become so sexy? I'm afraid I might be drooling.

"I'm Dean," he says. "We met the other night."

"I remember." I smile.

Dean's eyes crinkle at the corners. He nods at Jacob. "What's up?"

"Hey," is all Jacob says before tugging on my arm again, a little more forcefully this time. "We've got to go, Stella."

I lay a hand on Jacob's arm. "Save a seat for me, okay? I'll be right in."

Jacob makes a sound that can only be described as Neanderthal-ish and heads into the lecture hall.

The double doors crash closed behind us, and Dean lets out a breath. "I don't think he likes me very much."

I wave a hand dismissively. "Ignore Jacob. He's just a little overprotective."

"Like an older brother?" he asks, brows raised.

Oh my god. He's totally hitting on me. This incredibly sexy guy is hitting on me. "Something like that," I say, surprised by the flirty tone of my voice. *Go, Stella.*

"So, is he going to get mad if I ask you out, then?"

"Does it matter?" *Who is this vixen and where the hell did she come from?*

He chuckles and runs his thumb back and forth along his bottom lip, his eyes on my mouth, and says, "Not at all."

He must have placed some sort of spell on me because, for a moment, I am mesmerized by the glide of that thumb across his soft pink lip. I don't even realize that I'm biting my own lip until I'm hit with a sting of pain. I release it, breaking the spell.

Dean lets out a breath. "How about Friday around six?"

"Friday sounds great." I extend my hand in the universal gesture for let me give you my digits, and he hands over his phone. I plug in my number and hand it back. I'm grinning so hard my cheeks hurt.

"Friday," he says.

I nod. "It's a date."

Thirteen
Commander Stardust and Her Rodent Steed
Jacob

HE ASKED HER OUT. I can tell by the shit-eating grin she's been sporting the entire class. Even so, when we're dismissed, I still find myself asking, "What did he want?"

"Who, Dean?" she asks, as if it wasn't obvious.

"Don't be a smart ass. Yes, Dean." I roll my eyes at his name because fuck that guy.

She hugs her laptop to her chest and sways like a little girl. I'm not going to lie, it's fucking adorable, but then she has to say, "He asked me on a date," and screw it all up.

"Are you going?" I ask because I'm a masochist and I have to hear her say it.

She stuffs her laptop into her backpack and swings it over her shoulder pausing only long enough to say, "Yep," before strolling out of the classroom.

"Oh-oh, I've got it," Stella says, bouncing on her butt like a three-year-old. "We can show Commander Stardust riding into battle—her face all berserker-like here." She sets a card at the top left corner of the page. "Then the rest of the page can be a long shot of her knights riding their rodent steeds into battle behind her."

I quirk a brow. "Rodent steeds?"

"It's my story. I can call them whatever I want," she says, folding her arms across her chest in a way that pushes her breasts out. The tips of her nipples press against the thin cotton of her dress. The urge to reach out and graze my finger along the point is verging on unbearable. I have to force myself to look away before the aching bulge in my pants becomes too obvious.

I am not looking at my best friend's boobs. I am not looking at my best friend's boobs.

Rubbing a hand over my face, I try to return my attention to the note cards we have strewn all over the floor of my living room.

So far, we've tried three different ways to sort Stella's book, a campy space opera, into panels that I can draw for our graphic novel class. First, we tried cutting up a print-up of her novel to organize it that way, but it only took us about 3 seconds to mix up the pieces and lose our place. Next, we tried using pre-made panel sheets which, in my opinion, amounted to creative suicide. So now, we're cutting up note cards and gluing them onto paper to represent the panels.

"Alright, rodent steeds. Got it." I quickly sketch a few lines to represent the army's position on the page.

Stella's already moved on to reading the next part of the story, her excitable demeanor not at all fitting for doing schoolwork. She's been like this since Dean asked her out yesterday morning, and it's getting on my nerves. She's gone out with guys before—maybe not for a while, but still. What makes him so fucking special? "I don't like him," I tell her for the five billionth time.

She doesn't need to ask who I'm talking about. "Yeah, you mentioned that," she says, not even giving a shit enough to raise her eyes and look at me.

"I'm serious, Stella. The guy's a player. Everybody says so." That's not exactly true but, considering ninety percent of the guys on the team are, it's a safe bet.

"First," she holds up her index finger, "I'm going on a date with him, not marrying him. And second," up goes another finger, "who's to say I'm not just in it for a little fun too?"

Wha-huh? She did not just say that.

My thoughts must have shown on my face because she shakes her head. "Guys always think every girl is on the hunt for their future husband, but that's just a bunch of misogynistic bullshit. Women like sex too, you know?"

An image of her and Dean flashes in my mind and something in my stomach twists. "So, you're planning to have sex with him?" I say, cringing at the panic in my voice.

She rolls her eyes. "I'm planning to have fun. That's all."

I let out the breath I'd been holding and sag against the edge of the coffee table.

"If we end up having sex, we end up having sex. I'll just wait and see how the cards fall."

And there goes my stomach again.

Stella groans and slaps her book on the floor, sending note cards flying. "I'm getting tired of re-reading this book. Can we do something else?"

"Sure." I start to stack all the papers and note cards into a pile. "What do you want to do?"

She slumps back onto the carpet and stretches like a cat.

Why is that so damn sexy? I must be losing my mind.

"I don't know." She rolls onto her side, resting her head on her hand. "What do you want to do?"

So many things, says my inner horn-dog. *Shut up.* "Can I draw you?"

She tilts her head and gives me a flirty smirk, though I doubt she realizes she's doing it. "You want to draw me?"

I shrug it off as if my fingers aren't itching to sketch her. It's an intimate thing, drawing someone—the way you peruse their body and recreate it on paper. It's pretty much as close to touching someone as you can get without actual physical contact. And I really want to touch her. Part of me expected this newfound attraction to Stella to be short-lived. That things would go back to the way they were. Not that I hadn't found her attractive before. I've always thought she was beautiful, but it was external—the recognition of something beautiful that I couldn't have in that way. But Malcolm's words the other day flipped some sort of switch in my head that I can't seem to turn back off. It's driving me crazy because this is Stella, my best friend since third grade. I can't afford to screw that up.

But I swear to god, if that asshole Dean touches her, I'm going to tear his fucking arms off.

"Sure," she says with a tiny, almost shy smile. "It's been a while."

Not as long as she thinks. I've had her pose for me in the past—portraits and such, but it's more fun to draw people when they're being themselves and not posing—so I get sneaky. Sometimes I'll go to the park with my sketchbook and do quick gesture drawings of people doing everyday things. It's sort of my happy place. I sketch Stella all the time, but it's usually after the fact, like I take a picture in my head of some expression or action that grabs my attention and sketch it out when I'm alone. It's funny, I probably have a billion sketches of Stella going all the way back to when we were kids, but I don't think I have a single one of Emma or any other girl I've dated. I'm not sure I want to unpack that at the moment.

I jump up and grab my big sketchbook and a tin full of pencils out of my room, then plop back down on the floor in front of her.

"How do you want me?" she asks.

"The way you are is fine, if you're comfortable."

She says it's fine and I begin. Most people get caught up in the details when they draw—working through an image section by section until they've pieced the whole thing together. But that's not seeing the forest for the trees. You want to start big—lay out the overall form and proportions—and work your way down to the details. So that's how I begin—sketching out her structure, the shape of her body, the tilt of her head. It isn't until I begin adding the details to her face that I realize she's let her head fall, so it rests on her arms and closed her eyes. I'm not sure if she's asleep, but being able to study her like this is kind of freeing, even if I am feeling like a bit of a creeper. She looks peaceful. Her hair is fanned out behind her like a dark halo, and her lashes are so long they graze the dusting of freckles along her cheekbones. Her lips are slightly parted as if she was about to speak when sleep overtook her. I spend the longest time on her lips, fighting to capture every nuance. It's a long time before I set my sketchbook and pencils down on the coffee table.

I stretch and pop my neck. When I turn my attention back to Stella, I'm shocked to find her awake and looking at me. Our eyes lock and my breath catches in my throat. It's as if she's seen into the heart of me and is reflecting my longing and fear back at me in her gaze. We don't speak or smile and the longer we stay this way the harder my heart is pounding. I'm breathing so hard I'm practically panting, but I can't seem to get enough air. Across from me, Stella's chest rises and falls as rapidly as my own, telling me, I'm not the only one affected.

"Jake," Stella says, the word barely a whisper, but it breaks the spell all the same.

"Yeah."

She pushes up onto her knees. "It's getting late. I should go." She moves to get up, but before I can think better of it, I'm standing in front of her, my hand outstretched in a silent offer for help. She places her palm in mine, and the brush of her soft skin against my calloused fingers sets off fireworks in my chest. As soon as she's up, I release her hand and let mine fall back to my side, fingers flexing as the memory of her touch settles like a ghost upon my palm.

Neither of us speaks as Stella stuffs her things into her backpack, and I walk her to the door. Pausing, she turns around to face me. This is when I'd usually give her a hug and say goodbye, but that seems wrong now somehow. God, I hate this awkwardness. I want to kiss her so badly it's like an ache in my chest. I can't stop myself from imagining how soft her lips would be, how she would taste. Without thought, I run the pad of my thumb along her smooth lower lip. They part on a sharp intake of air, and I have the urge to slip my thumb into her mouth so she can wrap those beautiful lips around it and suck it like she would my cock. Fuck if that isn't getting me hard just imagining it. Instead, I move my hand so I'm cupping her cheek. At some point, I stepped closer, or she did. I'm not sure. Our bodies are still inches apart, but the space between them is charged.

Our eyes meet, and I'm not sure if it's fear or shock or something else that I see there, but it's like she's grabbed my heart and squeezed. Her eyes fall to my lips, and back again. Does she want me to kiss her? I lean forward, closing the gap between us so our lips are almost, but not quite, touching. Her moist, hot breath is like a caress. I turn away from her mouth, so my lips graze her cheek. My mouth's gone dry, and my cock is pressing painfully against my zipper. I want her so badly right now I can't think straight. If I don't put a stop to this, it's going to mess everything up. I can't just throw away ten years of friendship because I'm horny. Kissing Stella would be a mistake. I think… maybe… I have no fucking idea.

I back away, gaze still fixed on hers, and huffing air like I just ran the bleachers. She blinks as if coming out of a dream, then lowers her eyes and says, "Uh… Bye," before spinning around, hauling the door open and dashing down the stairs.

"Bye," I reply, but it's too late. She's already gone.

Fourteen
Getting a Little Help from My Friends
Stella

This feels wrong somehow, like after what happened last night, by going out with Dean, I'm sort of cheating on Jacob. Which is crazy because nothing actually happened—well, something happened, but hell if I know what. What I do know was that was possibly the single hottest experience of my life, and we didn't even kiss.

But he wanted to. At least, I'm pretty sure he wanted to.

What's driving me crazy is trying to puzzle out why he backed away.

Did he think I didn't want to kiss him? Did he have a change of heart? Did he suddenly realize he was making a mistake?

Ugh, I'm such a mess.

"Stella?"

Charlie's voice is firm, like she's been trying to get my attention for a while and is getting frustrated.

"Yeah, sorry," I say.

"What's going on with you today? I expected you to be excited, but you just seem..."

"Distraught," Emma supplies.

Charlie points a finger at the other woman and nods. "Distraught."

Nobody knows about what happened last night. I didn't tell Emma, for obvious reasons, but I'm not sure why I didn't say something to Charlie. Probably because I don't really understand what happened myself. It's a moot point because I can't talk about it now anyway, so I'm going to have to lie. "I'm just super tired. I didn't sleep well last night."

Emma nods, intent on whatever she's reading on her phone. Charlie tilts her head and squints her eyes like she doesn't quite believe me but is letting it go for now. "How do you like the dress?" Charlie gestures toward the blood-red sheath dress she brought for me to try on.

I turn around to look in Emma's full-length mirror, and run my hands down the front, marveling at the way the dress hugs my body. It's a gorgeous satiny material with straps that crisscross down the open back to just above my ass. Problem is, that ass may fall out the other end because the skirt is so short it barely covers it. "You don't think this is a little skimpy?" I ask.

Emma scoffs. "There's nothing wrong with letting your inner ho-bag out to play once in a while. You hide your body too much. You're hot. Own it."

Charlie giggles while I give Emma the evil eye.

She doesn't even flinch. "Listen, when we act like we're ashamed of our sexuality, we're just buying into the puritanical bullshit invented by the patriarchy to take away the power it gives us. Don't let the man hold you down."

"Word," says Charlie, and the girls fist bump.

I shake my head because what do I even say to that? "Seriously, Emma, are you sure you want to be an actress and not a politician or something?" I'm only half-joking. Emma could talk Hitler under the table.

"Nah." She waves a hand in dismissal. "Being an actress will be much more fun. Anyway, have you seen those awful she-suits female politicians wear? No, thank you."

"So, we have the dress," Charlie says, handing me back my clothes to change back into. She taps a finger against her bottom lip. That's Charlie's code for "I'm about to shake things up."

I freeze, dread curling in my gut.

"Now about your hair…"

I have been primped and plucked and powdered to within an inch of my life, and gazing at myself in the mirror, I have to say… I don't look too shabby.

And my hair looks fucking fabulous. I run my finger along the ends of my now shoulder-length dark auburn hair. I would have never picked this color myself, but Charlie was right. It adds a little color to my pale skin and brings out the amber in my eyes. Honestly, I can't remember the last time I felt so pretty.

Charlie claps her hands excitedly. "Dean's going to pee himself."

"Uh, thanks?" I reply with a smirk.

Emma laughs. "Not exactly what she was going for, Charlie." She grips me by the shoulders and turns me around. "Text us to let us know things are okay. Code words are 'Do we have homework in psychology?'"

"I don't think that's going to be necessary."

"Just because he's charming and has a pretty face doesn't mean he isn't a total douchebag one-on-one. Trust me."

I nod, bowing to Emma's expertise because she's probably dated more guys in the past year than I have in my whole life.

Emma continues, "I have to babysit tonight, but I'll keep checking my phone."

"Me too," says Charlie.

Emma nods. "Just keep texting if you don't hear back and need some saving."

A knock sounds on the door and all three of us jump. Laughing, I give them hugs and make my way to the door. When I open it, Dean is waiting in jeans and a gray button-down that complements his eyes.

His face breaks into a smile that is nothing short of predatory when he sees me. "Wow, you look amazing." He runs a finger along my now auburn locks. "And I love your hair."

"Thanks," I say. My cheeks are hot and I'm grinning so hard it's liable to break my face, but I look amazing, so who the hell cares.

"Milady," he says and extends his arm for me to take. I giggle like a doofus and want to smack myself, but I can't help it. I'm all hopped up, like I drank twenty espressos in the past five minutes, and it's taking all my willpower not to bounce around the parking lot like a sexed-up version of Tigger.

Dean's car is a Ford SUV the size of my living room. It's also so high off the ground there is no way I'm climbing up there without flashing my panties to the world. I'm about to tell him so when Dean opens the door, wraps his hands around my waist, and lifts me up onto the seat as if I weigh nothing.

"Thanks," I say, my voice embarrassingly breathy.

One corner of Dean's lip tips up into a smirk, and he gives me a wink. Then, he shuts my door, jogs around the front of the SUV and hops up into the driver's seat with ease. He gives me a smile that says, "Yeah, I'm the shit," and I can't help but call him out on it.

"I could have jumped in that easily too if I was six feet tall and not wearing a mini dress."

He throws his head back and laughs. It's deep and throaty, and I'm glad I'm sitting down because I'm not sure my legs would hold me up right now. "Most definitely," he replies. He throws an arm around my back and pulls me across the seat, so I'm crushed up against his side.

"I don't like you so far away," he says, with another wink.

Part of me wants to rally at the presumptuousness of the gesture. The other part wonders if I'd fit on his lap.

The restaurant Dean takes me to is Korean barbecue, which I didn't even know was a thing, but Dean says it's awesome, so I'm willing to give it a shot. We order at a long counter and take one of those little stands with a number to set on our table so they can find us when the food is ready. He grabs us a couple of waters and leads me through the double doors and into the most beautiful outdoor space I've ever seen. Seating areas are set up into clusters, some on platforms others on the grass. There are planters brimming with flowers and ivy and a simple stone fountain in the center with lily pads and actual koi fish swimming in it. The best part though, is the hundreds of white lights strung overhead that lend the space an ethereal ambiance.

"Pretty awesome, right?" Dean asks and all I can do is nod. He takes my hand and leads me to a round table, then pulls out my seat before taking his own.

Is this guy for real? I scan the courtyard for a camera crew that must be filming this elaborate joke, but besides the girls across the way, making duck faces at their phones, there isn't a camera in sight.

Dean rests his chin on clasped hands. "Are you looking for somebody?"

"Uh, Ashton Kutcher?"

"What?" he asks, shaking his head as if the words might make more sense if he scrambled them up.

"Nothing." I wave a hand. "Just a bad joke. This place is really gorgeous. I can't believe I'd never heard of it before."

"Yeah. It's my favorite restaurant. Sometimes I'll come out here during the day and order a coffee just so I can sit out here and study."

I probably look like a psycho, but I can't stop smiling. This is all so perfect. "So is the food as good as the decor?" I ask.

"Better." He gives me one of those smirks that I'm quickly learning is his trademark, as he fans out a napkin and drapes it over his lap.

I chuckle. "He opens doors, pulls out chairs and places a napkin in his lap at dinner. Dean Taylor, you are a mother's dream."

"I will attribute the napkin to my mom. She was like a tiny tyrant, that woman. I am twice her size, and she still terrifies me." He fakes a shiver.

I can't help but laugh. "Maybe it's a mom thing because I swear my dad is terrified of her. I suspect that was a major reason behind their divorce; the man got tired of never winning an argument."

The smile he gives me is warm and open, and a knot tightens in my chest at how beautiful it is. *But it isn't Jacob's,* whispers the nasty little voice in my head. The same one who has pushed away every guy who's ever tried to get close.

Not this time.

If he wants me, he needs to let me know—like actually make a move. I can't keep putting my life on hold waiting for him to get a clue.

"The opening of doors and all that is because of my dad," Dean continues, obviously oblivious to my inner turmoil. "He beat that shit into my head from the time I could walk. It used to drive me crazy, but I've learned to appreciate it as I've gotten older."

"Hmm," I say, tapping my chin in mock contemplation. "I wonder why?"

He ducks his head, gaze meeting mine from beneath dark lashes, and fidgets with his utensils. "Would you believe me if I said, it was for the satisfaction I get from being a gentleman?"

"Uh, no," I sputter.

He huffs out a laugh. "Well, then let's just say it has served me well with the ladies and leave it at that."

"Now that, I believe."

The server brings our food, and it smells like heaven—sort of spicy and sweet at the same time. We both got the pork because Dean was adamant that it was the best thing on the menu. I pick up my fork because I'm humiliatingly bad at using chopsticks, take a bite, and moan. It tastes even better than it smells.

Dean grins. "See, I told you."

"I will never doubt you again," I say and dig in.

Fifteen
Here Comes Mister Neanderthal
Jacob

Why did I let these guys talk me into going out? I'm miserable and making everyone else around me miserable by association. I've been sitting at this table in Melvin's—a bar plus old school arcade and usually my favorite place to go—for ten minutes with close to a dozen people, and I couldn't tell you a single thing anyone has said. It's all a little overwhelming: the noise and colored lights blinking from all corners as if vying for attention. There's nowhere I can look to get away from it. Stand-up arcade games line the walls and are set up in clusters between tables. The bar looks like something snagged right out of an old spaghetti western, but the shelves behind it, where all the liquor bottles and glasses are displayed, are lit with LEDs that constantly shift from one color to the next.

I'm still getting dizzy spells so drinking's off the table, and just the thought of getting up to peruse the arcade games turns my stomach. The whole point of coming out tonight was to get my mind off Stella's date with Dean, but that's been a complete bust because even here surrounded by all these people, I can't think about anything else. I keep wondering where he took her and if she's having a good time. And of course, being the asshole I am, hoping she's having a terrible time, so she won't ever go out with him again. It's like a song I can't get out of my head, playing over and over and driving me crazier by the minute.

Malcolm pats my shoulder, breaking me from my spiraling thoughts. "You want a beer, man?" he asks.

"No. I'm good, thanks."

Malcolm pushes out his chair, its legs screeching across the wood floor. He turns for the bar, and stops cold. "Whoa," is all he says, and I follow his line of sight to the front door where Stella, looking like a fucking goddess, is waiting to show her ID and holding Dean the dick head's hand.

"Son of a bitch," I say a little too loudly because it draws the attention of pretty much everyone at our table.

A couple of the guys whistle, and I snap at them to shut up, while Charlie jumps from her seat and runs over to greet her. Stella's all smiles as she hugs her friend, which blows my hope that she wouldn't have a good time to smithereens. I don't think I've ever seen her like this—all dressed to the nines, except at prom, and I was too focused on getting into Maddy Peterson's pants that night to remember much about it. She's wearing a slinky red dress that is entirely too short and tight, and so damn sexy, it's melting my brain. She changed her hair too—cut and dyed it a mahogany brown that looks amazing next to her pale skin.

I scrub a hand over my face. All this time. I had so many chances with her and never even considered making a move, and now that I've started to consider it, she's with another guy. Figures.

Stella's chatting with Charlie as she steps up to the bar, Dean's hand resting a little too low on her back. The jealousy is like poison bubbling through my veins and setting my whole body on edge. I'm clenching my fists so tightly, my nails dig into my palms. It's taking everything I have not to race over there and deck him for touching her. The intensity of my feelings is a little frightening. I've been jealous before, sure, but I've never wanted to rip a man's hand off just for touching a girl I like.

But she's not just any girl. She's Stella. The one constant in my life since I was ten. She belongs with me, belongs to me. And if that makes me a domineering bastard, so be it. I don't care. Because I belong to her too.

"Hey," Malcolm says, snapping me back to the present. He's facing me, shoulder to shoulder, his expression unreadable, but his voice is a soft warning. "You're staring." I drag my gaze away from Stella to him. "And you look about five seconds away from murder. Breathe."

I squeeze my eyes shut and take a few deep breaths. Fuck, did anyone else notice? When I open my eyes to meet Malcolm's again, they're creased with concern.

I rub my temples to ease the ache building there. "Thanks."

"Are you alright?" he asks.

I laugh, but it's hollow and joyless. "I feel like I'm going crazy."

"Over Stella?"

I nod.

"Kind of picked a bad time to start being interested in her." He bumps his shoulder into mine just hard enough to throw me off-balance, and I bump him back.

"It's your damn fault." I scrub a hand through my hair—if I keep this up, I'm going to be bald before I'm thirty. "I never thought about her that way until you and Ryan told me she was into me. And now I'm losing my frigging mind over her being with another guy."

He shrugs. "Sorry, not sorry. You're an idiot for not seeing it sooner."

"I'll agree with that," I reply.

Charlie hurries back to our table, and that's when Stella finally turns her gaze my way. Our eyes lock and a shock of electricity jolts through my chest. She feels it too. I can see it in her eyes and the way her lips fall open on an inhale—just like they did the other night. I think I've regressed 10,000 years in the last ten minutes because all I want to do is walk over there, throw her over my shoulder, and carry her off like a goddamned caveman.

She looks away first—of course, she does—turning back to Dean as he presses another hand to the small of her back. They head our way. It's obvious Stella's looking everywhere but at me. She's got her hands clasped together so tightly her knuckles are turning white. I'm fairly sure I'm the cause of her discomfort, though

I can't decide if that's a good or bad thing. By the death glare Dean's giving me, I'm guessing he's not too happy about it. So, I'll go with good.

They greet everyone with hugs and friendly pats on the back, and I just sit here because I truly have no idea how I'm supposed to act right now. Ignore them? Plaster on a fake smile? Wave? Can I give Stella a hug, or would that be too weird since I'm pretty sure Dean's on to me?

Indecision has me frozen in place. Jesus, I am not this guy. I don't get all moony and nervous with girls, period. And I sure as hell don't worry about whether Stella's dates think I'm stepping into their territory. Anyway, it's just a date—their first date—and I'm her best friend, so I should just hug her because I always hug her and—

Shit, she's walking over here.

"Hey, Jake." She gives me a tiny wave.

I search for Dean. He's still standing with Malcolm and some of the other guys. I can tell by Malcolm's wild hand motions he's telling a funny story, and keeping Dean occupied, no doubt to give us a couple of minutes.

"Hey," I reply, shooting to my feet a little too fast. I freeze, close my eyes and breathe through the dizziness.

Stella grips my shoulders. "You, okay?"

"Yeah. Just stood up too fast." I move to run my fingers through my hair and stop—Stella will read that move in two seconds flat. Instead, I reach out and tug a lock of her hair. "I like this."

"Yeah?" She smooths down her waves and beams at me, making my heart lurch and my chest ache.

I have this sudden urge to run a finger down her bare arm and take her hand. And maybe it's because I'm so focused on controlling my body that I lose control of my mouth and say, "You look beautiful."

As soon as the words are out of my mouth, I know I've fucked up.

Stella takes a step back, her eyes wide, fingers gripping the fabric of her skirt. Is she breathing?

I'm not.

I've overstepped. Fuck. Why can't I keep my stupid mouth shut? Especially after what happened yesterday. I'm probably messing with her head at this point. And she's on a date—with Dean the douchebag, sure—but still. I want to say something to break this tension, but my mind has gone blank. I just stand there gaping at her like a giant idiot.

"What's going on?" Dean says, breaking our stand-off, and for once I'm actually happy to see the guy because that was intense.

"Uh... Nothing," Sella answers. "Jacob reminded me we have a test on Monday that I completely forgot about." She gives him a convincingly sheepish look, and I have to say, I'm impressed. I never realized she was such a good liar.

Impressive acting notwithstanding, Dean doesn't appear convinced. Brows furrowed and the muscle in his jaw clenching like he literally wants to bite my head off, Dean's gaze volleys between the two of us. Finally, he turns back to Stella. "Did he say something to upset you?"

Not missing a beat, she says, "Yeah. That we have a test Monday. I told you that." She claps her hands. "So, are we going to play some Donkey Kong or what?"

"Sure," Dean replies with a smile, but his voice is strained. "Give me two minutes and I'll meet you there, okay?"

Stella looks between the two of us warily, then takes a hesitant step back. "Oh—okay," she says. Lips drawn into a thin line, she crosses her arms and heads toward the machines on the other side of the bar.

In a blink, Dean is on me, his fist curled in my shirt, face so close I can smell the peppermint on his breath. "What the fuck, Gonzales?"

Now, I'm facing a dilemma. I really want to bash his face in, but if I do, I'll get suspended from the team. Worse, if *he* gets a hit in... Well, I can't imagine that's good for a concussion. But backing down isn't really in my DNA, so I try to play it cool. I point a finger at the hand clutching my shirt, give him a smirk and say, "I suggest you take your hands off of me, Taylor, before this gets ugly."

Thank god for our friendly neighborhood Super Malcolm, who flies to the rescue. "Whoa," he shouts, shouldering his way through the crowd. He presses between us and lays a hand on Dean's shoulder, but when he speaks it's to the both of us. "I am not losing to fucking Duke next week because you two dumb asses got suspended. Hand's off, Dean. I mean it."

Dean hesitates a moment, his eyes flitting from me to Malcolm. "You stay the fuck away from her," Dean says with a shove and releases my shirt.

I laugh. "Whatever, man. Stella's been my best friend since elementary school. You've known her for like—what—five minutes? Don't start making demands, bro, 'cause if she has to choose, it'll be me." I jab a finger into his chest, just hard enough to give him a little push. His center of gravity's off, so he has to take a step back. It's petty, I know, but I get the tiniest bit of satisfaction from that, even more so from the stunned expression on his face. Obviously, he wasn't aware of Stella's and my history.

Ignoring him, I take my seat, trying to appear unfazed, though the room is spinning again. My vision's all blurry and my head is getting heavy.

I rub my eyes, and when I look up, Malcolm's standing over me, brows furrowed. Dean's already crossed the room and is standing beside Stella at the bar. Got to give it to the man; he's quick.

Malcolm ducks his head into my line of vision. "Jake, bro. You okay? I called your name like three times."

"What? Yeah," I say, trying to blink the cobwebs from my mind. I think I've hit my threshold for the night. My head is pounding again, and bone-weary exhaustion has swept through me. I need to go home. Taking out my phone, I put in a request for an Uber, and luckily, there's a guy nearby. I rise slowly in the hopes that the dizziness won't get worse and take a few deep breaths to clear my head before turning my attention to Malcolm. "I'm gonna cut out early. See you at the apartment."

He's eyeing me suspiciously. "Headache?"

"Nah," I lie, because he's like a mother hen, and while I appreciate his concern, I'm not in the mood for all his clucking right now. "Just tired."

He nods and we fist bump, and I wave goodbye to some of the others. Dean and I glare at each other as I pass, but no more words are spoken. I'm almost at the door when the urge hits me to turn around. My stomach flips at the sight of Stella standing across the bar, watching me. She doesn't smile or wave, just examines me as though I'm a puzzle she's afraid she'll never solve. Every cell in my body is telling me to go talk to her and explain myself. But this isn't the time or the place, and I've caused enough trouble for the night. So, I give her a smirk and a lazy two-fingered salute, then turn back around and head out the door.

Sixteen
Oh, No, He Didn't!
Stella

"Tonight was fun," I say as we reach my door.

"Yeah." Dean smiles, but something's off. He rests a hand on the door next to me. I think he's going to kiss me, but instead, he asks, "Is there something going on between you and Gonzales?"

I blink, confused. "Jacob?"

He nods.

"We're friends. Why? Did he say something to you?" I ask. If he threatened Dean or pulled some other overprotective bull shit, I'm going to kick his ass.

"Just friends?"

"Yes. Why?" I ask again.

Dean cocks his head, eyes squinting slightly as if he's trying to read my mind. Finally, he replies, "Because he doesn't look at you like a friend, is all?"

I snort out a very unladylike laugh.

"You think that's funny?"

"I think it's absurd," I reply. Though considering what happened the other night and Jacob telling me I looked beautiful, I'm not as sure as I pretend to be. He's never once said that to me. I might look cute or even great, but never beautiful. "Jake and I are just friends," I continue, not knowing if I'm trying to convince him or me. "If he's giving you shit, I'm sorry. He can be an overprotective ass at times, but he's just trying to watch out for me." Which isn't really true. For as long as we've been friends, Jacob has always jumped in to protect me if a guy was being a jerk, but he never seemed to give a damn about my relationships before. Not that I had many.

Dean's posture relaxes somewhat, so something I said must have eased his mind a little—though now mine is blowing up with questions. "Did he say something nasty?" I ask because I really need to find out what set off this line of questioning.

Dean stuffs his hands into the pockets of his jeans and shrugs. It makes him appear younger and a little vulnerable. "Just that you've been friends a long time and…" he hesitates.

Oh hell no. He is not stopping there. "And?"

Dean reaches up to scratch the back of his neck. Gaze fixed on the floor, he says, "He said that if you had to make a choice between him and me, you'd choose him."

Asshole. I grit my teeth to hold back the string of expletives ready to explode from my mouth. I'm trembling. My whole body is drawn taut, like a guitar string on the verge of snapping. And though I'm aware that Dean is still speaking to me, I can't hear a word through the whooshing of blood in my ears. Jacob's so sure that I will follow him no matter what, like a puppy dog gobbling up whatever little scraps of attention he's willing to give me.

Fuck him!

I get up on my tiptoes and pull Dean in for a kiss. His eyes flare wide in surprise, but he doesn't stop me. His lips are soft and teasing, giving me a taste, then pulling away, leaving me wanting more. When his tongue flits against the seam of my lips, I eagerly open for him. Our tongues stroke and caress, and he tastes so good, like peppermint. I lose myself in his kiss, my anger dissipating with each sweet nibble and stroke. Then he ruins it by gripping my ass and thrusting his erection against my belly.

I jerk away, my spine cracking into the door panel. The flash of pain clears my head further. "Thank you for tonight," I say and grasp the door handle.

Dean's eyes are hooded, his blue gaze an inferno ready to set my loins on fire. He leans a shoulder against the wall. "I could come in," he says, all smooth and self-assured.

"Another night," I say, hoping I don't sound too eager to leave.

"Another night then." He gives me a peck on the cheek. "I'll call you?"

"Yeah."

He nods and smiles, though his eyes still have the droopy lusty air about them that's making me a little nervous, though I couldn't say why. "Alright. Talk to you later."

"Bye," I say and step through my doorway. I wait until I hear his car pull out and grab my keys. I think it's time I had a conversation with a certain egotistical football player.

Seventeen

Sabotage!

Jacob

I'M WOKEN UP BY someone pounding on my front door, and I don't know whether the building's on fire, or somebody's dying, or what, but my neighbors are going to flip their shit if I don't put a stop to it quickly. Hopping out of bed, I slip on a pair of jeans, not bothering to zip them up, and sprint for the door. I'm not sure what I expected to see when I opened it, but it was not Stella, still wearing her slinky dress, glaring at me like some pissed-off pixie.

I rub the sleep from my eyes. "Jesus, Stella. What's your problem?"

"What's my problem? What's my problem?" Her face scrunched up and beet red, Stella clenches her hands into fists at her sides. And that's when it hits me; she's *really* pissed, like when Margo Evan's spread a rumor in tenth grade that she slept with half the football team, pissed.

Not wanting to hash out whatever issue she has in my apartment entryway, I usher her inside. "What's going on?"

"You are an asshole," she says, punctuating each word. "That's what."

I open my mouth to speak, but she cuts me off.

"How dare you talk about me like that to Dean."

I try to run back over the conversation in my head to figure out what I said that would have gotten her so angry, but I'm coming up blank. Meanwhile, she's pacing the room and cursing up a storm.

"I am not your lapdog," she says. "You don't get to keep me bottled up for yourself only to bring out when you want someone to stroke your ego. Not anymore."

"Stella, sweety," I grip her by the shoulders, forcing her to stop and face me. "You're not making any sense."

She wrenches herself from my grasp. "I am not your 'sweety,' and I am not your girlfriend," she says, her voice breaking on the last word. "And you have no right to interfere in my relationships when you have made it abundantly clear that you don't want to have one with me." Tears stream down her cheeks and her hands are shaking, and I'm so goddamned confused.

I splay my arms in surrender. "Please, Stella. I don't understand."

"You told Dean that I'd choose you."

I pause for a second, trying to make sense of this, but I'm still coming up short. "You're my best friend. He's a guy you just met who was telling me to stay away from you. So yeah, I told him if anyone was going to get kicked to the curb, it would be him."

"Why? Why would you say that? Are you so threatened by another guy in my life that you feel the need to sabotage it?"

"That's not what I was—"

"Bullshit. That's exactly what you were doing. I should have known the minute you told me I was beautiful. You have never—in the ten years that I've known you—said that word about me. Not once," she says between sobs. Stella grabs hold of her midsection, curling around it as though it pains her. "God, I'm so pathetic."

I shake my head, trying and failing to dislodge a memory of me telling her she was beautiful or even pretty. "I've always thought you were pretty."

She laughs, and it's so heartbreakingly cold, it's like a punch to the gut. "Yeah, right."

I reach a hand out to her, but she backs away. "It's true."

She raises her head, and for all that her eyes are red-rimmed and puffy; they're also determined, and I know what she's going to say before the words even leave her mouth. "Stay away from Dean and stay away from me."

She turns to leave, and I grab her by the arm, stalling her escape. "Please, Stella. Wait."

"Let go of me, Jacob," she says, not even turning her head to look at me.

"Please. Don't go. I'm sorry."

"I said let go of me."

"We can talk about this."

"I'm done talking." She tugs her arm from my grip and grabs the doorknob. I don't know what to do. My heart is trying to punch a hole in my chest, and I can't breathe. I dive for the door, slamming it back into the frame just as she opens it. "I was jealous. Alright." She turns her head away, refusing to look at me, but I continue anyway because if she leaves now, I'm afraid I'll never get her back. "You looked so beautiful, and he was touching you like… like you were his to touch, and I was so insanely jealous, I wanted to rip his goddammed arms off. Is that what you want to hear?"

Stella's head whips back around, her eyes two angry slits. "Do I want to hear that you were jealous? After pining over you for ten years, watching you fuck every pretty girl in sight and wondering," she takes a ragged breath, "wondering, what's so wrong with me?" she says, hand pounding her chest. "Why don't you see me? Now, someone else is interested in me, thinks I'm worth something, and I'm suddenly desirable."

"Stella—"

She slams both hands into me and I stumble back. "You fucked Emma, and I had to listen to it every night. Every fucking night I cried myself to sleep because I wasn't pretty enough." She shoves me again. "Because I would never be good enough for you." And again. "And now you're jealous? Fuck you."

She goes to shove me again, but this time I snag her wrists and clasp them against my chest. "I didn't know."

She glares at me. "You didn't care."

"Stella—"

She twists and tugs her arms, trying to break my grip. "Let go of me."

"Stella—"

"Let go of me, dammit," she screams.

But I don't let her go. I push her against the wall and crush my lips into hers.

Eighteen
That Took a Turn Toward the Unexpected
Stella

My head's such an emotional mess; it takes me a second to process what's happening. Jacob's kissing me, and I want to push him away. I should push him away. But I don't. I can't. I've wanted this, dreamed of this, for so long that my brain has short-circuited. I'm like a woman starved—desperate for his touch, his kiss, his warm body pressed up against mine. My arms slide up his torso and I wrap them around his neck, and this sets something off in him. His kisses become rougher, his touch frantic. The tip of his tongue teases my lips and I open for him, gasping as he thrusts his tongue into my mouth. This isn't sweet; it's carnal. Ten years of unrequited need pouring out of us in a rush of hands and tongues and teeth. I'm shaking. My body is on fire. I might implode from the overwhelming sensations.

Grasping my ass hard enough to bruise, he hauls me up, and I wrap my legs around him. Trapped between Jacob's body and the wall, I'm rendered immobile, unable to give or take anything more than he will allow. I happily relinquish control. In this moment, he owns me body and soul, and I can't get enough. He trails kisses across my jaw and down my neck. I lift my chin, a silent plea for more, and he gives it to me, licking and sucking and nipping. Reaching the curve where my neck and shoulder meet, he bites me, hard. I yelp from the pain, and he quickly soothes it with his tongue. My core is molten and slick with arousal. He grinds his erection against my sex, teasing my clit with every thrust. Already, the pressure is growing in my core, and with it my need. I need him inside of me now. But Jacob has other plans.

"Lift your arms," he whispers into my ear, his low voice sending shivers down my back. I do so without hesitation, and he sweeps my dress off over my head, leaving me in only my lacy black bra and thong panties. "Fuck," he groans as his eyes and hand roam over my torso. He doesn't even bother to remove my bra, only pulls down the cup to free my breast. Wet heat envelops my nipple as Jacob takes it into his mouth, first sucking it then lathing it with his tongue. He pulls down the other cup and does the same to that nipple while he kneads my other breast, rolling and pinching the hard bud between his fingers. Each sensation sends a jolt of electricity straight into my sex.

He's kissing my lips again, one hand still clutching my ass while the other moves down my stomach, pausing at the waistband of my panties. He's giving me a chance to object, but I'm too far gone for that now. I grasp his wrist and shove his hand beneath my waistband and further until his fingers skim my sex and he curses at discovering how wet I am. He pushes a finger into me, and I cry out at the invasion. Then he pulls it out again and slides my arousal up my center, eliciting another cry when he uses it to circle my clit, teasing and coaxing, keeping me on the edge and driving me crazy. Again, he slips a finger inside of me and out to circle my clit, back in and out and around, and in and out and around until my climax is hanging by a razor's edge and I'm begging him, "Please."

"What do you want, Stella?" he asks, breath hot against my ear, his voice taunting even as his fingers continue their torturous assault. "Tell me."

"I want to come," I beg. "Please."

"I like it when you beg," he says, pressing two fingers into me—filling me up. And it's so intense yet so frustrating I want to cry. He pumps his fingers into me, my climax building higher and higher with every thrust. "Come for me, Stella," he says, and presses his thumb into my clit.

And I detonate. My vision flashes white as I'm assaulted by waves of pleasure so intense, they're almost painful.

"I'm going to fuck you," he says, his fingers still pumping inside of me, milking every ounce of pleasure from my orgasm. "Say, yes."

"Yes," I gasp. He removes his fingers and fumbles with his back pocket, all the while kissing me. I reach between us and free his cock. It's thick and perfect, and I want it inside of me now. There's a drop of pre-cum leaking from the tip. Jacob lets out a hiss as I drag my finger across it and use the wetness to circle the head. He's pulled a condom out of somewhere and quickly sheathes himself. Pressing me hard against the wall, he pushes my panties aside and guides himself into me, slowly, as if he knows it's been a while and is trying not to hurt me. It feels so good, but I'm impatient, and I want him to pound into me right now, even though I know he's right to be careful. Once he's seated fully inside of me, he pauses and takes a breath. "Are you okay?" he asks, his voice raspy.

I nod. "Yes."

And he begins to move, slowly at first, pulling out almost to the tip and sinking back inside of me again. Out and in. I groan, savoring the sensation, at the same time about to crawl out of my skin—wanting more, needing more. But I'm at his mercy, pinned in place and unable to meet his thrusts.

"Please," I say, not caring that I'm begging, and he obliges, increasing his speed and power. He rolls his hips, rubbing my still sensitive clit, and another orgasm swells inside of me. It's all too much, overwhelming. I'm like a balloon ready to burst.

"Jacob," I yell, and whatever tether was holding him back snaps. He pounds into me furiously, our panting breaths and slapping skin echoing through the empty apartment. The pressure builds and builds. I can feel my release, taunting me, just out of reach. Then, I tip over the edge and fall. My climax crashes into me with such force, it ricochets throughout my body. Jacob's thrusts grow more erratic, drawing every last drop of pleasure from me even as he works to find his own. One final thrust and he roars as he comes, his orgasm so powerful I feel his cock spasm inside of me.

We stay like that for a time, holding each other as he grows soft inside of me. He pulls out and sets me on my feet but doesn't let go. He continues holding me and I wish I could stay like this forever.

"Hold on," he says and steps away to remove the condom.

Without his warmth enveloping me, I'm suddenly exposed and vulnerable. My hands tremble as I put my bra and panties to rights and drag my dress back over my head. Jacob comes back from the bathroom, his pants zipped and buttoned. He stops at the end of the hallway, and looks at me from across the room, not speaking or smiling, just staring at me as if he has no idea what to do with me. My eyes sting, and I blink rapidly, trying to stem the onslaught of tears. He opens his mouth. "Stella... uh...," he begins and then stops and scrubs a hand through his hair. "We should... probably... talk. Fuck." He leans over, hands on knees like he might get sick.

"It's okay," I say, my throat swollen and aching from holding back tears. "You don't have to say anything." Because it's all right there on his face, plain as day—regret. It's funny. I never really thought of heartbreak as a physical thing. It was only an expression, a metaphor for mental pain. But looking at Jacob right now, I swear I can feel my heart shattering into thousands of tiny shards that shred my insides.

The sound of laughter echoes down the entryway and I quickly comb my fingers through my hair and wipe my cheeks.

A moment later, Malcolm and Ryan come staggering through the doorway. Ryan has his arm draped over Malcolm's shoulder, and by his red face and glassy-eyed expression, it's clear he's trashed. "Hey, Jacob," Malcolm calls to his friend, a little too loudly. "Ryan didn't want to pay for an Uber, so he's gonna sleep here tonight, alright?" He obviously hasn't noticed me yet since he's facing away from where I'm partially concealed by the door.

But Ryan does. "Heyastella," he says, the words slurring into one.

Malcolm spins around to look at me, his smile dying, to be replaced by a creased forehead and drawn brow. He glances back and forth between Jacob and me and asks, "Everything okay?"

"Yep," I say before Jacob can reply. My voice is overly bright and forced, but it's the best I can do at the moment. "I was just leaving. See you guys later." I move for the door.

"Wait, Stella," Jacob calls from behind me, but I'm already walking out the door. "Goodbye, Jacob," I say, not turning to see if he followed and shut it behind me.

The last thing I hear before I storm down the stairwell to cry my eyes out in my car is Malcolm's voice asking, "What did you do?"

Nineteen

Hindsight is an Evil Bitch

Stella

I DON'T KNOW IF Ryan called her or not, but Charlie's sitting on the curb when I pull up to my apartment. She doesn't ask questions or even console me; she just wraps me up into a rib-breaking hug and helps me inside. The apartment is quiet. It's got to be close to two in the morning, which means Emma's asleep and Kat is probably still out partying or won't be coming home at all. Charlie sits me down on the couch and crosses to our dinky kitchen. "Tea?" she asks. I nod. I'm usually more of a coffee drinker, but right now I'll accept anything warm and comforting.

A few minutes later, she returns with two steaming mugs and hands one to me.

"How much did they tell you?" I ask, shoulders slumped, eyes on my lap, my humiliation like a physical burden weighing me down.

She plops down next to me on the sofa. "Not much. Ryan was pretty hammered. He just said you were upset, and Jacob wanted me to check on you."

At the mention of Jacob's name, my eyes begin to sting. My throat's swelling up again and it's like I'm trying to breathe through a straw. "I'm... So... Stupid," I say, between strangled breaths.

Charlie blows on her tea, the steam temporarily dissipating, then reappearing. "You are not stupid," she says and takes a sip. Charlie is a tea maniac and would drink it twenty-four/seven if she could. She sets the cup down on the table and turns her full attention on me. "So, spill."

I take a deep breath. I want to tell Charlie, and I don't. It's like, I want her advice, but I'm afraid of what it might be. "We had sex."

She draws back as if slapped, her mouth forming the surprised "O" that I thought only toddlers and cartoon characters made. The wide-eyed shock on her face would be comical if my life wasn't the punchline. "Don't screw with me, Stella."

"You know I'm not."

Charlie shoots to her feet, hands covering her mouth as she lets out a shocked, "Oh my god," and sets about pacing the room. "Oh my god."

"You already said that."

She pauses and faces me. "I'm trying to process, okay? Give me a minute." More pacing. "I thought you went over there to confront him about Dean."

"I did," I say, explaining about our fight and how Jacob admitted he was jealous.

"And you had sex?"

"No." I throw my hands into the air. I hate that I have to rehash all of this for her. Maybe I shouldn't have said anything to begin with.

"I'm sorry. I just don't understand."

"I was pissed, okay—called him out for stringing me along. I told him everything. Everything. I just wanted him to see how much he hurt me and…"

"And?" she says, finally halting her pacing and resuming her position next to me on the couch.

"And he kissed me."

"Then things moved on from there?"

I nod.

"Okay. I know his timing sucked, but you still love him, right?" She clasps our hands and ducks her head trying to catch my eyes which are currently exploring my lap. "Maybe he needed to see you with another guy to realize his feelings."

"You didn't see his expression, Charlie—afterward." I drop my face into my hands and shake my head. "He just stood there and stared at me with this look of mortification on his face. And you know what the worst part is?" I raise my head to meet her eyes. "It was the best sex I've ever had. So now I have another thing to compare every other guy to and no one will ever measure up, and I'm..."

There's a soft knock on the door and both our heads snap up. My heart immediately goes into overdrive, and though I can feel my lungs expand and contract, I'm suffocating. "I can't breathe, Charlie." I manage to say between gasps. "Oh fuck, I can't—"

"Shh," Charlie coos and rubs my back. "It's just a panic attack. You need to try to calm down."

I bob my head in agreement. Yes. A panic attack. It's just a panic attack. I'm okay.

"Stella," Jacob's voice calls through the door and my heart is pounding so hard, I think I might faint. "I know you're in there. Answer the door. Please."

A sleepy-eyed Emma shuffles into the living room, wearing only her night shorts and tee, and scratches the rat's nest forming on her head. "What's going on?" she asks, then seems to notice me and Charlie on the couch. "What's wrong?"

Another knock at the door followed by, "I'm not leaving until I talk to you."

Emma gestures at the door with her thumb. "Is that Jacob?"

Ignoring her, because I can't deal with anything else right now, I tell Charlie. "I can't talk to him."

She simply nods and heads for the door.

Emma moves to sit next to me and rubs my back. Her eyes are creased with concern, and it kills me because when she finds out what happened, I know she's going to hate me. "Are you alright?"

I shake my head but don't elaborate.

Charlie opens the door, just enough to block it with her body, and dropping all pretense, she says, "You need to leave, Jacob."

"Not until I talk to Stella," Jacob replies, his deep voice like a warm glove wrapping itself around my heart and crushing it.

"Excuse me," says a female voice coming from outside. Kat. She squeezes past Jacob and Charlie, who promptly steps out the door and closes it behind her. Kat looks almost as haggard as Emma but in a "just had sex" kind of way—her clothes are askew, and her hair looks like she stuck a finger in an electrical outlet. Pausing when she sees Emma and me on the couch, she jerks her head toward the door. "What's going on?"

Emma shrugs. "They got in some sort of fight."

"Stella?" Kat asks. "Are you alright?"

I nod even though it's a total lie. I am most definitely not alright, but Kat isn't someone I want to talk to about this. In fact, when she hears about Jacob and me, she'll probably want to kick my ass.

Charlie's voice snaps our attention back to the door. Her words are too muffled to make out, but Jacob's deep voice comes through clear as day.

"I... I don't know," he stammers. "I just need to make sure she's alright."

My hands tremble as I fidget with a bit of string that's pulled free of my skirt, an obvious ploy to avoid meeting Emma's and Kat's eyes. Even so, I can sense them watching me, their gazes like lasers boring a hole into the top of my skull.

More murmuring.

"Stella," Emma says, the concern in her voice making me feel even more like shit than I did before. "What's going on?"

I don't know what to say. Do I lie and hope she doesn't find out? Do I tell her the truth? If I do, she's probably going to hate me. Tongue frozen by indecision, I glance at her out of my periphery but don't respond.

Emma hops to her feet. "Well, I'm going to see—"

"No," I say, gripping her arm. She stops cold and stares down at me, accusation in her eyes. She tugs her arm free and strides to the door.

Grabbing the handle, Emma swings it open right as Charlie blurts, "Well, maybe you should have figured that out before you fucked your best friend."

Charlie whirls around, face panic-stricken when she sees the open door. She groans and rubs a hand down her face. "Goodbye, Jake," she says over her shoulder as she steps inside and slams the door in his face.

"You bitch," Kat yells. She lunges for me, and I jump from my position on the couch and race for the other side of the room, narrowly avoiding a face plant when I trip over an errant throw pillow. Fortunately, Charlie manages to grab her around the midsection and drag her away before she can murder me.

I lower my gaze, afraid of the hurt I'll see in Emma's eyes.

"You slept with Jacob?" she asks, her voice barely a whisper.

"Yes," I reply, eyes glued to my lap.

"W-why would you..." Emma's voice cracks and I don't have to see her to know she's crying. "I don't... how could you—"

"Because I'm in love with him. Alright?" I interrupt. "I've been in love with him since I was ten. And the first time he shows any fucking interest in me, I have sex with him, screwing you over and throwing ten years of friendship down the fucking drain. So, yeah, I fucked everything up. Okay? I'm sorry."

Emma doesn't move. She just stares blankly into space. A single tear escapes her eye, drawing a path down her face, and the fragmented pieces of my heart crack just a little more at the sight of it. "You said you two didn't think about each other that way. You said—"

"I lied," I shout, my voice hard and tremulous. The room goes silent. Three pairs of eyes stare back at me, their expressions a mixture of pity, shock and anger. I take a calming breath and swipe a hand across my wet cheeks. When I speak again, my voice is softer, if not any kinder. "What should I have said, Emma? You're my friends. Should I have stood in the way of you two potentially being happy together, when I knew I didn't have a chance? What kind of asshole would that have made me?"

"An honest one," she says through gritted teeth.

I swallow around the lump in my throat and meet Emma's eyes. "If I'd realized giving you my permission meant I'd have to listen to the two of you going at it for three months, trust me, I wouldn't have." I turn to Kat, whose murderous stance has deflated somewhat. "You still going to kick my ass?"

Her lips thin, but she doesn't reply.

I nod. "Well, you know where to find me if you change your mind." I shoot a tight-lipped smile at Charlie. "I'm going to bed," I say to no one in particular and head to my room, so I can cry myself to sleep.

Twenty

Where's the Rewind Button On This Shit?

Jacob

I feel like utter shit, and I mean that on many levels. I got pretty-much zero sleep this weekend, so I'm like a walking zombie. Stella never showed up to drive me to class, which I kind of expected to be honest, so I had to ride the bus. It was packed, standing room only, and I ended up wedged between some guy who smelled like he'd been rolling around in garbage, and a white-haired old lady whose hand kept "accidentally" grazing my junk.

Seriously, I feel violated.

Then there's Stella. Now that's a whole other level of shit. Charlie was right. I didn't think; I just acted, and afterward… I froze. Not that the sex wasn't good—it was incredible. I think that's part of what freaked me out. It wasn't just sex, it was something more, and I'm not sure I'm ready for more. What I do know is that I don't want to lose her. But there's no way to tell her all of this because she refuses to see me and won't answer my calls or texts. I thought about writing everything I was feeling down in a text, but that would probably take two hours, and for all I know, she's blocked my number. Instead, I wrote her a letter. It took me two days to fill one page, and it isn't nearly good enough, but I'm not like Stella. I'm not good with words, and I can't exactly convey my feelings in a drawing. So here

I am, waiting in class and hoping she'll show, so I can hand her my really crappy letter, and maybe she'll talk to me again.

Problem is, I want to do more than talk.

That night keeps running on a loop in my head and it's making me crazy. I want to see her and touch her and kiss her and fuck her. Just thinking about it gets me hard and no amount of cold showers and jerking off is making it any easier. I'm a mess. I rub my eyes, trying to quell some of the exhaustion weighing me down. The doctors cleared me to start back training today so hopefully I'll be able to work off some steam on the field. I glance at my phone. Class starts in three minutes. She probably decided to skip it. I wouldn't blame her but come on. She's going to have to talk to me, eventually.

The double doors swing open and my heart somersaults when I see her step into the classroom. She's wearing jeans and a forest-green sweater that molds to her body and the reminder of that gorgeous body pressed against me, gets my dick going.

Down, boy. It's not the time.

Her eyes immediately find mine and we freeze there a moment, watching, waiting. I can't tell if she's waiting for me to make the first move or not, but I'm determined not to screw this up again, so I stand and start working my way across the aisle to her when she spins around and goes right back out the door.

Shit.

I race down the steps and am almost to the doors when a voice calls, "Mr. Gonzales." I skid to a stop. It's the professor. I should have pretended like I didn't hear him, but I was raised to mind authority and my body stopped before my mind could think better of it.

"Sorry, sir," I say. "Uh... I've had a bit of an emergency. I need to go."

"And what might that emergency be about?"

Now, I'm aware that being a guy has definite advantages, but if there is one thing girls got on us, it's the ability to excuse themselves from literally anything, by claiming period issues. Now, I have to make some crap up and hope it's good enough to get me out of class. "Got a text that my mom's sick, sir."

He eyes me askance, obviously not convinced. "And it has nothing to do with Miss Leone, who just ran through those doors?"

Damn, someone's been paying attention. "No, sir."

He makes a humming sound as if considering, then gestures toward my seat. "You should probably take along your book bag, don't you think?"

I glance back at where I was sitting. Sure enough, I'd left my backpack on the floor. "Yes, sir. Thank you." I rush back up the steps, grab my bag and race out the door. Stella's got a sizable head start on me, but I'm praying she hasn't gone too far. I breathe a sigh of relief when I see her across the courtyard, and suck it right back up again when I realize why she's stopped.

She's talking to Dean. I start across the field. God, I hate that guy. Maybe hate isn't the right word.

Loathe.

He's a world-class asshole, but of course, Stella doesn't know that. She's only seen what he's allowed her to see. She isn't around when he acts like an ass on the field or when he talks smack about girls in the locker room—which will get him a fist to the face if he so much as breathes a word about Stella.

I make it across the quad in record time. Stella's back is to me, but Dean sees me coming and takes on a defensive posture: arms crossed, feet slightly apart, chin tipped up like an arrogant prick.

Yeah, we all see how tough you are, douchebag.

Stella must notice the change in his demeanor because her back stiffens, and she pivots around to face me. Her lips are drawn into a straight line and her eyes are glassy. It's my fault. I haven't even spoken to her yet, and I'm already pissed at myself for getting her upset.

"Hey, Stella," I say, ignoring the jackass posturing behind her.

"Hey," is all she says, but it's like music to my ears because it's the first word she's spoken to me in three days.

"Can we talk?" I ask, then tack on a "Please," for good measure.

"I don't think that's a good idea," she says.

"Hey. Gonzales." Dean starts in, and I'm already vibrating with the need to knock that smug smirk from his stupid wanna-be-Ken-doll face. "Stella and I were having a conversation. Why don't you get lost?"

"And why don't you go fuck yourself," I reply, which, yeah, I was trying to piss him off, but it isn't my fault he's got such thin skin.

He jerks at me like he's actually going to do something about it. We both know he won't because he's not that stupid—fighting on school grounds won't just get you suspended from the team; it could get you expelled. Of course, Stella doesn't know these things, so she jumps in front of him, hands on his chest to hold him back, exactly the way he wanted.

When she turns around, Dean smirks at me, and I have to ball my hands up into fists so tight my nails dig into the skin to stop myself from pummeling him into the dirt. If there was a benevolent God, he would send a tornado to sweep this guy up and dump him in the middle of the Atlantic—preferably in shark-infested waters.

Turning my attention back to Stella, I simply say, "Please."

She glances back at Dean, who drops the smile and stuffs his hands in his pockets in a lousy attempt to appear innocent. Stella raises a brow at him, and to me says, "Not here. If you want to talk, you can come by tonight."

"Are you going to let me in this time?"

She's avoiding my eyes, still uncomfortable I guess, but I can see the corner of her lip tip up into a ghost of a smile when she says, "Maybe."

A lock of hair has fallen into her face and my hands itch to reach out and touch it, tuck it behind her ear. Instead, I stuff my hands into my jeans' pockets. "I can work with maybe." I reach into my back pocket and pull out the letter I wrote. "Here."

She looks at the letter warily. "What is it?"

Dean lays an arm across Stella's shoulder. "Yeah. What is it, Jakey?"

I shut my eyes and breathe.

I will not kill Dean. I will not kill Dean.

When I open them again, Stella's leaned into him, and something twists inside my gut. "Just read it, please." I hold the paper out to her again, then snatch it back. "Not with him," I add on, and extend my arm again.

"I wouldn't do that," she says and reaches out to take the letter from me. Our fingers brush for only a moment, but it's like my whole being zeros in on that point of contact, her soft heat burrowing beneath my skin like a brand. My mind goes blank, and I forget to breathe. All I see are golden-brown eyes, a perfect heart-shaped face and soft pink lips that I want to kiss.

She steps back, and the spell is broken. Stella whispers, "Thank you," turns around and leaves with him, taking my heart with her.

The locker room reeks of BO and muscle cream, but to me, it's like coming home. It helps that the NU locker room is state-of-the-art and fucking incredible. On one side of the room, aisles of glossy crimson lockers jut out into the space, each bearing a life-size action photo of some of the best players to ever grace these halls. Coaches' offices line the other wall, while oversized leather chairs run along the interior beneath the massive silver and crimson eagle, our mascot, painted on the ceiling. Down the hallway are the video room, weight room and the like—all state-of-the-art, and all I've been allowed to use for the last week. I need this, a chance to get some energy out on the field. Free weights and jogging are all fine and good, but they're no substitute for the rush you get running plays.

"Meeting in five minutes," calls out Coach Reed. He runs the defensive line, so I don't work with him that much, which is good because he's a sadistic bastard. Not that Cheeny, our offensive line coach, is much better, but at least he stops being a dick when you get off the field. Reed's a dick full-time.

I finish throwing on my gear and gather around the play board where Coach Snowden, our Head Coach, is waiting, clipboard in hand, to rip into us for whatever latest offense we've committed. The man is perpetually pissed off, like red-faced, spitting, tears the skin from your bones furious, all the time. He's fairly young, late forties, but about thirty pounds overweight, with a belly that looks ready to give birth. Rain, shine or cold as shit, the man is wearing an NU polo—tucked in—shorts and a cap to hide his bald spot. This has, of course, led to the worst farmer's tan known to man, but the way he's going, heart disease will do him in way before skin cancer has a chance.

We gather around him while he rants about some missed plays and lazy blocking during the last game, which I missed, and I've mostly tuned him out until I hear my name. "We're playing tackle scrimmages today, except for Gonzales."

Ahhh, fuck me.

"He's still recovering, so no hits on him today. Got it?"

"Yes, Coach," we all shout—military style.

"Taylor," Coach says, and Dean's head pops up, grinning like an idiot. "You find something about that funny?"

"No, Coach." Yeah, right. He was calling me a pussy or some other middle school-level smack down he thinks will damage my fragile ego.

I'm shaking in my cleats.

Coach points at the tunnel doors. "Twenty laps. Go."

Dean grumbles under his breath as he shoves his helmet on and starts off.

It takes some serious self-control to hold back my smile.

"Henderson, you'll fill in till he's finished," Coach says, and claps his hands. "Alright men. On the field."

We break and head up the tunnel.

An hour and about a thousand routes later, my head is pounding, and I'm at the line of scrimmage facing off against—wouldn't you know it—Dean. This should be fun.

"Hey Gonzales," Dean calls, trying to mess with my focus.

"Fuck off, Taylor," I reply, because I'm incapable of ignoring that shit.

"Got a date with your girl tonight."

The ball is snapped, and I charge straight down the field and bank to the left, and because Malcolm's the man, the ball's right where I need it. I snatch it out of the air and haul ass down the field, Dean eating my dust, when the left cornerback pulls up beside me and taps me out. I give the kid, a newbie freshman, a fist bump, toss the ball to Malcolm and make my way back to the line.

Dean takes his place across from me, and I can't help but ride him a little. "Hey, man, what happened to you back there? You get lost in my dust?"

"No, but I'm looking forward to getting lost in Stella's—"

"Hike." The call hits me out of nowhere.

Son of a bitch. I'm down the field a second too late and the ball flies right over my head. Incomplete.

"Damn, Jakey. That went right over your head." Dean cackles and, tapping a finger on the side of his helmet, says, "You need to be keeping your head in the game, bro, and forget about me being balls deep in your girl tonight."

I lurch forward off the line, ready to kill the bastard. He backs up, hands in the air and a smug grin plastered over his ugly face.

The whistle blows.

"Offsides," Coach shouts. "What the hell are you doing, Gonzales? Get your ass back in line."

I move back into position, wishing I wasn't wearing this goddamned helmet, so I could rub my temples to ease the pressure before my head explodes. My hands are shaking; I'm so pissed.

I will not kill Dean. I will not kill Dean.

The asshole literally struts back into position. "Touchy, touchy. What? You can't take a joke?" He moves into a crouch. "Well, not exactly a joke. I will fuck her tonight. Does that make you sad?" He pouts and rotates a fist back and forth next to his eye like a whiny baby.

Something in me snaps, and I blurt out, "You tell me, Taylor. How does it feel to know I was the one fucking her after your date on Friday?"

That smile drops like an anvil, and I only get to enjoy a second or two of satisfaction before the ball is snapped, and I shoot off the line. Ten yards out, I curl back, my eyes on Malcolm. He beams me right in the chest. I tuck the ball under my arm and spin for the end-zone, my focus razor-sharp.

I don't even see Dean coming until he slams into me like a fucking bulldozer and sends me sprawling onto the grass.

My body barely hits the turf and suddenly half the team is standing over me—staring like I'm some sideshow act. I roll onto my knees, but I'm off balance. I don't know if I can get up.

Coach is on one side, a grad assistant coach—I can't remember his name—is on the other and they're helping me to my feet. There's a din of chatter behind me and I'm vaguely aware that Coach and the assistant are asking me questions, but it's all kind of surreal and dreamlike. They walk me through the locker room and sit me down on the couch in Coach's office. The blast of A/C is amazing against my hot skin, and I let my body sink into the soft cushion. Wait, I pat my head. I'm not wearing a helmet. Where the hell did my helmet go?

Before I have a chance to ponder that question further, Coach hands me a water bottle. "Drink," he says, and I obey. The water is freezing to the point of hurting my throat, but I guzzle it down anyway, drinking half the bottle in one go.

"Feel better," Coach asks, once I've set the bottle down.

"Yeah," I reply, though I'm not really sure if that's true. "Sorry. I..." I rake a hand through my hair and down my face as if I could scrub the cobwebs from my brain. Coach sits on his desk, watching me, his forehead scrunched with something like concern. Which means, either I look even more fucked up than I feel, or I'm hallucinating because Coach only has two settings: irritated and angry. Neither scenario is particularly appealing.

"You remember what happened?" Coach asks.

"Yeah," I say, not even trying to hide my annoyance. I slump back into the sofa and close my eyes. "Dean hit me."

"Alright," Coach says, shoulders relaxing a bit. "Coach Cheeny is going to give you a ride home. Get some rest. I don't want to see you on the field for the rest of the week. We'll reevaluate on Monday."

I blink my eyes open. "So, no game this Saturday?" I ask, even though I already know the answer.

"Sorry, kid." Coach scratches the stubble on his jaw. "You're a good player and I want you on the field as much as you want to be there."

I doubt that.

"But the way you took that hit," he shakes his head as if trying to dispel the memory. "I'm not a hundred percent sure you're ready yet, and if we put you out there too soon, it could fuck you up for good."

"I can handle it."

His face reverts to the surly asshole we all know and love. "I didn't ask. Now get the fuck out of my office and go home."

Twenty-One
Give a Girl a Baseball Bat
Stella

I CAN'T SAY HOW long I've been sitting here staring at this sheet of paper, thirty minutes, an hour. It's like this stupid piece of paper may possibly have a huge impact on my life, and I can't seem to bring myself to take that leap.

The patter of footsteps coming from down the hall tells me Emma's approaching. She passes without a word and heads into the kitchen. A glass clanks on the countertop. The fridge opens, liquid is poured, the fridge is closed, and I'm still staring at this piece of paper, wishing I could ask my friend to do this with me. We've barely spoken since she found out I slept with Jacob. She's angry at me right now, and I don't blame her. I probably could have saved us both a whole lot of suffering if I'd just been honest with her.

"Are you going to open that or stare at it for another two hours?"

I jump at the sound of Emma's voice and have to laugh at my own ridiculousness. It's not like I didn't know she was there. "I'm thinking another two hours might not be long enough," I reply.

She leans a hip against the peninsula and takes a sip of her drink. "What is it?"

"A letter from Jacob."

"Oh." Her posture stiffens, and she bites her lip nervously. We're both quiet for a few minutes, looking at Jacob's letter. Then Emma finally says, "You want some water?"

That's as close to an olive branch as I could hope for right now. The pressure in my chest eases a bit. I didn't realize how much this tension between us was affecting me. "That would be great."

She gives me a tight smile and heads back into the kitchen.

I take a breath and slip the scrap of paper off the table. My hands tremble a little as I unfold it, making the task harder than it should be. When I finally have it open, I am greeted by Jacob's typewriter-perfect penmanship.

Stella,

It's kind of weird, writing to you like this. I don't think we've written each other notes since sixth grade, but since you're avoiding me, I had to resort to drastic measures.

I want to start by saying that maybe I never told you before, but I've always thought you were beautiful. Why do you think I like drawing you so much? I've just always considered you like a sister which made you off-limits. Then, that day at my place when you ran off, you gave me this look, and it was like a switch got flipped in my brain. All of a sudden, I wanted to kiss you so badly it hurt. After that, it was all I could think about and—I'm not going to lie—it scared the shit out of me. My track record with girls isn't exactly stellar, and you've been a part of my life for so long, that I don't think I'd know how to live it without you if I screwed things up.

Then Dean asked you out, and I was afraid I missed my chance. And I know I screwed everything up that night at my place. I know you think I regretted it and that's why I acted like a jackass, but that wasn't it. I was just overwhelmed—like all the cylinders in my head were firing at once, and I froze.

Anyway, I really suck at writing letters, if you haven't figured that out, so please can I talk to you?

Jacob

I drop my head into my hands. What the hell does any of that mean? Why all the dancing around? Why couldn't he just say, yes, he wants a relationship, or no, fuck off?

Emma steps up next to me and hands me my water. "Look, Stella—"

A long, somewhat dramatic yawn comes from the hallway, followed by a disheveled Kat in a T-shirt and sleeping shorts. "Damn you guys are loud. I was trying to sleep."

Emma pulls her phone from her back pocket. "Uh... It's 5:30 Kat."

"And?"

"And it's 5:30."

"Yeah. So?"

"P.M.," Emma continues, "as in... at night."

"I have a late gig tonight and an early class tomorrow, so I was trying to squeeze in a little extra sleep." Covering her mouth with her hand, Kat lets out another monstrous yawn. She looks back and forth between Emma and me. "Everything okay?"

Emma and I grunt out noncommittal answers.

Strangely, this seems to placate Kat who simply nods and steps into our pathetic excuse for a kitchen. Pausing to lean on the kitchen peninsula she says to Emma, "Let me know if I need to kick her ass?"

Emma sputters out a laugh, but I don't think Kat's joking—not entirely. She's protective of Emma, which is a little strange because she's the younger of the two. One thing I can say for certain is, if Emma ever killed someone, Kat would totally help her bury the body.

Emma peruses her phone, and I watch Kat as she pulls out slices of bread, removes the crust and rolls them into tight balls before eating them.

So, that's normal.

A pounding on the door has us all jumping out of our skin. "Stella," a voice calls through the door. "It's Dean. Open up."

Dean? What the hell is Dean doing here?

"Stella. Open the damn door," Dean hollers and he's pounding on our shitty door so hard, I'm worried he might break it.

"I'm not liking his tone," Kat says. "I'm going to get my bat." She pops a bread ball into her mouth and heads back into the hallway.

"Is she serious?" I ask Emma.

Emma laughs.

More pounding.

"What bug crawled up his butt?" Emma asks.

I shrug. Hell, if I know. I push myself off the couch and make my way to the door. He's still pounding like a complete psycho so the first thing I say when I open the door is, "What the fuck, Dean?"

He has one arm propped up against the door frame, shoulders hunched. His head snaps up when I speak. "What the fuck to you, Stella? Let me in. We've got to talk."

Emma pops up behind me, her head visible over my shoulder. "Looking a little stressed there, Dean. You should probably see a professional for that."

"Shut up, Emma," he says and pushes past us and into the living room.

"Sure. Come in. Make yourself at home," Emma deadpans.

He jabs a finger toward the hallway. "Get the fuck out, Emma."

Excuse me? "Don't talk to my friend like that," I say.

"Get out," he hollers. His chest rises and falls in heavy panting breaths, and his eyes are wild.

My heart's thumping a manic rhythm and my hands are shaking, but if Emma's frightened, she shows no sign of it. She plants her hands on her hips and, in a tone that brooks no argument, says, "I live here asshole, so if anyone's getting out, it's you."

He makes a growling sound deep in his throat but doesn't argue further. Hands stuffed into his pockets, Dean begins pacing the living room. "You going to close the door?"

Some instinctual part of me says to keep that method of escape open. "No. I think I'll leave it open. Now, are you going to tell me what's going on or what?"

He doesn't stop to look at me as he speaks; just a quick glance my way and he continues pacing a hole into my carpet. "Is it true?"

I'm getting pretty pissed off at this point so, of course, I give him a snarky reply. "Yes, Dean. It's true. The lunar landing was a fake. It's all a government conspiracy—"

He cuts me off. "I'm not fucking playing, Stella."

"Well, I'm afraid you're going to need to be a teeny-weeny bit more specific, Dean."

He quits pacing and steps up to me—almost nose-to-nose—and it takes all my self-control not to back away. His jaw is tight, body ridged, like he's getting ready for a fight. "Did you fuck, Gonzales? Is that specific enough for you?"

The words strike me like a hammer to the chest, knocking the wind out of me. "Who told you that?" I ask, on a gasped whisper.

"He did. Who the fuck else did you think?"

Jacob told him? Why? No, that can't be. "Why would he tell you that?"

"Does it matter? Is it true? Did you fuck him after our date?"

I don't respond and that's answer enough.

"Mother..." He spins around and punches my wall, ripping a hole in the drywall.

Emma and I shriek and turn to run down the hall, but Dean's too quick. He snatches me up by the elbow and hauls me back. "You fucking whore—"

He's gripping my arms so tightly, it's painful. I'm in full panic mode now, screaming at him, "Please stop." Tears are streaming down my face; I'm tugging against him with all my strength, but he's too powerful and he won't let go.

"Hey, asshole."

We both spin around to find Kat, a solid wood baseball bat perched on her shoulder, her face beet red and scrunched up in rage. "You like putting holes in walls? Well, here you go." She swings. The bat barely skims Dean's head, hairs flapping in its wake, and smacks into the wall with a thud right above Dean's hole.

Dean releases me and backs away, his expression a mixture of shock and confusion. "Whoa. Okay. Calm down." He raises his hands in surrender, but Kat is way past giving a shit.

She wrenches the bat from the wall and stalks toward him, swinging it in a circle at her side like a player coming up to the plate.

Behind me, Emma whoops like this is, indeed, a sporting event and not a case of demonic possession. "You're in deep shit now, Dean," she shouts. "You better run."

I spin around to glance at her. Emma is grinning maniacally, and now I'm wondering if I somehow got shacked up with the Florida equivalent of the Texas Chainsaw family.

A shiver snakes down my spine and it is not from the cold. Kat looks like every horror movie killer that has ever haunted my dreams at night—her movements confident and relaxed, her eyes bat-shit crazy. If I were the one she was going after, I'd probably pee myself.

"Who the hell do you think you are?" Kat says. "Coming into my place, putting a hole in my wall, calling my friend a 'whore.'" She swings again, narrowly missing Dean's ribcage as he jumps backward. "How many people have you slept with Dean? Because I'll bet it's a fuck load more than Stella."

Dean stumbles to the door. "Jesus Christ. You're fucking crazy. You know that?"

Kat stalks him out the door, and Emma and I follow close behind. Beside me, Emma's cackling like a goddamned supervillain, and it's almost freaking me out more than Kat.

"Oh, you haven't seen crazy yet, asshole." Kat cracks the bat against the brick wall, sending bits of white dust flying. "You come near my friend again, and I'll show you crazy. Got it?"

"Yes. Okay. I'm going." Dean takes hold of the handrail and starts backing down the steps. His toe slips and he barely catches himself before careening to the bottom of the staircase and runs like his ass is on fire.

"Okay. Show's over," Kat says, and I didn't realize until that moment that a bunch of our neighbors came out of their apartments to see what all the commotion was about. Kat struts over to Emma and me, the bat perched on her shoulder and a smug grin on her face. Emma gives her a high five and a hip bump and all I can do is stare at the two of them, mouth gaping. Kat lays a hand on my shoulder, and I have to fight back a shudder.

Then she shoves the bat into my hands and gives me a wide, not-at-all-crazy grin. "Something to remember, my friend. It doesn't matter how big or strong a person is; everybody's afraid of crazy."

Twenty-Two
And Now I Can Breathe
Jacob

Now that my head has cleared and I'm feeling halfway human again, the reality of what I said to Dean at practice is sinking in. "What the hell was I thinking?"

"I'm pretty sure we've established that you weren't thinking," Malcolm replies, unhelpfully, from the kitchen. He returns with two beers and hands one over to me while swigging the other.

"I'm such a dumbass," I say. "Stella's going to kill me."

Malcolm looks at me over the top of his bottle while he downs half of it in one go. The man's an enigma. As long as I've known him, Malcolm's been able to guzzle beer by the gallon, yet I can't remember the last time I saw the guy more than mildly tipsy. "Yeah. I wouldn't put money down on you surviving the next twenty-four hours, that's for sure."

"Damn, Bro, you could at least pretend to be supportive."

"I got you a beer, didn't I?" Malcolm tips his bottle toward the unopened one in my hand. "If you're looking for a hug and a chat about feelings, you've been hanging out with chicks way too much. I'm a man and men don't express their feelings. We suppress them with alcohol and violence. I provided the alcohol, but if you're looking for a fight, you're going to have to go elsewhere, because no way am I damaging this pretty face." He pats his cheeks and purses his lips in what, I'm assuming, is a poor attempt at imitating a cute little girl. In truth, he just looks like an exceptionally ugly drag queen.

There's a knock on the door. I set my unopened beer down on the coffee table and push off the couch to answer it. "I wouldn't take that face on the road yet," I say over my shoulder.

Malcolm makes a motion like a knife jabbing him in the chest and blood gushing out of the wound. I'm laughing when I open the door and stop cold.

Stella's standing in my entryway, those sorrowful brown eyes looking up at me. The laughter dies in my throat and along with it my ability to speak, to breathe.

She shakes her head. "Please explain to me," she says, her expression more tired than angry, "why you felt the need to brag about us having sex."

I take her gently by the arm and pull her inside, closing the door behind us. Malcolm has made himself scarce, thank god. "Stells," I begin. I try to take her hand, but she rips it away.

"I mean, is this a football thing where you guys announce your conquests and stupid shit like that?"

"No. Of course not. I wouldn't do that."

She plants a hand on her hip. "Well, yeah. You kind of did."

Shit. She got me there.

I scrub a hand through my hair. I need to head this shit off at the pass before it turns into another catastrophe. "Look, it's no excuse. I was an idiot, I can admit that, but the bastard was taunting me, okay? Saying how you two were going out tonight and he was going to f—" I pause, and she cocks a brow, obviously aware of what I was about to say. "Have sex with you. I just wanted him to shut up. So yeah, I told him, but I wasn't bragging so much as—"

"Having a pissing contest?"

I wrinkle my nose. "When you say it like that, it sounds so…" I pause, searching for the right word.

"Immature," she supplies. She folds her arms across her chest and leans back against the door, waiting.

I'm so frigging in over my head right now. I have no idea what to do or say. An apology isn't going to be enough. I know that much, but what else can I do? What I want to do is grab her and kiss the living shit out of her, but that would probably just piss her off more. Instead, I stuff my hands in my pockets, hoping that will be enough to keep me from doing something stupid. "I'm sorry?" I say, but it somehow comes out sounding more like a question than a response.

"Is that supposed to be an apology?"

Groaning, I rub a hand down my face. "What do you want me to say, Stella? I'm sorry, okay? This has all been a giant shit show. Can we please just start over?"

"You know what's funny?" she says, her tone making it clear that it is not at all funny. "He was lying. We didn't have a date. Today, outside of class, was the first time I'd spoken to him since we went out. He was screwing with you."

Of course he was. I bow my head. "I'm such an asshole."

"You said it. Not me."

We both go silent. She turns her head away from me, amber eyes trained on the floor, but she's not trying to leave, so that's a good sign.

It's taking all my self-control not to pull her to me right now. She's so small and delicate and beautiful. We're so close; I can feel her presence in the space between our bodies. It dances along my skin, almost like she's in my arms already. "Tell me what to do, Stells," I beg.

She stands there quietly for a few moments, watching her fingers as they fidget with the hem of her blouse. Finally, she looks up at me through dark lashes. "I don't want to fight anymore," she says, her voice a raspy whisper. "I just want to be with you."

And I can breathe.

I close the distance between us, take her face in my hands and crush my lips to hers. This time, there's no hesitation. Her lips part, tongue darting in to sweep mine and it sends a shock wave through my body. I tilt her head, deepening the kiss, pulling her closer. She wraps her arms around my neck and presses her body against mine. She feels so fucking good. I'm losing my damn mind. We need to get in my room before I strip her naked and fuck her in the living room.

I'm only vaguely aware of Malcolm pushing us aside and shaking his keys, saying something about heading out. I barely manage to pull away long enough to lock the door behind us before Stella's in my arms again. She lifts her arms. I drag her shirt over her head and make quick work of her lacy white bra. I knead her breasts, fingers pinching and tugging on one perfect pink nipple while laving and sucking on the other. She moans and arches into me, and it's the most beautiful thing I've ever seen. I grip her ass—god, she's got a great ass—and lift her. Her legs immediately go around my waist. She grinds against my aching cock then slips a hand between us and begins stroking up and down my length. I groan against her lips. "Fuck." I want to pound her into the wall again, but I walk her to my bedroom, only pausing our kiss long enough for her to tug the shirt over my head. I use my heel to push the door shut and toss her onto the bed.

She lets out a shocked laugh, but quiets as she notices my eyes roving her body. Her face goes all red, and she lays her arms over her breasts. It's fucking adorable, but not what I'm going for at the moment.

I crawl onto the bed and straddle her. "Don't cover yourself," I say, lifting her arms over her head, leaving her upper half exposed. "Keep them like this. No cheating."

"Why?"

Arms on either side of her head, caging her in, I lower myself onto her, pinning her to the bed with my body. I nuzzle her neck, breathing in her scent—a mixture of her vanilla soap and something that's just Stella. Teasing her with warm breath and the brush of my lips, I trace the line of her neck and up and around the curve of her ear. "Because I'm going to devour you, now, and these," I tap a finger against her open palm, "are in my way." A shiver snakes through her at my words, and it's like she grabbed my cock and squeezed. I brush my lips against hers. "Do you like that?"

"Yes," she says on a breath, the words barely audible. I pull her into another kiss, this one harder and more demanding. Our tongues stroke and dance and she tastes so fucking good, it's hard for me to stop. She whimpers when I pull away, making me smile. I move down her body, hands roaming her curves. Her skin is creamy and baby soft against my rough fingers. Last time, we were so desperate, I never got a chance to really look at her. I'm looking at her now, and she's so beautiful. Her breasts are perfect handfuls, as if they were made for me, and I take them into my mouth, one then the other nipping and sucking. Stella groans and wiggles beneath me, wanting more, but my body holds her in place. She's beautiful. She's mine. And nothing in my life has ever felt more right.

Twenty-Three
Everything I've Ever Wanted
Stella

HE HAS MY BODY pinned down so I can't move, my arms over my head so I can't touch, and I'm so turned on I'm practically vibrating. Jacob's trailing kisses down my stomach, coming to a stop when he meets the waistband of my jeans. The look he gives me is mischievous as hell as he slowly, painstakingly unbuttons and unzips my jeans, exposing the front of my pink cotton panties. They're not at all sexy, but Jacob doesn't seem to care. He hooks a finger on the waistband and tugs it down, his fingertip grazing my sex. He plants a kiss there, his hot breath seeping through and under my panties. I try to raise my hips, a silent plea for more. His tongue darts out, teasing just below the waistband as his finger delves lower, brushing my clit. I cry out in shock or frustration, or both. I don't know. Moisture pools along my sex and I press my legs together in a useless attempt to gain some friction there.

If it's possible for someone to die from getting turned on, I may be on my way out. Finally, Jacob takes mercy on me and shimmies my jeans and panties down my legs and tosses them aside. He parts my legs, spreading them wide, my sex on display. I'm embarrassed and excited and hot as hell all at the same time. The embarrassed part of me tries to close my legs, but Jacob's holding them firmly apart, a hand on each thigh.

He drags a finger down my center, and I gasp.

"Fuck, you're wet," he says, then sweeps the flat of his tongue up my center, tasting me like he would an ice cream cone. He dips a finger inside me, pumping twice before dragging it between my folds to circle my clit. I buck and arch my back, wanting more, needing more. But he just continues his methodical torture.

"Please," I hear myself beg, past the point of shame.

"What do you want, baby?" he whispers, breath hot against my sex.

"More."

And he responds, unleashing himself on me. He licks and sucks my clit, pumping one finger inside me, then two. Lowering my arms, I grip his hair and ride his fingers and mouth, faster, harder, my whole being fixated on the coiling sensation building in my core. My climax barrels down on me like a train slipping the rails, and rips through my body with a ferocity that has me seeing stars. I cry out, no longer caring if anyone hears. Jacob continues his assault until he's wrung every last spasm out of me.

He removes his pants, and a jolt of heat fires through me at the sight of his engorged cock. I need it in me now. Jacob crawls back up the bed, positioning himself between my legs. He kisses me and I can taste my arousal on his lips. Then Jacob reaches into his nightstand, pulls out a condom, and rolls it down his length. He leans over me and nuzzles my neck. "You, okay?" he asks, and if I didn't already love him, that small measure of concern would have done the trick.

"Yes," I say, the weight of that word so much more than a simple reply.

Jacob kisses me again, as the tip of his cock teases my entrance. Slowly, he pushes into me until he's fully seated. He pauses, giving me time to adjust, and kisses me again—slow and deep—as he begins to move. His pace is unhurried, gentle, pulling out almost to the tip then pushing back into me, and driving me out of my mind.

"Jacob," I say between kisses. He pauses to look at me. "I don't want sweet."

A grin spreads across his beautiful face. "Thank, fuck." He wraps an arm under my leg, tugs me closer. His thrusts come increasingly harder and faster, hitting that perfect angle that has my eyes rolling into the back of my head. I start to cry out, but then his mouth is on mine, swallowing my cries as he sets a brutal pace. It's fucking glorious. My climax builds and builds until my orgasm slams into me out of nowhere. Like a tidal wave, my pleasure crests, then recedes over and over again while Jacob's movements become more frenzied as he nears completion. He comes with a roar and collapses on top of me, his arms taking the majority of his weight. I stroke his back while he catches his breath, exploring the broad expanse of his shoulders and the curve of his spine into his hips and ass.

Jacob kisses my forehead, then hurries into the bathroom to dispose of the condom. He returns quickly and slips into bed beside me and pulls me tight against his chest. It's warm and comforting and everything I've ever wanted.

Twenty-Four
Never Said I Promise
Jacob

Waking up to Stella all naked and snuggled in my arms—awesome.

Waking up to Malcolm pounding on my door and bitching about weight training—not so much.

Groaning, I roll out of bed. "I'm coming. I'm coming. Jesus."

The pounding stops and Malcolm's voice calls from the other side of my door. "You have five minutes, then I'm going without you."

I hold up my middle finger with one hand while searching the laundry basket with the other.

"You better not be flipping me off either, you lazy bastard."

I spit out a laugh. The guy knows me too frigging well. "Then stop being an asshole," I yell back.

"Learn to use a fucking alarm clock, and I won't have to be an asshole. Five minutes." The crappy floor creaks like something out of a haunted house, telling me he's headed down the hallway.

"Yes, Mom," I call after him and he grumbles something that sounds suspiciously like, "If I was your mama…" before he goes out of earshot.

Stella rolls onto her back and rubs her eyes. "What time is it?"

"Way too early," I say, slipping on my socks and grinning like an idiot. I haven't got the heart to tell her her boob's peeking up over the top of the bedsheet. "Just stay in bed. I'll be back in a couple of hours, and we can go to class."

Eyes still closed, she gives me a half-assed salute. "Aye, aye, Captain."

I lean down to kiss her forehead, then follow up by sucking that bare nipple into my mouth, because how could I not?

"Hey." Grinning, she swats me away and lays a hand over her boob. "Pervert."

"You know it."

It isn't until I go to kiss her a second time that I notice the bruises circling her upper arms. I have to pause a second to gather all the thoughts whirling around in my head. I've seen those bruises before, more times than I can count on my mom, my sister, myself. "Stella?"

She hums in reply.

"What happened to your arms?"

She squints up at me, then raises her head and lifts each arm to examine the bruises. "Fuuuck," she says and drops her head back onto the pillow. "Promise me you won't make a big deal out of this?"

That was not what I wanted to hear. What I wanted to hear was, "Emma and I were wrestling" or "I had an allergic reaction to some Egyptian arm bracelets." Telling me not to make a big deal about it means it's definitely something worth making a big deal about. "Sorry. Not going to happen."

She moves to sit against the headboard, and I might have laughed at the way she drags the blanket up with her to keep her tits covered if I wasn't on the verge of losing my shit. "Look, Kat took care of it. He's not going to bother me again, okay?"

I swear I can feel my blood pressure rising, and with it, a throbbing in my skull. I have a pretty damn good idea who "he" is, but I need to hear her say it. "Who?"

"Jacob," she warns.

I grit my teeth and ask again. "Who?"

"Dean."

"Son of a..." I snag a coffee mug off the nightstand and hurl it across the room. It cracks against the wall, but surprisingly, doesn't shatter. It does, however, leave an ugly brown stain dripping down the wall.

Stella lunges for me and wraps her arms around my chest. The only way I could get her to let go would be to shove her away, which she knows I won't do. "Stop it." She plants her hands on either side of my face and forces me to look her in the eyes. "Kat ran his sorry ass off with a baseball bat. The guy nearly peed his pants, alright? He will *not* be bothering me again."

"He shouldn't have put his hands on you."

"No, he shouldn't have," she agrees, "but it's been handled and no good will come from you going after him. Promise me you won't go after him."

I start to pull away, but she plants a kiss on my lips and presses her still-naked body against me, effectively dousing my anger.

After a few seconds, she pulls away and, jackass that I am, I almost fall over following her. "Promise me," she says again.

I give her a side-long look. "You're an evil genius, you know that?"

She makes what must be the worst maniacal laugh ever, "Mwahahaha," then slaps me on the butt. "You better get moving or Malcolm's going to leave you."

The entire drive to training, Malcolm rambles on about some garbage I couldn't give half a shit about, while I replay what Stella said to me in my bedroom over and over in my head.

"It's been handled."

"No good will come from you going after him."

"Promise me you won't go after him."

I didn't actually promise, though. A technicality I doubt would make much of a difference to Stella, but as much as I plan to try not to beat the ever-loving crap out of Dean, I'm not sure I'll be capable of keeping that promise. I could have forgiven angry words or name-calling. Though it would still piss me off to think he upset Stella, I would have most likely given him some shit and warned him to keep away from her.

But when he put his hands on her, that crossed the line.

Guys like Dean think *might makes right*. It's acceptable to manhandle someone half your size—so what if it leaves a few bruises? It's not like they're actually hitting that person... yet. That's how it starts for assholes like Dean, like my father. The only memories I have of the man are of him hurting someone—my mom, my sister, me. But he wasn't always that way, not at first. It was years before he graduated from yelling and belittling to grabbing and shoving, then hitting my mom, and ultimately, hitting us.

The day we ran away was the best damn day of my life.

Now, I'm supposed to just let this go—to see this guy at practice every day, knowing he hurt Stella and do nothing. How am I supposed to do that?

"Hey," Malcolm says, breaking me from my internal freakout. "You awake?"

I shift uncomfortably in my seat. "Yeah, man. I'm just kind of in my head, you know?"

Malcolm steers us into the athletic complex, going too damn fast over the speed bumps, then parks and kills the engine before turning to me. "Sure. I was just prepared for you to get all gushy on me about you and Stella, who I'm guessing spent the night, so this," he waves a circle in front of my face, with his index finger, "scrunchy thing you've got going on here seems out of place."

"It's fine. Stella's good—she's great."

We climb out of his top-of-the-line Supra, stretch because that car is about two sizes too small for us, and move around to the back. Malcolm pops the trunk for us to grab our workout bags. "So? What?" He slams it shut and swings the bag over his shoulder. "You pissed about Dean tackling you yesterday?"

"No," I say, holding out the word in a way that really says, "not exactly" and Malcolm picks up on it immediately, of course.

He sighs. "So, what did he do now?"

"He grabbed Stella and left nasty bruises on her arms."

Malcolm jerks back as if slapped, his eyes about to bug out of his head. "Did he hurt her? Emma?"

"No. They're okay." We start heading back to the weight room again, but now Malcolm's giving me weary looks out of the corner of his eye—like he's afraid of what I might do. I don't blame him. I'm afraid of what I might do too.

"Thing is," I continue, "Stella's roommate, Kat, supposedly went after him with a bat—"

"No shit?"

"No shit. Kat's a little crazy, so I wouldn't put it past her. Anyway, Stella says it's been handled and doesn't want me to confront him about it, which is…" How the hell do I describe the shit show that is my mental state right now? "Difficult," I finish, massaging the back of my neck. I can't think with these frigging headaches. The way I'm going, it would be cheaper to buy stock in ibuprofen.

Malcolm doesn't really mention anything again until we're selecting dumbbells off the shelves. "I get it," he begins. "I think I'd be ready to kick his ass if I were you too, but I can also see Stella's point of view. You get in a fight and the both of you could get suspended, and she'd probably feel bad if she was the cause."

"I'm benched for the next week anyway, so I don't see how it matters."

"Cause we need you out there ASAP, man. Danny's a great guy, but he can't catch for shit."

I laugh, even though he's full of crap. Danny's a good receiver, good enough to replace me permanently if I don't get back in the game soon.

A commotion sounds from the hallway, and I don't have to see him to know it's Dean. His ridiculous SpongeBob SquarePants laugh is like a live wire attached to my nerves. That fucker is laughing. He scared the shit out of the girls, grabbed Stella so hard it left bruises, and he's laughing it up with his buddies like nothing ever happened. I'm shaking—fucking shaking. There's a pressure building in my head like someone's beating it with a goddamned mallet and the blood pounds in my ears. I'm clenching my jaw so hard I'm liable to crack a tooth, and my hands ache from squeezing the dumbbells.

Fuck it. The dumbbells hit the floor with an earsplitting clang, and I march across the room, through the double doors, and into the entryway. "Hey. Asshole," I shout. He spins around, that stupid grin on his face replaced by shock as I barrel toward him, fist upraised and ready to pound him into the floor.

He throws his hands up to guard his face like a wussy, and I swing.

But my fist never connects.

Three guys grab me around the arms and waist and drag me away from Dean. I thrash and yell at them, "Get the fuck off me," but they've thrown me up against the wall—pinning me.

Coach blows his whistle—the piercing screech shocking everyone into silence—and stomps into the center of the room, directly between Dean and me. "What the hell is going on here?"

And this is why Stella told me to leave it alone. Fuck. I stop fighting and let my head fall back against the wall. The guys release me but position themselves between Dean and me like human walls.

"That crazy fucker tried to jump me." Dean points at me, eyes blazing like he has the right to be pissed.

"You're lucky I don't rip your goddamned head off, you bastard."

"Enough," Coach shouts. "Both of you in my office. Now." His gaze sweeps over the crowd that's formed. "The rest of you, get back to work. The show's over." He turns around and strides away without even checking to see if we've followed.

Twenty-Five
Just When You Think You Know Somebody...
Stella

I can't believe I'm here waiting for Jacob. What does all this mean? Are we together now? I mean, if he had sex with me to ignore me again, I will literately kick his ass or set Kat on him. That chick is crazy. I'm starting to think Emma might have a few screws loose as well. She was downright giddy watching her sister go after Dean.

My phone buzzes in my back pocket. I glance at the clock. Who the hell is calling me at seven-thirty in the morning? I pull out my phone, fully prepared to rip whatever telemarketer had the audacity to ring me at this time a new one. But when I check the caller ID, instead of seeing the ubiquitous "Unknown Caller," it's Emma's name on my screen.

And now I'm worried. Nothing short of a full-scale alien invasion would get her up before nine.

"Hello."

"Oh, thank God," Emma says, between panting breaths. "Kat's got the car and she's not answering her frigging phone, and I need to get to my mom's like right now, and I'm starting to panic."

"Okay. Calm down. I'll be there in five minutes."

"Thank you. Thank you. Thank you. I'll be waiting out front."

We hang up and I shoot a quick text to Jacob telling him that Emma had an emergency, and I'll have to meet him at school. Then I throw on my sneakers, grab my keys, and go. Emma never talks about her mom—her dad, sure—but I don't think I've heard more than two words about her mother since we met. It's obviously a sore subject, so I don't bring it up. If she's swallowed her pride enough to ask me for help with her, it has to be really bad.

I pick up Emma, and she directs me to a trailer park on the outskirts of town. And when I say trailer park, I don't mean one of those places where people mostly keep their areas clean, and you might see some pots of flowers here and there. Nope. This place is a total shithole—and that's probably putting it nicely. There is trash everywhere—everything from rusted bikes to fast-food wrappers. The area is so overgrown, it would take a hack saw to free some of these trailers from the weeds and ivy entangling them. Many of the trailers look deserted, their windows or steps broken, their walls crumbling. One trailer is actually lying in a heap on its side. I can't even imagine the story about how that happened. We rumble down the gravel road winding through the center of the park, coming to a stop in front of a rusted beige trailer, I might have thought was abandoned as well, were it not for the woman lying sprawled across the steps.

Emma's mom. Jesus.

Emma practically leaps out of the car, and I follow. "Is she alright?" I ask.

"I don't know," she replies, her voice low but gritty like she swallowed sand. She crouches beside her mom and rolls her onto her back. That's when the smell hits me—vomit and urine. I reel back, lifting a hand to cover my nose and mouth.

"Mom," Emma says as she tries to shake her awake. "Mom."

"Already tried that," says a voice from behind, startling me. I spin around to find an old woman with stringy white hair, wearing a pink bathrobe and slippers, standing on the gravel walkway. "Found her like that this morning. No telling how long she's been there."

"Thank you, Ms. Fitzpatrick," Emma says, then shifts her attention to me. "I'm going to need help."

"What do you need me to do?" I ask Emma. It probably makes me a horrible person, but I really don't want to touch her mom. She has dried vomit on her face and shirt and a dark stain on her jeans that I'm sure is where the pee smell is coming from. If Emma needs me to help lift her or whatever, I'll do it, but I can't guarantee there won't be two piles of puke to clean up afterward.

"Hold the door for me, please."

Relieved to be doing something that doesn't involve vomit, I scramble up the steps. There is an outer screen door and an aluminum door, masquerading as wood, leading inside. The screen door is coated in rust and looks one good rainstorm from disintegrating. The damn thing squeals like a fire truck siren as I pull it open, and it takes me a minute to move the rusty slider into place to keep the screen from closing before I can open the, only slightly better-looking, interior door.

It's obvious Emma has done this many, many times. She grabs her mom under her arms and drags her up the steps and into the kitchen/living area with a proficiency that speaks of a great deal of practice. Except for the kitchen, where dirty dishes have overflowed from the sink to cover the counter, every conceivable surface, and even sections of carpet, are piled with empty beer cans and liquor bottles. "The shower's over there." Emma points to the opposite end of the trailer. "Can you get it started for me?"

"Sure." I sprint across the room, careful to step around the stacked beer can landmines and slide a flimsy plastic door into the wall. Inside, the tiny bathroom is crammed tight with a slim shower, toilet and half-sized sink, all of which are in as good of shape as the rest of the place. I open the shower door, turn on the water, then attempt to skirt the edge of the space to get out before Emma starts undressing her mom. Using strength I didn't know she possessed, Emma somehow wrangles her mother into the shower—clothes and all.

"I can take it from here," she says. I just nod my head and shut the door behind me.

Back outside, I find a hose and spray down the steps. I guess I know now why they don't like to talk about their mom. I wonder when it started—the drinking?

If I had to guess, I'd say when Emma's dad got sick or shortly after he died. How many times had Emma or Kat gone to "run errands" when really, they were having to deal with their alcoholic mom?

There's a semi-clean lawn chair set up amongst the weeds, and I consider waiting there for Emma, but it seems wrong to leave her to handle all of this by herself. So, I decide to put on my big-girl panties and go back into the trailer to pick up a bit. Without the foul stench of vomit and urine overwhelming my senses, the stagnant scent of stale beer, mildew and body odor fills my nostrils. I search under the sink—ignoring the scratching sounds coming from the back of the cabinet. I really do not want to know what's making them. Unfortunately, if there are trash bags in this place, I can't find them. I do, however, find a decent-sized box stuffed into a corner and I set to work picking up cans and placing them in the box.

It's so nasty. I'm fighting some serious whole-body cringing right now. I've lost count of the times I've picked up a can to have a roach skitter out from beneath it. But I am nothing if not stubborn and by the time Emma helps her mom into her bedroom, I've cleaned up most of the empty cans and bottles and thrown them in the trash bin outside.

Emma doesn't seem to notice what I've done, or maybe she does but is too embarrassed to admit it. She won't meet my eyes as she moves to leave, just gives me a curt, "I'm finished," then heads outside. Not a word is spoken the entire thirty-minute drive back to our place. I drive and Emma sits quietly in the passenger seat, picking at her nails. I have about five million questions running through my mind, but I don't voice them. If she wants to talk about it, she will.

It isn't until I've parked in front of our apartment that Emma speaks, though she still won't meet my eyes. "Don't tell anyone about this alright."

"Of course not," I say, and I mean it. If I were in her position, I wouldn't want anyone to know either—half of them will pity you and the other half will scorn you. It's a no-win situation, no matter what you do. I take her hand in mine. "I'm your friend, and I'm here for you no matter what. Okay?"

"Okay," she says, and though her head remains bowed and her assault on her poor cuticles unceasing, I can see the corner of her lip tip up into the beginnings of a smile.

Twenty-Six
Who's Afraid of the PDA?
Jacob

MAYBE MY HEAD IS all screwed up because the reaming Coach gave me after I tried to punch Dean was one for the history books, and I couldn't care less. I'm not going to lie; I'm happy as hell Dean got suspended—I probably would have too, if I wasn't already benched—but right now, all I care about is getting to class so I can be with Stella. It's only been about four hours since I left her this morning, and I'm already jumping out of my skin to see her.

Is it possible to be addicted to another person? That's how this feels right now, like an addiction. It's not just that I miss her. I've always missed Stella when she's not around. I've always looked forward to seeing her because she has a way of cheering me up just by her presence. But this is so much more intense. I crave her. Maybe it's because this is all new, and things will settle down over time, but I've never felt this way about a girl before. It's kind of terrifying and super weird when I think about it because this is Stella—the girl I've known most of my life. At the same time, when I'm with her, it feels totally natural. And that's probably the weirdest part of all—that it really isn't weird.

Jesus, I'm even confusing myself. Maybe that concussion did screw up my head. It would explain why I'm falling for my best friend.

I step into the lecture hall and Stella's waiting for me in our regular seats. She doesn't see me at first, but when she does, the smile that lights up her face is so beautiful; it's like she's the sun shining only for me.

I am in so much trouble.

I slide into the seat next to her and her bright smile turns shy. "Hey," she says, dipping her head and not quite meeting my eyes. If I didn't know Stella so well, I might think she was embarrassed—but that isn't it. She's unsure. Something in my chest twists at the realization. After all of this, she's either not truly convinced that I want to be with her, or worse, that I want to be seen with her. It's such utter bull shit, but Stella's never been one to see her own worth.

The hair has slipped from her shoulder to conceal the lower half of her face—like her own private wall. I tuck the hair behind her ear and rest my forehead against her temple. "Don't cover yourself," I whisper. They're the same words I said to her the night before and by the blush spreading across her cheeks, I'd say she remembers.

She tilts her head up and meets my eyes. "Sorry." There's a tremor to her voice and her hands fidget nervously on her desk. It kills me to see her like this so I do the only thing I can think of to reassure her. I lean over and press my lips to hers.

The kiss is soft and chaste, nothing compared to the way we devoured each other the night before. Still, my stomach dips as if in free-fall and my cock begins to harden like I'm a thirteen-year-old again having his first kiss. Though, in my cock's defense, the past two times with Stella were so beyond anything I've experienced before, I can't blame it for being a little overly enthusiastic.

We break the kiss and her eyes flutter open, the light filtering in the multitude of windows setting off the flecks of gold so they almost glow. Then she rests her head against my shoulder and all the tension eases out of her with a sigh. Good. I kiss the top of her head, but can't seem to pull away. Her vanilla scent, mixed with a floral aroma I can only assume is her shampoo, is intoxicating. I might have stayed like that, sniffing her head for the next two hours like some psycho if Professor Gibson hadn't given me the look of disapproval when he entered the room.

He's about twenty minutes into a rant about the differences between graphic fiction and manga before I'm convinced his attention has moved away from us. I lean into Stella and whisper, "You free after class?"

She presses her lips together in a failed attempt to hide her smile and nods. Excellent.

Twenty-Seven

Haven't I Seen This Horror Flick?

Stella

"So, this isn't one of those scenarios where the innocent girl is lured into the woods by the evil killer, where he murders her and buries the body never to be found again, is it?" I say, my eyes trained on my feet as I pick my way through the pine needles, broken branches and prickly underbrush blanketing the forest floor. I'm regretting my choice of attire—jean shorts, a burgundy tank and sneakers. Considering it's eighty degrees in the middle of October—hello global warming—my clothing made sense until I found out I was going for a hike through the woods on what barely qualified as a trail. Now, it'll be a miracle if I don't come out of here without my legs looking like something out of a horror movie.

Jacob takes my elbow, steering me around a tangle of thorny vines. "And you're the innocent victim? Riiiight," he says, the sarcasm rolling off him in waves. "If anyone here should be afraid, It's me. Who knows what you could be hiding in here." He hooks a finger in the neckline of my tank and pulls it out to peek at my breasts.

I bat his hand away. "Oh please, we both know my boobs aren't big enough to hide a pocketknife, much less anything substantial."

"I'm not sure." Jacob grabs me about the waist and pulls me into him, so his front presses against my back, then brushes the hair back over my shoulder and begins kissing his way up my neck. "I think a full body cavity search may be in order."

The image of him stripping me naked and exploring every inch of my body, flashes through my mind, and a rush of heat floods my middle and pools between my legs. There's got to be something wrong with me if that turns me on, right? "Sounds kinky," I say, my attempt at humor coming out a little too breathy.

He chuckles. "You don't know the half of it."

"Okay, now I'm scared."

Laughing, Jacob doesn't release me but continues to press me forward, while hobbling around my feet like a penguin, so we don't face plant in the brush. "We're almost there."

"My gravesite?" I peek at him over my shoulder. Jacob's lips are pressed together like he's trying to hide his smile and failing terribly.

"Among other things."

Finally, the trees thin, and we come across what at first glance looks like a clearing. As we move closer, I realize this isn't a clearing at all but a small lake with water so blue, it's like someone dropped a hundred gallons of bright-blue dye in it. At the same time, it's so clear, I can see straight through to the beige rocks lining the bottom. "What is this place?"

"It's a sinkhole. The area's chocked full of them." He edges us closer to where the ground falls off several feet above the water. "One of the guys on the team is a local and told us about them. You see that stone?" He points to the beige stone visible around the edge of the sinkhole. "That's limestone that's basically collapsed in on itself. The water is straight from the aquifer."

"That's why it's so clear."

He nods. "And so cold. Come on."

The incline is steeper than it looked from above, so our descent is slow. Jacob holds my hand the entire way down, pointing out areas to step and others to avoid. He's being overly cautious and protective, but that's Jacob, and I'd be lying if I said there wasn't a small part of me that didn't secretly love the way he's always looking out for me.

Jacob must have scoped this place out ahead of time because he leads us straight to a mostly-flat stone right beside the water and drops his backpack, with a plunk, onto the rock. We remove our shoes and I'm expecting the stone to be baking, but it's only a little warm against the soles of my feet. I make my way over to the water's edge and dip in a toe to test the temperature.

"Shit." I jerk my foot back. "It's freezing."

"I told you," he says, his expression more amused than smug. "Cool, right?" He sits down, pulls a couple of waters from his bag and hands me one.

I take a seat next to him, twist off the cap and down the water. The walk wasn't that long, but it's so frigging hot and humid, I feel like I've been through a marathon. I'm covered in a sheen of sweat, droplets rolling between my breasts and along my spine.

"So are you ready," he asks, standing up. Employing the universally accepted sexy-guy method of striptease, Jacob grabs the back of his shirt and tugs it off over his head.

I squint up at him, "Ready for what?"

There's a mischievous glint in his eyes that I'm all too familiar with. It's the same look he gives me every time he's about to rope me into something that's going to get me in a crap-ton of trouble. "To swim," he says as if it's no big deal.

Now, I know exactly what he's getting at, but I'm going to play it dumb because it's the best stalling tactic I can come up with at the moment. "Uh, we didn't bring suits."

He tilts his head and raises his brows to me as if to say, *"I know you're not this stupid,"* so I quickly jump to Plan B—whining.

"But it's so cold and what if we leave our clothes and some animal comes along and snatches them away?"

He gives me a knowing smirk, "Suit yourself," then strips down right in front of me like it's the most natural thing in the world. I'm pretty sure my heart has shut down completely, and I'm definitely not breathing, possibly drooling, because

Jacob naked is a sight to behold. The bright light accentuates his broad shoulders and sculpted pecs dusted with hair, which narrow to abs I want to trace with my tongue. He has that V along the hips that I thought only existed in romance novels and Calvin Klein ads, which basically forces the eyes down to his... thingy. And okay, I probably sound like a four-year-old, but does he have to just wave it around like that? God, even his thighs are sexy. He knows it too, the bastard. While all of my bodily functions have shut down, except for my eyes which scan him in a purely involuntary response, he just winks and dives in.

He pops back out of the water, flicking his head so the water sprays from his hair. The smile he gives me is devastating, and I groan before I can stop myself. He hears it, of course, and his smile ticks up another notch. "Come on, Stells. You know you wanna."

I press my lips together and shake my head. "No, I don't think I wanna."

He freestyles over to me and rests two very sexy arms on the rock at my feet. "Please?" He bats his lashes playfully, and something about the way the water clings to the fine hairs has me reaching out to sweep my thumb across them. He closes his eyes, lips parting on a soft intake of air. I lean over and brush my lips across his. They're freezing cold and yet, I'm melting.

I pull away and his eyes blink open. He gives me the strangest look then, like he's never seen me before. "Turn around so I can undress," I say.

He wraps icy fingers around my ankles, his smirk returning. "But that's the best part."

I cock a brow. "You sure about that?"

He releases my legs and wades backward. "One of them, at least."

I'm terrified and turned on in equal measures. Part of me wants to give him the show he's obviously waiting for and part of me wants to shy away. But I'm tired of hiding, of being embarrassed. I want to be brazen and adventurous, not just for Jacob, but for me too. I stand, locking eyes with Jacob as I grip the bottom of my tank top with trembling hands and whip it over my head, revealing my white cotton bra that does nothing to hide my hardened nipples. Biting my lip, I unbutton and unzip my shorts then slowly shimmy them down my legs and step out of them. Jacob's eyes track every motion, his breaths coming more rapidly. There's an intense hunger in his eyes and the fact that I'm the one who put it there makes me feel so fucking beautiful and sexy. I slip a strap from one shoulder, then the other. Then, I reach around my back to unlatch my bra and being a complete tease hold it to my chest for a few seconds before letting it fall to the ground. I lower my arms, resting them at my sides, giving him a full view of my breasts.

There's something so hot and freeing about standing here half-naked in front of him in broad daylight and allowing him to look his fill. I feel like a goddess, and I am so turned on, I'm sure I'm soaking through my white cotton panties. Finally, I roll those down my legs and step out of them, but I don't jump in—not yet. "Happy," I ask.

Jacob's Adam's apple bobs as he swallows and nods. Now, it's my turn to smirk. Never in my life have I ever felt more powerful than I do in this moment.

I raise my arms above my head and dive. The icy cold water is a shock against my overheated skin, but it is also invigorating. I paddle to the surface, take a breath of blessedly warm air and laugh a bit from the wonder of it all. Closing my eyes, I run my hands over my face and scalp to wick away some of the water. When I finally open them again, Jacob is wading so close that all I would need to do is reach out a hand to touch him. He grips me by the hips and pulls me closer until my body is flush against his. A hand cups my cheek, thumb gently stroking my icy flesh. Jacob's eyes flash with something like astonishment. "Wow," he says on a breath, then presses his lips to mine, setting off a tingling in my extremities—or maybe that's hypothermia. It doesn't matter. We're making our own heat. Jacob kisses me slowly, thoroughly, as if he's trying to memorize every touch and taste. Tilting my head, he deepens the kiss while calloused hands slide around to my ass and back. Jacob releases my mouth to nip and suck his way down my chest, and I arch my back urging him on. He takes my nipple into his mouth and drags his teeth along the tender flesh—sending a bolt of pleasure straight to my clit. I cry out. I'm losing my mind. I need him inside of me now.

"Jacob," I say with a gasp, as I reach between us to wrap my hand around his cock. Against the freezing water, it's so hot and engorged. I squeeze and stroke him up and down his length.

"Fuck," Jacob says then drags a hand down my backside until he reaches my center, his fingers teasing my entrance.

"Please," I beg. "Please, Jacob. Fuck me."

He swears again. "I don't have a condom."

"I'm on birth control. I promise. It's fine. Now fuck me." I smack his ass and he growls in my ear. Gripping my ass, Jacob lifts me to straddle him and walks us into shallower water, his mouth never leaving mine until we're only ankle deep. He lowers me to the ground and whips me around, so my ass is pressing against his cock. He palms my breast and rolls my nipple, the cold sharpening the sensation and making me wet. His breath is hot against my icy cheek, his voice deep and gravely like he's been screaming when he says, "On your hands and knees, baby." I don't hesitate. I drop into the shallow water, only my hands and knees submerged, and Jacob kneels behind me. Running his hands over my ass and up my spine, he positions himself at my entrance, the tip of his cock pressing into me and out again. Pressing and retreating, pressing and retreating each time a little further—teasing until I finally scream, "Jacob," and he slams all the way into me.

Gripping my hips, he pumps in and out of me faster and faster, hitting that spot inside me that makes me crazy, ratcheting my pleasure higher and higher until I'm screaming his name. He wraps a hand around my hair, tugging my head back and riding me like a fucking animal. I love it. I want him to use me, own me. I'm scaling the edge of my orgasm, the pressure building until I think I might explode. Then Jacob reaches around me and gives a hard slap to my clit, and I see stars. My orgasm pounds through my body. On and on my sex spasms and squeezes his cock. His control slipping, Jacob slams into me once and again and again, his cock jerking inside me as he finds his release. We push against each other milking the last waves of our orgasms before toppling into the shallow water in a tangle of limbs.

Twenty-Eight
Busted!
Jacob

THE SILENCE SETTLES OVER us like a blanket, my raspy breaths and the twitter of birds the only sound. I pull out of Stella, and she whimpers but doesn't budge. Jesus, that was intense. I don't even know how to wrap my mind around it, right now. All I can think about is getting Stella out of the cold water. I kneel beside her, and she smiles lazily up at me as I lift her into my arms, carry her to our rock and set her down on a towel. Then I lay behind her, pulling her back against my chest and close my eyes as we bask in the warm sunlight.

I awake to the sound of voices overlapping and drawing closer.

"Shit." I am instantly sitting up and awake. "Stella. Wake up." I shake her by the shoulder.

She blinks up at me. "What?"

"Get dressed."

She must hear the voices then because her eyes get huge, and she scrambles for our clothes. "Shit. Shit. Shit. Shit. Shit." She repeats the words over and over like a mantra, and I can't help but chuckle a little at her panicking. "It's not funny, Jacob. Help me." Her voice is serious but she's still smiling.

I've got my shorts on, but Stella's only managed her tank before figures start to emerge from the woods. Quickly, I throw the towel around her waist and pull her behind me. She has her face pressed against my back and she's shaking with laughter. Two guys and two girls about our age step out of the woods. A blond guy, tall and skinny, is the first to spot us.

"Oh, hey." He waves. His drawn brows tell me that he knows something weird is going on but not what.

"Hi." I begin to wave but realize at the last minute that I have Stella's underwear in my hand, and I shove it at her behind my back.

Stella just squeaks and is laughing so hard now, she's shaking my whole upper body. Keeping a straight face is impossible as the rest of the group takes notice of us. The other guy is shorter, with long brown hair pulled up into a topknot. The girls are both stick thin and petite with brown hair, but one is extremely pale while the other's skin is a dusky brown.

They're all looking at us like we're lunatics.

The guy with the topknot is the next to speak. "Are we interrupting something?"

"Nope," I answer while Stella yells, "Yes."

Grins spread across each of their faces as it becomes clear what's going on.

"We were just leaving," I say. "Just have to get our things together." I turn around to face Stella who is so red she looks like a tomato about to burst. "Let's just climb up," I whisper. "You can put the rest on when we reach the top."

"Are you kidding? I can't climb up like this." She gestures to the towel. "I'll be flashing my hoo-ha the whole way up."

A laugh bursts out of me. "Your hoo-ha?" I say a little too loudly.

She slaps my chest, and I clamp my mouth shut.

"It's a medical term," Blondie calls back.

Stella groans, "Fuuuck," and drops her head to my chest.

Drawing back, Stella forces me to turn around to face the others. The guys and the pale girl have waded into the water while the other girl sets up camp on a rock a little off and to our left. "Just cover me, okay?" she asks.

I can't help but mess with her at this point, so I reply, "I'll try, but that ass is pretty hard to conceal. I'm a pretty big guy, but even I can only do so much."

The swimmers are cracking up with us now, and I'm having too much fun to stop. "It's huge," I say, holding my hands apart at a span at least double Stella's actual size.

She slaps my back. "Fuck you, Jacob."

I peek over my shoulder as Stella is tugging up her panties. "It's okay, babe. You know I like them big."

"Shut up. Shut up. Shut up," she hollers, while literally jumping up and down. "And look away, you perve." She half-heartedly shoves the side of my head.

"Are you kidding? This is the second-best show I've gotten today," I reply, obviously alluding to the sexy-as-fuck striptease she did for me earlier.

She's pulling up her shorts, all the time ranting, "Oh my god, Jacob. I am going to kill you. I'm going to chop you up into little pieces and feed you to my neighbor's cat."

"I think that might be a bit too much for one cat."

"Not the part I'm talking about."

A chorus of "Ohhh's" sounds from the water.

"On no, you didn't." I spin around and Stella's lucky to have managed to zip up her shorts before I lunge for her. She squeals and darts away but gets about two feet before I have her pinned to my chest.

"You are in so much trouble," I say.

She smiles up at me and the pure fucking joy in that smile about sends me to my knees. It's the most beautiful thing I've ever seen, and I know, in that moment, that I would do anything it takes to keep that smile on her face. I cup her cheek, dragging my thumb back and forth along her cheekbone. Her skin is so soft. I didn't know skin could be so soft. She presses her face into my palm and closes her eyes. My whole body is buzzing and jittery, and I feel ready to bust out of my skin. Everything around us has fallen away, and it's just me and Stella and the words that keep repeating in my head. *I love you. I love you. I love you.*

Twenty-Nine
How Does She Do It?
Stella

Jacob had to do some evening football training thingy, so after what was by far the best date I have ever had, I dropped him off at the athletic complex and headed home. My head must have still been in the clouds because I had fully expected my apartment to be empty. Instead, I find myself walking into a clusterfuck of monumental proportions.

Charlie, Kat and Emma are all seated in the living room surrounding the coffee table, which is currently littered with open Chinese takeout containers. Kat sits on the floor, the other two on the couch, all stuffing their faces. The sweet, delicious scent of honey and sesame sets my mouth-watering, and I am suddenly ravenous. When was the last time I ate?

"Stella," Charlie calls. She pats the cushion to her left. "Sit down. Are you hungry?"

"Starving," I say and take a seat.

Emma gives me a soft smile. "We got way too much." I don't know what else to say, so I just smile back. Things have been strained with us since everything came out about Jacob, and I don't know how to fix it, or even if that's possible.

It's funny because out of the three girls, Kat is the one I'm the least close to, but damn if that girl doesn't take one look at me, points and yells, "You had sex," so loudly they probably heard it in the next town over.

I freeze. How the hell does she know that?

Charlie flattens her hands against my cheeks, squeezing them together until my lips pucker out, and forces me to look at her.

"Can you please let go of my face?" I mumble-spit between scrunched-up lips.

Charlie's eyes go three times their normal size. "Oh my god. You did."

There are two problems with this scenario, as I see it. First, is it really that big of news that I had sex? It's not like I was a virgin, though it had only been a few times and approximately two years ago, but geez, way to make a girl feel like a loser. And second, and more importantly…

"How can you possibly tell that by looking at me?" I ask.

"See," Kat's pointing that damn finger at me again. "She's not denying it."

Charlie waves a hand at my face. "You've got the whole post orgasm glow."

"And pine needles in your hair," says Kat. She pops a whole dumpling in her mouth and smiles, obviously pleased with herself for calling me out.

I glance at Emma, who's watching our exchange, her face devoid of any expression.

Charlie squeals and claps her hands. "I want all the details. Did he go down on you? Did you go down on him? Does Dean's body to dick ratio match up because if so…" Charlie fans herself.

Kat pivots to look at me, her expression incredulous, and raises both palms in a double-stop motion. "Whoa. Isn't that the asshole who punched the wall? Seriously, Stella?"

Charlie starts questioning Kat about the wall, but all I can think of is that I never told her about Jacob or everything that went down with Dean. Shit. She's going to be so pissed. Normally, Charlie would be the first person I'd go to with this sort of thing, but I've been so caught up with Jacob that I hadn't gotten around to telling her.

Unfortunately, before I can come up with a way to deflect her question until we're alone, Emma responds. "It wasn't Dean." The other two girls' heads whip around to look at Emma, who continues picking at her Kung Pow Chicken like she's searching for hidden treasure. "It was Jacob."

Kat and Charlie turn back to me so slowly, it reminds me of something you'd see in a corny family comedy. Not that I'm feeling particularly comedic at the moment. "Emma I—"

She cuts me off. "Don't apologize." Taking a breath, Emma sets down her food and meets my eyes. "Jacob and I were just a fling. It never could have been more than that. He was too hung up on you." She lowers her gaze and wrings her hands in her lap. "How much of a selfish asshole can one person be, huh?" I'm stunned silent, but Emma continues on. "I don't think it was him really as much as it was the idea of him. The way he looked at you like you hung the fucking moon. Nobody would think of messing with you because they knew Jacob would do anything, anything to protect you." A tear trickles down her cheek and she swiftly wipes it away. "He adored you in a way I'd never even known existed, and I wanted that for myself." She takes a shuddering breath. "It was so obvious he was in love with you and you with him, but I convinced myself you weren't. I fooled myself into thinking you two didn't see each other that way because I wanted someone to love me the way he loves you." Her voice breaks on those last few words and the tears that had been welling in her eyes sprang free. "And you are such a good friend. And you didn't deserve that. And I'm so fucking sorry."

I rush to Emma's side and wrap my arms around her, rocking her as we both cry. "It's okay," I say between hiccupy breaths. "I love you. You're such an amazing person, Em. So much more than you give yourself credit for and somebody will come along who sees that. I'm sure of it. You just have to give yourself time."

"Dammit, Stella," Emma says, studying her fingers as they fidget with the hem of her blouse and avoiding my eyes. "You're supposed to hate me."

"Truth is," I begin, "I knew if I said something, you'd back off, but I just figured," I shrug, "he's a good guy and why should I get in your way when there was no chance he would want me. Then when you did get together, all that logic went out the window, you know? I was angry and resentful and strangely pissed at myself for being angry with you. Who knows how things might have panned out if you hadn't dated him? All I know is, right now I am so happy, and I'm not going to ruin it by being angry about something that's over and in the past. I just want my friend back, okay?"

Emma nods. "Me too."

"Yay, girl power," Charlie hollers then plows into Emma and me, almost knocking us over with a full-body hug but succeeding in making us laugh, which was probably her intent. Then comes a much more subdued Kat. She wraps her arms around the three of us and kisses her sister on the temple, but when she speaks, it's so low that only I can make out the words, "Thank you."

Thirty
When Things Seem Too Good to be True...
Stella

NOTHING BEATS A PARTY after a hard-won game. The place is electric. All that adrenaline coming off the win is being funneled into dancing and drinking and getting crazy. A win against a top-tier team, even more so. So, when we beat the top-ranked team, for the division win, the shit pretty much hits the fan.

This party is being put on by a senior linebacker, Cory Haines, whose family obviously has more money than God and is decidedly absent for this momentous event. Every square inch of the kitchen countertop is covered with liquor. I've seen full-service bars displaying less alcohol. This doesn't include the two kegs or pot circle out back. The funny part is that, even though the party's in their honor, most of the players are sober—nobody gets to this level without a considerable amount of self-discipline. Once the season is over, these guys will go back to their party-animal ways, but until then, they're making sure not to do anything that could risk their chances. Jacob's no different and I'm glad because although I'm happy to celebrate the awesome plays he made today—two touchdowns, thank you very much—I'm not really in the mood to party. Not that I've ever been much of a party girl, but for the past six weeks that we've been together, Jacob's been so busy with school and football that I prefer to be alone with him any chance I get.

Fortunately, he feels the same. "Can we please leave now?" Jacob whispers in my ear. We're seated on a patio chair out back—Jacob on the chair and me on Jacob—with Malcolm and Ryan and Charlie, watching the games of chicken being played out in the pool and placing bets on how long it will take before people start taking off their suits. So far, nobody's gotten naked, leaving only Malcolm and Charlie in the running to win, since the time hasn't yet passed for their bets.

"There it goes," Malcolm shouts, when one of the girls playing chicken gets her bikini top pulled off. "Pay up suckas." The rest of us groan and hand over five dollars each. Malcolm counts it out like this is some major win and not a measly twenty bucks.

"I think that's our cue," Jacob says.

Malcolm splays his arms. "Awe, man. Come on. You two are getting to be like an old married couple. Stay." He raises a glass half full of some orangy concoction. "Have a mimosa," he says, nailing the snooty British accent.

Jacob rubs his chin as if considering; then holding his hands, palms up, like a scale he says, "Let's see, getting drunk," right palm goes up, "or getting laid?" right palm goes down, left palm goes up.

I slap his arm. "Hey."

Jacob laughs and shakes his left hand. "Gotta go with getting laid, bro. Sorry."

Malcolm waves us off muttering something about "goddamn couples."

We make our goodbyes and head to the car. I toss Jacob the keys and he snatches them out of the air, but when I lift the handle for the passenger side door, it doesn't catch. "Babe, you got to unlock—" I stop cold as I realize Jacob hasn't moved any closer to the car. An instinctual part of me recognizes that something is very wrong here. The hairs on the back of my neck rise, and my heart slams against my ribcage. "Jacob," I call out, my voice a trembling whisper. I stumble over to him and lay my hands on either side of his face. His gaze is vacant, but his eyes blink rapidly. "Jacob," I say more forcefully this time, "Jacob."

No response, just blinking, blinking.

"Jacob," I yell. I slap his chest, grasp him by the shoulders and shake him with all my terror-fueled strength. "Baby, please. Wake up," I say, tears reducing him to a dark, unmovable shape. "Help me," I scream at the top of my lungs, my hands never releasing his shoulders. "Help me."

Footsteps rumble down the driveway. Two boys come into view, then three more behind them, and just as they reach us, the rigidity seeps from Jacob's body, and he sags in my arms. The boys each grab one of his arms and help me lower him to the ground. Jacob slumps against the car bumper and looks at me, his eyes droopy and tired but aware. "Stells," he says, confusion marring his beautiful face. "What's wrong, baby?"

Thirty-One
And the World Turns Upside Down
Jacob

"Mr. Gonzales," the doctor begins and already I don't like the guy. He's a balding old fart who's looking at me like I'm an asshole, wasting his time. Like I enjoy scaring the shit out of my girlfriend and making my mom miss work and Ana miss school, so I can eat shitty food and wear a gown that leaves my ass hanging out the back. As if sensing my rising hostility, Stella squeezes my hand.

"It says here," the doctor continues, "that when you were last diagnosed with a concussion, you told the doctors that it was your first concussion. Is that correct?"

What is this a fucking interrogation? "Yes. That's correct," I reply, trying to match the snide tone of his voice.

He purses his lips but continues. "Well, your MRI says otherwise."

I'm trying to process his words, when my mom asks, "What does that mean?"

"That means that there is evidence of significant scarring on your son's brain, most likely from a previous event or events."

My mom chokes back a sob.

"Esta bien, Mama," I lie because in no way is this alright.

Turning his attention back to me, the doctor sighs and says, "From your girlfriend's description and these tests, it's most likely you experienced a focal impaired awareness seizure. Unlike grand mal seizures, they can be easily missed because they're so subtle. You've probably had them before and weren't even aware. If I had to guess, I'd say they were probably triggered by your most recent concussion."

I tip my head back against the mattress and close my eyes to hold back the tears blurring my vision. My mom's sobbing in the chair next to me and as much as I love her, I kind of wish she wasn't here because the last thing I want to do right now is comfort her.

As if that wasn't enough, the doctor continues chastising me like a total asshole. "You're lucky your girlfriend realized what was happening. Playing football with this sort of condition is extremely dangerous."

"So, no more football, then?" I ask. It's a stupid question. The minute Stella told me what happened, I knew, but some delusional part of me has to hear the words.

The doctor removes his glasses and rubs his eyes. "Mr. Gonzales, I understand that football is important to you, but we're talking about your brain. Lying to your doctors so you can keep playing—"

"I wasn't lying, damn it," I say, cutting him off. My blood pressure is rising, blasting through my veins as if trying to break free. I almost hope it does. I hope I fucking drown in it.

"He wasn't lying," my mom says, her voice trembling like an old woman. "He just doesn't remember." All four of us turn stunned gazes on her. Her head is bowed so low that I can't even tell if her eyes are still open. She twists the tissue in her lap like it did something to piss her off, but that's it. She drops a fucking bomb on us all then stops speaking.

"Mama?" I can barely get the word out of my aching throat because I know what she's about to say, and I can already feel the fissures forming in my chest, waiting for that one, two punch that will shatter me.

My mom lifts her gaze to mine. Her face is tear-stained and splotched with red and there's so much regret in her brown eyes that I almost feel guilty for being furious with her at the moment. "Tu Padre. El—"

I explode.

"Fuck," I roar and throw the nearest object, a soda can, across the room. It smashes against the wall spraying Canada Dry all over the mint-green paint and vinyl floor. I don't care. I wish there were more. I wish I had twenty cans to throw, that I could demolish this room if it would stop me from feeling like a dam bursting. Splotches of colors stain my vision as I press my palms against my eyes in an idiotic attempt to stop the torrent of tears streaming down my face. It's about as effective as trying to hold back a dam with a band-aid.

She lied. My mom fucking lied. He beat me so bad I got a concussion or two or three or who the hell knows how many, and she never even took me to the hospital, never even told me it happened.

I can't stand it. This feeling like I want to crawl out of my skin. He's still hurting me, after all this time. He's like a ghost I can't get rid of, destroying my fucking life. It wasn't bad enough that he made my childhood a living hell. No. Now he's taking away football and left me with epilepsy to boot. What am I going to do now? Everything I've worked for is shot to shit because my own father hated me.

It hurts to breathe. I'm sobbing like a fucking three-year-old, curled up into a ball on my side, facing away from Stella. My arms are slung over my head to hide the sad sack of shit I've become. I don't want her to see me like this. I don't want anyone to see me like this, but I can't stop.

Stella's at my side, trying to comfort me. She's rubbing my arm and calling my name, and I just need her to stop. I need her to stop because it's making it worse. I jerk my arm away. "Stop, Stella. Please."

But she doesn't stop. "Jacob," she says. I can hear the sob in her voice and it's like she's stomping on my already shredded heart.

"Goddammit, Stella. Stop!" I wrench my arm from her grasp. "Just go away. Please. Just fucking leave me alone." I'm screaming at her and it's wrong and totally unfair. I'm like an injured dog, lashing out because I'm so goddamned scared and angry and a hundred other emotions I can't even put words to.

And then I hear the door snick shut as she leaves the room, and I don't even have the energy to hate myself for pushing her away.

Thirty-Two
What Just Happened?
Stella

Stepping into the hall, I'm a big blubbering mess. I don't know what to do or where to go. I can't even see with the tears clouding my vision. People are staring, I'm sure of it, and all I can do is hide my face against the wall and sob. I don't understand what I did wrong. I just wanted to comfort him, and he threw me away.

A warm hand rests on my shoulder. "Come on, love." It's a woman's voice, soft and soothing. I turn my head to see an older, dark-skinned woman with curly silver hair giving me a sad smile. She's wearing blue scrubs and a nurse's badge, though my vision's too blurry to make out the name. "Let's get you settled somewhere private, alright?"

I don't have the energy to speak, so I simply nod. She leads me down the hallway and into a small room with about six chairs lining the walls and a small coffee table covered with magazines in the center of it all. "You stay here and get some rest. If anyone comes looking for you, I'll send them this way."

I nod again, even though it wasn't really a question. My eyelids are heavy with exhaustion, and I don't fight it. I close my eyes and welcome the oblivion of sleep.

I'm awakened by the sound of my name and a hand gently shaking my shoulder. "Stella." I don't need to see her face to know that soft, sweet voice belongs to Jacob's sister, Adriana.

I'm all achy from sitting curled up in this chair for so long. I sit up and stretch and rub my eyes. "How long was I out for?"

Adriana smiles. She's so pretty—basically the female version of Jacob—except with fuller lips and porn star boobs. "It's been about an hour. How are you doing?"

I shrug. "Is Jacob okay?"

She takes a seat in the chair next to mine. "He's calmed down, if that's what you're asking. The doctor gave him some sleeping pills. They're keeping him overnight so they can monitor him with some machine to see if it can catch him having a seizure."

"Good," I say to the floor. I can't look her in the eyes. I have no reason to be embarrassed, but after what happened, I can't help but feel exposed.

"What happened in there, that had nothing to do with you, Stella. You get that, right?"

"Yeah," I say, even though I don't really get it, but I'm not about to bother her with my problems. She has enough to deal with right now.

"Did Jacob ever tell you about our father?" she asks.

I look up at her for the first time and realize she's as big of a mess as the rest of us—body stooped from exhaustion, eyes all swollen and red from crying. "Not really," I say. "He just said he was an asshole and didn't want to talk about it. It didn't feel right to press him on it."

Adriana rolls her eyes. "I figured. Jacob thinks he can just bottle everything up and not deal with it, so when the levee breaks," she waves a hand in the direction of Jacob's room, "It explodes." Tears well in her eyes and her hands shake, but her voice is steady when she speaks. "Our father was extremely abusive—not the drunk asshole kind either. He was just an evil, angry son of a bitch who got off on hurting others. It would usually start out with him beating up on Mama. Jacob and I would hide in my bedroom closet whenever he went into a rage and sometimes Papa would beat Mama and stop there and sometimes, he would come for us." Something twists in my gut, and I feel like I might be sick.

Adriana looks at me out of the corner of her eye, then raises a trembling hand to her mouth as if afraid to let her words spread too far. Tears spill down her cheeks and her voice cracks when she says, "Jacob would tell me to stay put and go out to meet my father. He would let himself get beaten to protect me."

The bottom drops out of my stomach. Jacob was eight when he moved to Orlando—just a little boy. What kind of damage could a grown man do to such a tiny body? I shiver and rub my arms, not from cold but from revulsion. I pull Adriana into a hug, both of us crying—Adriana for her guilt over the pain her brother endured and me for that brave boy who protected his sister in the only way he could.

We stayed like that a little while, both of us crying, while also trying to comfort each other. Adriana pulls back, takes a deep breath and wipes her cheeks with the back of her hand. "So, the whole point of telling you this is so you know he wasn't angry at you. He was angry at my father. You just happened to run into his crosshairs is all, and maybe he knows you love him enough to forgive him for it."

"Thanks." I give her a small smile, which she returns with one of her own, before popping out of her seat

"I should get going. My mom's waiting for me to go back to the hotel."

I follow her out and back to Jacob's room. Inside, Jacob is sound asleep. His mom, Gloria, sits on the reclining chair with her head in her hands but looks up when we approach. Her face is tear-streaked and haggard, just like the rest of us, but her eyes appear haunted. I can't imagine what it must have been like in that situation, constantly afraid for your life and your children's. It must have taken so much courage for her to escape that and start over on her own, but she'll only blame herself for not doing it sooner. The corners of her lips tip up slightly when our eyes meet like she wants to smile for me but just can't.

"Ready," Adriana asks, and Gloria nods. She crosses to where Jacob sleeps curled up on his side, brushes back the hair that's fallen across his forehead and leans over to kiss his temple. "Good night, mi cielo." Gloria blinks back tears as she rights herself, then pulls me into a bone-crushing hug. A few seconds short of me passing out, she releases me, only to lay her hands on my cheeks and kiss my forehead. "Thank you for looking out for him."

"Always," I promise.

Pressing her lips into a line, she gives me a curt nod, then takes one last look at Jacob before grabbing her purse and heading out the door. Adriana waves and follows her mom out.

I blow out a breath, letting go of some of my pent-up tension and relax into the ugly leather recliner. Checking my phone, I see that I've got twelve missed texts—most of those from Malcolm, who was really upset when Jacob told him not to visit and hasn't stopped texting me all day. A couple are from Emma and Charlie, checking in. I haven't talked to either of them since this morning, so I should probably reply. Maybe I could ask Charlie to stop by my place and pick up some clothes and a toothbrush for me. I run fingers through my tangled mop, stopping every few seconds to work out a knot—a hairbrush might not be a bad idea either.

I shoot a text to Charlie and wait for a reply.

There are also two missed calls from my mom. I love the woman, but she is a heart attack waiting to happen the way she worries about everything. I sigh. If I don't call her back soon, she'll probably phone the police or worse, decide to make a road trip up here. Taking one last look at Jacob, I step just outside the hospital door to phone my mom.

She picks up on the first ring. "Stella, I've been trying to reach you for hours."

"Hi Mom," I reply because I enjoy being a pain in her ass.

"Don't you give me that, Stella. I was worried. Are you doing alright? How's Jacob? Have the doctors told you what's going on yet?"

I sag against the wall. I am way too tired for this, but I answer anyway. "Jacob's doing better." I pause, not sure how much Jacob would want me to share with her. I decide to keep it simple. "The doctor said he had a seizure."

My mom sighs. "That's what I was afraid of. And football?"

I shake my head even though she can't see me. "Over."

"Jesus. He's going to lose his scholarship."

"I don't know."

"How'd he take it?"

"Not good," I reply, choking back tears. Even over the phone, my mom can tell, of course.

"It'll be alright, baby. We'll figure something out."

"Yeah," I reply. We're both lying and we know it, but sometimes lying to yourself is better than the alternative.

After that, we make a little small talk and say goodbye. When I enter the room, I'm shocked to find Jacob awake and watching me as I enter. My breath catches in my throat and my chest tightens. It occurs to me then that I can't remember a time when I greeted Jacob and he didn't smile at me. For his sake, I try to smile and sound somewhat cheery when I say, "Hey," but my voice is shaky and too high-pitched to be convincing.

Jacob squeezes his eyes shut as if he's in physical pain. When he opens them again, they're glassy with unshed tears. His throat bobs as he swallows and when he speaks it sounds hoarse and gravely, so unlike his normally smooth, deep timbre. "Hey."

He's still curled up on his side. I sit down and prop my arms up on the side of his bed so I'm looking at him through the gap in the handrails. I ache with the need to touch him and attempt to reach between the bars to run my fingers through his hair, but his hand catches mine. "Don't."

My heart stutters and tears start to well up in my stupid eyes again. "Why?"

He drops my hand and rolls onto his back, so he doesn't have to look at me. "I'm sorry about earlier—" he begins.

"Don't apologize. It's fine."

"No, it's not," he snaps, and I startle at the sudden change in tone.

"Jacob—"

Sighing, he says, "You should go home, Stella. Get some sleep."

The words settle in my chest like a dead weight. He's kicking me out again. Maybe his tone is kinder, but it amounts to the same thing. "I don't want to leave," I say.

He still won't look at me. "I'll be fine. Really. There's no reason for you to stay here another night."

It's taking everything in me to keep my tone calm, even though inside I'm screaming. "Why don't you want me here, Jacob?"

My question must have caught him off guard, because he turns his head and looks at me. "It's not that."

I'm struggling to breathe around the lump in my throat, but manage to keep my voice calm and ask, "Then what is it?"

He goes back to looking at the ceiling. *Great.*

"I just want to be alone."

Those six words settle like a wall between us. I nod, not trusting myself to speak without completely breaking down. I can't even look at him as I stand, the sting of his rejection leaving me raw. It isn't until I'm almost at the door that I realize there's a question I need to ask. I take a deep breath in and blow it out—not that it does a damn thing. "Do you want me to pick you up tomorrow?" I ask. My words are breathy and strained and there is no possible way he could hear them and not know that he's fucking crushing me. A small part of me holds on to the hope that the sound of my pain will wake him up—spur him to tell me to stop, ask for a kiss goodbye, or at the very least, apologize, but he does none of those things.

He simply answers in the same indifferent tone. "My mom will get me."

And that's the end of that.

Thirty-Three
Now What?
Jacob

EVERYTHING'S SORT OF SURREAL—LIKE I'm a ghost walking around in someone else's body. I answer questions when asked and follow instructions. I even eat and sleep and shit as per usual, but there's a weight hanging over me like a wet blanket. It drags me down so that every word, every step is a slog, and all I really want to do is sleep.

The doctors prescribe some medication and tell me to see a specialist—whatever, that's fine. They tell me not to drive, that I'll need to be careful for a while and not go anywhere alone until we get things under control—that's fine too. It's not like I have anywhere to go anymore. Football's out of the picture and school might as well be, at least for the foreseeable future.

And Stella. Yeah. I fucked that up really good. She sent me a text this morning asking how I was doing. I just answered that I was "Okay." What the hell else was I supposed to say? Sorry to be such an asshole, but I kind of just want to crawl into a hole and die. I'm sure that would go over well. What's funny is, on top of everything else, I'm pissed at myself for being so weak and pathetic. I made a colossal ass out of myself at the hospital—completely lost my shit. I've never broken down like that before, and it kills me that Stella was there to see it. Maybe that's part of the reason I'm avoiding her, because I'm embarrassed by the way I acted and afraid that she'll look at me differently now.

My mom and Adriana have been jabbering all morning about me—talking like I'm not even here—and what I should do now. I should probably be paying better attention, but all I can think about is Stella and the way she looked at me last night when I asked her to leave.

Adriana plops down beside me on the sofa and smacks my shoulder, breaking me from my depressing as fuck thoughts.

"What?" I say.

My mom comes out of the kitchen holding three plates—with what I'm assuming are sandwiches—balanced precariously in one hand and a bag of chips in the other. I hop up and grab two of the plates before setting them down on the coffee table and returning to my position on the couch. Mom drops into the recliner with a huff. "Have you heard a word we've said?" she asks in that tone that makes me feel like a frigging ten-year-old.

"No," I say and take a bite out of my ham and cheese. It needs mayonnaise.

Adriana blurts out a laugh. "At least he's being honest."

I get up and head back over to the fridge.

"I understand that you're upset..." my mom begins.

You have no fucking idea how I feel.

"But this is important."

I grab the mayonnaise and slam the fridge shut. "No shit, Mama."

"Hey. Watch the language."

I roll my eyes but don't reply. It's not worth the fight.

"Anyway." She pauses, watching me as I squirt half a pound of mayonnaise on my sandwich. "That's really bad for you, Papo."

Another "no shit" is on the tip of my tongue, but I give her the truth instead. "It's not like I have to stay fit for football anymore."

"Well, I'm sure Stella would appreciate it if you didn't have a heart attack before thirty," Adriana says. I get that she's trying to lighten my mood, but if she thinks talking about Stella will cheer me up, she hasn't been paying very close attention.

"Anyway," my mom says again. "I think you should come home. Just for a little while," she adds quickly, hands raised like she's trying to ward off a wild animal. "Until you get your meds worked out."

I take another bite of my sandwich. I'd expected this. There's no real way around it. I can't ask my friends to watch me 24/7, cart my ass back and forth from the doctor and take me grocery shopping. It's too much. "I know," I say through a wad of sandwich.

"Oh," my mom says, clearly shocked by how easily I gave in. "Good." She pours some chips onto her plate and hands the bag to Adriana.

I can feel my sister's eyes on me, like if she stares at me long enough, she'll discern what I'm thinking.

At least one of us would.

Giving up her mind-reading act, Adriana asks, "When are you going to tell Stella?"

I bite back the urge to tell her to fuck off and mind her own business. I wouldn't hesitate if I thought for an instant, she asked just to get a rise out of me. But it's only out of concern for Stella. When we were kids, Adriana followed us around like a puppy. It annoyed the hell out of me, but Stella always insisted we include her. She said I was lucky to have a little sister who loved me and since she didn't have any siblings, Adriana kind of became hers too.

Finally, I say, "I don't know."

"Have you even spoken to her today?"

I scrub a hand over my face. "Don't start this shit, alright."

"You can't just shut her out."

"I know."

"The longer you keep this up, the worse it's going to get."

"I know," I say, more harshly this time.

"She was really upset yesterday and—"

I spring off the couch, fists clenched at my sides. "I know, alright."

Adriana follows suit. A whole foot shorter and the girl somehow makes me feel small. "Do you? Because she was a wreck yesterday."

"Adriana—" my mom cuts in.

"No." Adriana shoots a glare at my mom. "He needs to hear this." Then back to me. "She loves you, you idiot, and you threw it in her face. You're dealing with a world of shit right now, I get that, but did it ever occur to you that she is too?"

"I don't have to put up with this shit." I spin around and stomp for my bedroom door, slamming it shut behind me. If Adriana understands that I meant for her to leave me the hell alone, she certainly doesn't care because she just follows me inside. I'm left with two choices: physically throw her out the door or lean on my dresser with my head on my arms and listen. I listen.

"First," she says, "she finds you unresponsive and staring into nothing. She had no idea what was going on or if you would *ever* recover. Do you have any idea how terrifying that must have been?" I squeeze my eyes shut and swallow hard. I do; I saw it on her face when I came to. "Then," Adriana continues, her volume rising as she speaks, "when she tries to comfort you, which is also comforting herself let's be honest, you kick her out of your room. Twice. She's fucking devastated and now, you're talking about leaving her behind like it's no big deal—"

My tenuous hold on patience snaps, and I round on her and scream, "Of course it's a big deal."

"Then talk to her, you asshole."

We just stand there, staring each other down and panting like dogs. My mom hovers in the doorway, her gaze full of concern, but if she has an opinion on the matter, she's keeping it to herself.

"Fine," I say and shove past her, "but you'll have to drive me."

If I had to guess how upset Stella was by the way Emma greets me at the door, I'd say Adriana went easy on me.

"You're lucky you have a head injury because I really want to hit you right now," Emma says, and my heart sinks in my chest.

"Can I see her, please?"

She steps back and opens the door for me to enter. "She's in her room."

"Is she asleep?" I ask, the wimp in me searching for any excuse to avoid this conversation.

Unfortunately, Emma knows me well enough to see through my bullshit. She glares at me and points to the hallway. "Go."

I tap on Stella's door and wait a beat before letting myself in. She's lying on her bed, back to the door, and for a moment, I think maybe she is asleep. I close the door and take a step toward the bed, noting the way her shoulders tense. She's awake. She just doesn't want to look at me. Fuck. I'm such an asshole. I sit beside her on the bed and lay a hand on her shoulder. "Stella?" I whisper because something about this moment feels solemn—like when you enter a church or library.

"What?" she replies. Her voice is strained and raspy, no doubt from crying on my account, and here I thought I couldn't hate myself more. Adriana's right; I am a selfish asshole.

I brush the hair from her face and my hand comes back wet. "Baby, can you please turn around and look at me?"

She shakes her head.

"Stella—"

She flips over and it's like a sucker punch to my chest. Her face is tear-stained, her eyes are bright red with dark purple bruising underneath. When she looks at me though, there's a sadness there, but also defiance. Good. She should be angry.

I just want to pull her to my chest and hold her, but I don't have the right to do that at the moment. "I'm sorry," I say.

"You already said that."

I crawl across the bed and lay down across from her, tucking a hand under my cheek. "I was really upset, and I didn't want you to see me like that. I didn't mean to hurt you."

She shakes her head. "You forget, I know you, Jacob. Maybe being embarrassed had a little to do with it, but you were angry and wanted to punish me."

I draw back in shock. "Why would I want to punish you?"

"I don't know," she shrugs, "Maybe because I was the one who saw your seizure and made you go to the ER, or because I called your mom and told your friends, or maybe it was because it was easier than punishing yourself. You tell me."

I stare at her in stunned silence. Is she right? Was I trying to punish her? "If I was doing that, it wasn't intentional."

She nods and runs the sleeve of her hoodie under her eyes.

I take her hand in mine, kiss the knuckles and hold it against my chest. Closing my eyes, I draw in a breath, her warm vanilla scent soothing in its familiarity. If only I could bottle it up and take it with me to Orlando.

Am I doing the right thing?

Stella's busy with school and my friends all have practice and classes. They didn't sign up to take care of my pitiful ass. How can I place that sort of burden on them?

"Tell me," Stella says. I open my eyes to see her watching me.

"Tell you what?"

"Whatever's putting that expression on your face."

Sometimes I wish she couldn't read me so well. Rationally, I know it's better this way, better to tell her now than spring it on her at the last minute, but that doesn't make it any easier. Taking a shaky breath, I say, "I'm going back to Orlando."

I'm not sure what reaction I was expecting: shock, anger, something visceral and expressive. Instead, Stella goes completely still and closes her eyes.

"Why?" she asks. The word a breathy whisper.

At least I have an answer for this. "We still don't know exactly what we're dealing with. We don't know how often it's happening, or if I'm a risk to myself. Until we get the seizures under control, I have to be super careful. I need to have someone available at the drop of a hat. I can't drive. I can't go out by myself. I can't even take a bath."

She smiles, though it doesn't reach her eyes. "You never take baths."

I give her a tight smile in return. "You're missing the point." I roll onto my back and rub my eyes. "I'm fucking scared, Stella. It's like someone ripped the ground out from under me, and I'm in a free fall. One minute I'm a regular guy in school, playing sports, going to the grocery store, gym or wherever without anyone's help or permission and all of that's just gone. Hopefully, the meds will work, and I can eventually get back to something like a normal life, but even that isn't certain. It's a really shitty place to be." I laugh, but there's no joy in it.

"How long?" she asks. She's being so calm about all of this. It's kind of freaking me out. She's supposed to be crying or yelling, Something. Not this detached acceptance.

"Christmas. Maybe. I hope. I don't know. That may just be wishful thinking."

"Then you'll come back? You still have your scholarship. Even if they take it away, I'm sure we can get you financial aid."

Her eyes are glassy, which means she isn't taking this as easily as she's letting on. It also means I'm a selfish prick because it makes me feel better that she feels bad. "I don't know, baby. I hope so."

"I'd take care of you. We could get our own place. We'd go everywhere together anyway, so it doesn't make any difference who's driving."

It'll never work. She's only one person, and she has her own life. She doesn't need to play nursemaid to my sorry ass. I can't say that, of course, I've already hurt her enough, so I just tell her, "We'll see how things go, okay?"

She nods and snuggles into me, and for a little while, I can pretend that everything is as it should be.

I had two days. Two days to pack my things, say goodbye to my friends and leave my life behind. And two days with Stella. We tried to remain upbeat, but my impending departure hung over us like a dark cloud, casting a shadow over everything we said or did.

And now that our time is over, I'm wishing I could do it over again. I should have gone out and had drinks with Malcolm and Ryan and fucked Stella until she couldn't sit down because now it was over. That was my life before and this is my life after.

God, I never realized how good I had it.

My mom and sister are already in the car waiting for me to say goodbye. Malcolm, Ryan, Charlie and Emma all came to see me off. We hugged and promised to text or whatever, and I can handle that. I'm okay. It's Stella holding me back, which is stupid. I'm going to see her again. She'll be down in less than a month for Christmas, regardless, but I can't help worrying that this is going to be the end of us. After ten years of bullshit, we got two months. Two months. If there is a God, he's a giant asshole.

I think, for my sake, Stella tried not to cry, but she only held out for about five minutes before the tears started to fall. I don't mind. It's like she's grabbed hold of my heart and is squeezing the life out of me, but it's also kind of nice to know she'll miss me. I'll sure as shit miss her.

"Text me when you get there?" she asks, smoothing down my shirt like I have somewhere important to be. "And FaceTime... When you can."

"Sexy FaceTime?" I waggle my eyebrows suggestively.

That gets a laugh out of her. Good. Laughing is good. "I'll think about it," she says.

I press my lips to hers for one last kiss and almost lose it when I taste her salty tears. When I start to pull back, she tightens her grip, unwilling to let me go just yet.

Then, pressing a soft kiss to my cheek, Stella leans in to whisper in my ear. "I love you."

Her words set off a flurry of emotions—elation, and fear, and excitement, and hurt.

And guilt. Lots and lots of guilt.

My emotions are still in free fall when she releases me and moves to stand with our friends, a sad smile on her face. I tip my chin in one last farewell and slip into the back seat of my mom's ancient blue Corolla. Ana scrolls through her playlist and soon Led Zeppelin's "Babe I'm Gonna Leave You" is blasting through my mom's shitty speakers. I lean back and settle in for the four-hour drive while my mom and Ana argue over the noise level. It isn't until we've pulled away and are halfway down the block that I realize. I never told her I loved her back.

Thirty-Four
Put Some Vodka on That
Stella

I REALLY TRIED TO hold it together for Jacob's sake, but my stupid eyes did not get the fucking memo, and now that he's gone, I've completely stopped trying. If I didn't have Emma on one side and Charlie on the other holding me up, my ass would be a sobbing lump on the pavement.

The girls deposit me on the couch, and I listen while Charlie gets down to business. "Ryan," Charlie points at her boyfriend.

Being a smart ass, Ryan salutes with a, "Yes, sir."

Charlie gives him her patented, "Don't fuck with me," look, and I have to laugh a little as the man slowly lowers his hand, his eyes searching the ceiling like a little boy caught misbehaving.

Charlie continues, "We need alcohol." She ticks the list off her fingers. "Bailey's, Kahlua, Vodka—orange and regular.

Malcolm scratches his chin. "Exactly how much are we planning to drink here?"

"Not we," Charlie replies, pointing between herself and the boys. "We," she says, now pointing at herself and us girls. "And Kat. If she can make it."

Emma plops next to me on the couch and pats my leg. "Sorry, guys, but this is a girls-only shindig."

Ryan makes a face like he smelled a fart. "Then why am I the one getting all the alcohol?"

"Because you're the only one over twenty-one," Charlie replies.

"I'm twenty-one," Malcolm chimes in.

"Yes, but you're not my boyfriend, so I can't make *you*."

Malcolm laughs, while Emma makes a "Whup-ah," sound and mimes cracking a whip.

"Hardy-har-har," Ryan says to Emma, crossing his arms. He adds to Charlie, "You can't *make* me do anything."

Lips spread into a sly grin, Charlie saunters over to her boyfriend and wraps her arms around his neck. "You're right, baby." Charlie leans in and places a soft kiss on his cheek. "But I can ask," she moves to kiss the other cheek, "very," and down his neck, "very," back up to his lips, "nicely."

Ryan's eyes narrow. "You are evil."

"And you love it." She bites her lip and smacks his ass. "Now hurry up."

He groans but heads out the door. "I'll give him a hand," Malcolm says, chuckling as he follows his friend outside. The door clicks shut behind them, but Ryan can still be heard telling Malcolm to "Shut the fuck up." To which Malcolm's laughs only get louder.

"Kat," Emma shouts, though her sister is five feet away. "I can't feel my face." Glancing up from checking my texts for the five hundredth time, I find that Emma is, indeed, pressing on her face and squishing it around like silly putty.

"I told you not to smoke so much," her sister replies, still taking hits off the joint the rest of us gave up on thirty minutes ago.

Charlie jumps to her feet, empty glass raised in the air. "Who wants a refill?"

"Me," I say, swigging down the last of my white Russian and handing the empty glass to Charlie.

"Coming right up," she says. Glasses raised in the air, Charlie sashays over to the peninsula where we've set up our makeshift bar and goes to town making our drinks.

She returns quickly with my white Russian. I take a sip and gasp as the overabundance of alcohol hits my tongue and throat. "I'd say you should get a job as a bartender," I say to Charlie, because, damn, the girl can make a mixed drink, "but no one would ever hire you because you make them sooo strong." That is also true, as is the fact that I am a known lightweight and white Russians are my weakness. Combine those two with Charlie's extraordinary bartending skills, and only one drink in, I already have a good buzz going. Normally, I'd leave it at that, but tonight, a buzz isn't going to cut it. Nope. I'm in the market to get thoroughly, utterly and supremely wasted. If I have to skip class tomorrow, so be it. Whatever I can do to stop my brain from rehashing what happened when I told him I loved him, over and over. Every time I think about it, I feel nauseous. I purposely didn't give him time to say it back because I didn't want him to feel pressured, but now, I'm all unsure and questioning whether I should have waited. It wasn't so much the way he reacted as much as his total lack of reaction—just a tip of his chin like I was one of the guys, and he got in the car. He didn't even turn around to see me standing there as they drove away. Acid starts to burn in my throat at the thought, and I try to chase it away by slugging down the white Russian Charlie so generously made for me. Probably not super effective, but whatever.

"So, I have a question," Kat begins, which draws my attention because when Kat starts out a sentence with "I have a question" it's usually not one anybody wants to answer.

"Proceed," Emma's stoned ass says with a wave of her hand, like she's the queen of the living room.

"Uh, thanks," Kat deadpans. "Anyway, I'm gonna start with Stella but all you chicas are on the chopping block, so be warned. And I know when you lie."

Emma fake coughs into her fist. "Bullshit."

Kat scratches her temple with her middle finger and continues. "Stella, who's the best sex you've ever had—be honest."

"Jacob."

"You said that too fast," says Kat, squinting at me like the truth is written in tiny print on my forehead.

"That's because there's no contest. I've been with two other guys, in high school, who probably knew less than me and lasted all of five seconds."

"Fair enough. Fair enough," Kat replies. "Emma?"

Emma jabbed a thumb at me. "Sorry to mooch your man, but same."

Kat laughs, "Stella and I can both attest to that."

"Yep," I add with a pop on the "p."

Emma grimaces and covers her face with her hands. "Ugh, sorry. You guys should have said something."

"Oh, yeah, sure." Kat nods her head, lips pursed and brow furrowed as if in agreement. "Yo, sis. Can you please fuck more quietly? Other people are trying to sleep."

Emma smacks her sister's shoulder good-naturedly while Charlie and I crash into each other, laughing.

Kat turns to Charlie and rubs her hands together like a cartoon villain. "And Ms. Charlotte?"

"I plead the fifth," she says and the rest of us boo.

"I'm sorry, but that doesn't compute," I argue. "You plead the fifth as to not self-incriminate. So what? Are you protecting your hand?"

"Shut up, Stella," Charlie says and chucks a pillow at my head, which I defend spectacularly, by hiding behind Emma.

Emma, on the other hand, gets smacked right in the face, yells, "Bitch," and proceeds to throw the pillow back at Charlie, missing her mark by at least five feet.

Charlie doubles over with laughter. "Damn, girl. You suck." Emma responds by giving her the finger, which only makes her laugh harder, and soon Charlie is rolling on the floor, clutching her stomach and saying, "Oh god, it hurts."

Kat, being her perpetually cool self, simply takes a sip of her white Russian and smirks at her sister. "Emma's not what we'd called athletically inclined."

"Oh please, you couldn't throw a ball to save your life," Emma retorts.

Charlie sits back up, runs a finger under each eye, and sighs.

It occurs to me then that she never actually answered our question. "Charlie, is there something going on with you and Ryan?" I ask.

She immediately deflates. "No. Not really."

"Uh-oh," Emma and Kat say simultaneously. They grin at each other and high-five. I swear sometimes those two act more like twins than sisters.

"It's just... Ryan is sweet and hot, and I love him to pieces, but..." She wraps her arms around her legs and rests her chin on her knees, while the rest of us wait on pins and needles. "Sometimes he's too sweet. Does that make sense?"

No. It doesn't make sense, at least not to me, and by the way Emma's eyebrows have gone all scrunched up, I'd say the same goes for her.

Kat, however, nods sagely. "I get it. My girl likes it rough. Looking for some Dom/sub play, bondage, spanking, anal—"

Charlie makes a face. "Eww, no."

Kat's grin is nothing short of diabolical. "Ahhh, so that means you're into the first four."

"Oh, she got you," Emma says, bouncing in place and pointing a wobbly finger at Charlie. How many drinks has she had?

Charlie groans and covers her face with her hand. "This is so embarrassing."

"Tell you what," Emma cuts in. "You tell us about this, and I'll tell you something juicy about me."

Charlie looks up at her friend and purses her lips. "Which probably means you were going to do that already."

"Definitely. But now you won't feel so alone. So, spill."

Charlie groans again but doesn't hide her face this time, which seems like progress. "He's just really sweet, like too sweet. It's like he thinks I'm breakable or something, and everything has to be planned out and is always so sickeningly romantic." She rolls her eyes. "Which is a shitty thing to say because what girl wouldn't like her guy surprising her with candlelight dinners and rose petals all over the bed?"

Kat leans over and pretends to throw up in Charlie's lap.

Charlie chuckles. "Exactly."

"Sounds like he's trying a little too hard," I say.

"It's like the Madonna-Whore Complex," Emma says, and we all stop to look at her. "It's when a guy sees a woman as either a 'good girl,'" she makes air quotes on good girl, "that's the Madonna or a whore. They want to marry the Madonna and fuck the whore." The girl's slurring her words and barely sitting up straight, yet she's talking about the Madonna-Whore complex like a psych professor.

Charlie cocks her head. "I don't understand. What does that have to do with Ryan and me?"

"You're the Madonna."

Charlie's eyes widen in understanding. She yells, "Fuck," and drops her head back into her hands.

"So basically, he's putting her on a pedestal?" I ask Emma.

She nods.

Charlie drags her hands down her face, making her all droopy-eyed. "What do I do?"

"Fuck if I know." Emma tips a shoulder and takes a sip of her white Russian as if she didn't just drop a bomb on poor Charlie. Some of her drink spills onto her flowery shirt and Emma cusses and scrubs at it with her hand, which I'm guessing in her current inebriated state, seems an effective way to clean it. Then, just as quickly, she gives up and drinks some more. Noticing all of us looking at her expectantly, she sighs and rolls her eyes like we're all a bunch of morons. "Talk to him. Maybe do to him what you want him to do to you—like tie him up or something kinky."

"Videotape it," Kat practically yells in poor Charlie's face, making her jump.

"Yeah and share it with your friends." Emma waggles her brows and the sisters high-five again.

"You two are serious pervs. Anyone ever told you that?" I say, glancing back and forth between Emma and Kat.

Emma sweeps a hand through her golden locks in a move that says, "You know it."

Groaning, Charlie stands up and heads for the kitchen. "I need a stronger drink."

I pick up my phone and check it again, even though the ringer's on, and I should hear it if Jacob texts me. Nothing. I look at the clock. It's almost midnight. He should have been in Orlando two hours ago. I want to text him, but things are so tenuous right now. I'm afraid of being too clingy. It's funny. If we were still just friends, I wouldn't have thought twice about texting him or giving him shit for not texting me. God, I hate this. I slap the phone down on the coffee table. "At least your boyfriend's still here," I say, then want to smack myself. The whole point of tonight was to get my mind off the fact that Jacob left. If I start thinking about it, I'm going to cry again, and I am so tired of crying. I sigh. "Please forget I said that."

Emma pats my knee. Her eyebrows are drawn together, and she's wearing a little pout. Shit. Here comes the sympathy train. "It's only temporary. He'll be back."

I breathe and blink away the burning in my eyes. "Charlie." I hold up my half-full glass. "I think this needs more vodka."

"On it." She bounces over, snatches up my glass and heads back to the quickly-diminishing collection of liquor on the peninsula.

Kat doesn't speak, just watches me with obvious pity.

"All right, Em," I say, attempting to change the subject. "Give us your gossip." I don't know if Emma was really itching to talk about this or if she's just playing it up for my sake, but I'm grateful when she perks up and starts talking.

"I'm pretty sure Malcolm's trying to get into my pants."

Charlie, who is sucking down her new and improved white Russian as she returns, chokes, and almost spits her drink out all over us. Kat jumps up to pat her back, and Emma laughs.

"Please don't spill my drink," I say, hopping up and snatching my glass out of her hand. I'm going to need every last drop of this. I take a large gulp and immediately regret it as what must be pure vodka burns my mouth and down my throat. Even my nostrils feel like they're on fire. "Jesus, Charlie," I finally manage to squeak out between gasps. "I said to make it stronger, not add the entire bottle of vodka."

Charlie waves her hand like my loss of taste and smell is inconsequential. "It's not that bad." She takes a sip, coughs into the back of her hand and blinks wildly to stop her eyes from watering. "Maybe just a little bit more cream."

I hand my glass over. "Just a splash," I say, holding my index finger and thumb an inch apart.

Charlie sticks her tongue out at me but heads back to the peninsula, anyway.

"Anyway," Emma continues, as if uninterrupted. "He keeps trying to touch me and asking me to do stuff and whatever. It's pretty obvious, to be honest. He's a cool guy, and I don't want to hurt his feelings, but I'm just not really into him."

"What's wrong with him?" Kat asks.

"What do you mean?"

"Is he ugly, stupid? What don't you like?"

Emma shrugs. "I don't know. He's really good-looking actually and is a political science major, so I guess he has to be pretty smart, right?"

"So, what's the issue?" Kat asks.

I totally miss what she says because the vodka has officially kicked in and I'm feeling all sorts of loose. "I know why?" I chime in. Even I can hear the slur in my voice. "Malcolm's used to girls throwing themselves at him because he's a quarterback, yadda-yadda, and Emma's not like that. Add into it the fact that she's insanely hot and Malcolm thinks he struck gold." My vision is going all wonky, splitting my friend into two identical Emmas, who are both watching me with droopy eyes and a smirk. Both Emmas open their mouths as if to speak and I lift a finger for them to shut up and let me finish. "Ironically, the reason Emma doesn't like him is because, like every other guy, all he cares about is how she looks."

Both Emmas nod their heads. "Yep, that about covers it."

"Ha-ha," I yell and point my finger at the Emmas, who keep splitting apart and merging together, making me dizzy. "You're not the only smart drunk person." Charlie hands me my drink again and now I'm thinking, this may not have been the best idea. I gulp it down anyway because fuck it.

Something like a boot jabs my side, and I hear Kat's unmistakable voice saying, "Wake up Sleeping Beauties."

The first thing I think, as I attempt to open eyes that seem to have been glued shut, is: did I get hit by a bus? Because there is no way I'm hurting this badly from just a hangover. My entire body is stiff and achy—my hip hurts, my shoulder hurts, and my head feels like an egg that got cracked open. If I open my eyes right now, am I going to see my brains spilled out onto the sidewalk? Am I on a sidewalk? The ground is way too hard to be my bed. So, I got hit by a bus and the girls left me on the sidewalk?

That's rude.

Next to me, somebody groans. "Let me die in peace." Definitely, Charlie.

Through my pain-filled haze, I hear the fridge open, the jangling of bottles, drawers opening and closing and the fridge shutting again. I pry one eye open, and immediately shut it because the light hits me like an icepick to the brain. Ugh, this isn't going to be pretty. On my second try, I manage to get both eyes open, but just barely. I scan my surroundings, but I can't see anything due to a wall blocking my view—oh wait, that's the peninsula. I roll over onto my belly and whatever was propping my head up slips free, and I end up with a face full of ugly brown carpet. Why am I sleeping on the floor in my living room? At least that explains why my shoulder and hip hurt so much.

My ears catch the faintest sizzling sound, and the scent of eggs fills the air. And, oh my god, is that bacon? The hickory-smoked deliciousness calls to me like a drug. My stomach's going haywire. It rumbles with hunger while simultaneously rolling like a hamster's wheel.

A shuffling sound approaches from down the hall, followed by Emma's sleepy voice asking, "Coffee?"

"In the pot," replies a way too perky Kat. "Eggs and bacon coming up," she calls out to Charlie and me.

Somehow, I manage to stand and plod to the kitchen like something out of a zombie movie. Kat tosses a plate of eggs and bacon on the counter in front of me. "Eat up, buttercup."

"What's wrong with you?" I ask Kat, then turn to Emma. "What's wrong with her?"

"She's a bitch who enjoys rubbing it in that she doesn't have a hangover?"

"Oh, so I guess you don't want breakfast then."

Kat tries to swipe Emma's plate, but Emma sees it coming and snatches it away. "Don't fuck with my eggs."

Kat gives Emma the evil eye and points at her with a spatula. "I think someone wants me to sing the Star-Spangled Banner. Oh-oh," she begins loudly and already horribly off-key.

"No," Emma screams, snatching up her plate and running back into her bedroom.

Kat winks, "Works every time."

A shower and a gallon of water later, I'm feeling well enough to drag my ass to class, though the fact that Jacob still hasn't texted me kind of makes me want to go right back to bed. I'm going through the motions, moving to and from class in a haze. It's quarter till noon, when I step out of comparative literature, that I give in and text Jacob.

I'm really hoping he isn't looking at his phone at the moment because I probably spend five minutes typing and retyping my text. I go through the whole gambit of questions from the accusatory, "Why haven't you texted me?" to the sweet and somewhat needy, "I miss you," and finally decide to keep it simple.

Me: Hey, you get in okay?

I take a seat on one of the picnic benches in the courtyard and watch the phone like a complete and total jackass, hoping he'll write back quickly because I'm going crazy. At the same time, if he does write me back quickly, I'm probably going to be upset that he was on his phone and didn't write me.

Great. I'm turning into *that* girl.

I shut off my phone and lay my head on the table. The air is crisp with the threat of winter, but the sun is deliciously warm on my back. My tense muscles begin to unravel, the warm rays like a soothing balm against my skin. A cold spot appears across my shoulders, warning me that someone is standing next to me well before he decides to speak.

"Someone sitting here?" Dean asks.

I raise my head to see Dean standing on my left, his massive body silhouetted in the sunlight. "Nope," I say, though I don't really want him to sit here, which has less to do with Dean than with the fact that I just don't want to be around people, in general, right now.

He sets his book bag on the table and sits down, elbows on his knees and hands clasped. "How're you holding up?"

I shrug because what do I say to that? "Well, Dean, I'm pretty bitter and depressed. Jacob is obviously pushing me away despite what he promised, and all I really want to do is cry and scream and beat the shit out of something until I stop hurting?" He doesn't want to hear that.

"That bad, huh?" He gives me a crooked smile.

"I'll be fine," I say.

"Yeah. I know, but right now has kind of got to suck." I can't tell if he's trying to be nice or trying to rub my face in it. Dean turns away from me, his gaze searching out some nebulous point in the distance, and says, "I'm obviously not his biggest fan, but what happened to Jacob," he sighs and drops his head. "It's got to be my biggest fear, you know? I wouldn't wish that on anyone."

All I can think to say is, "Yeah."

"Anyway." He scratches a stubbly chin. "Things went way off the rails with you and me." I choke out a laugh at that, and he smiles. "And for what it's worth, I'm sorry. I never should have gone after you like that." He smiles. "I've been wanting to say that to you for a while, but since Jacob already came pretty close to murdering me, I figured it was smarter to back off. Anyway," he says, hands slapping his thighs. "If you need anything..." I take a breath to reply, but he cuts me off, hands raised in surrender. "As friends. Let me know, huh?"

"Thanks." My phone buzzes and I snatch it up. Please be Jacob. Please be Jacob.

"I'll leave you to it," Dean says, gesturing to the hand holding my phone, and stands.

"Thank you, Dean. I mean it," I say, giving my best approximation of a smile.

He nods and starts off. I give him barely half a second before I check my phone.

My heart leaps to see that it's a text from Jacob, then plummets when I realize it only consists of one word.

Jacob: Yes.

Thirty-Five
What Goes in the Shed, Stays in the Shed
Jacob

Stella: Hey. How are you?

Me: Fine. You?

Stella: Good. I went out with Emma last night and watched her spend two hours fending off Malcolm. The guy really needs to learn to read the room.

Me: Yeah.

Stella: What are you up to?

Me: Not much.

Stella: Do you have something against sentences or is it just me?

Me: What do you want me to tell you?

Stella: I don't know. Whatever you're doing with yourself.

Me: I sleep ALL THE TIME. That's it. And once a week I get to go to the doctor. Not exactly exciting.

Stella: Fine. Sorry, I asked.

Two weeks since I came to live at home, and I'm going fucking crazy. At least now we've sort of figured out some warning signs that I'm going to get a seizure—headache, sometimes dizziness or blurry vision—and after, well, I generally feel like shit, so that's fairly obvious. Are the meds working? It's hard to say. Since I didn't know to keep track of the seizures before, there's no way to tell if they're decreasing or not. Kind of a big oversight if you ask me, but nobody did so...

Stella's pissed at me, and I don't blame her. I barely call or text and when I do talk to her, I'm not much of a conversationalist. It's not like I'm trying to be a dick. I just don't have much to talk about except how miserable I am, and that's the last thing Stella wants to hear. It's not only Stella, either. I barely speak to anyone. Not my mom or Adriana, not my friends from school. I mostly just lay in bed and try to sleep. Right now, that's the only thing that has any appeal at all. Yeah, I'm a sorry sack of shit, and I know it. I just don't know how to pull myself out of it. I've been sketching a little, mostly from memory, because I'm fucking alone all the time. And I write letters to Stella—it's a journal, really. Mom got it for me when I refused to see a therapist. I totally gave her shit about how stupid it is for a grown man to have a journal, but it actually does help to have something to vent to—not that I'm telling her that. The fact that nobody else can see it makes it easier to be honest and get shit off my chest. All of it is written to Stella, though I doubt I'll ever show it to her. Shit, the way I've acted, I wouldn't blame her if she told me to fuck off and never see her again.

I never even told her I loved her back, and I'm sure as hell not going to do it over the fucking phone, especially when I can't find anything to say to her that isn't depressing as hell, so I hardly even speak. Every time I get off the phone with her, I can tell how much I'm hurting her, and it kills me because I don't know how to fix that either.

I'm lying on the couch right now with a copy of *The Shining* draped over my face. It's one of my favorite movies, and I always meant to read the book, but I can't get into it. I can't really get into anything.

I hear my mom's car pulling into the driveway, and for a minute, I consider going to my room, so I don't have to see the way she looks at me, the same way Ana looks at me—all full of pity and worry. It just makes me feel even more like shit. But I stay put. I refuse to be such a loser that I can't even look my mother in the eye.

The front door creaks open and shut, followed by my mom's heels tapping across the tile floor and stopping just short of where I'm lying on the leather couch. She doesn't say anything, probably wondering if I'm asleep, as if anyone could sleep with those taps echoing through the little house. It's practical here to have tile floors, it helps to keep things cool, but it can create a hell of an echo in an open space.

"Yes, Mama," I say, hoping I'll get a simple hello and goodbye.

But I'm not so lucky. Instead, my mom asks, "What are you doing?"

"Reading."

"I wasn't aware you could read a book that way."

"Osmosis." I shrug. "I'm giving it a shot."

"And how's that working for you?"

I remove the book and sit up. "It's not." My mom is wearing one of the button-up blouse and pencil skirt combos that are her staple for her job teaching high school science. Today, though, she's holding a couple of bags with what looks like large rolls of paper poking out of them.

I point to the bags. "What's all that?" I ask, nervous about what she'll say but too curious not to keep my big mouth shut.

Her lips curl into a thin smile. Sometimes, I swear if I didn't know my mom better, I'd say the woman was an evil genius. "I'm so glad you asked."

Or maybe just evil.

"This is for you," she continues. "Your sister and I are tired of seeing you mope around all day. You need something to focus on, so I found some of your old sketchbooks out in the shed and got you all of this painting crap, the guy at the store said you'd need. I thought maybe you could turn a few sketches into paintings or something."

"Mom—"

"And don't even think about refusing because this stuff was very expensive and most of it isn't refundable."

That makes no damn sense. "Why wouldn't it be refundable?"

"Because I say so."

Wow, real creative mom.

I follow her down the hallway and into my room, where she literally dumps both bags out onto my bed. Smiling in that condescending mom way that makes you want to kick something, she pivots around on one foot like a fucking pro and tap-tap-taps past me back out in the hallway.

"Uh, what are you doing?" I ask, but she ignores me and heads back into the living room. Our house is an old 1970s-style concrete block ranch—great for hurricanes but little else. The interior's worn but clean. The kitchen is probably smaller than the one I had in my old apartment, which is saying something, and has never been updated.

Artistic folks, like myself, who are searching for the exact color of brown that most resembles dog shit, have to look no further than our fake oak cabinets and matching parquet-style vinyl floor. Add to that, the used-to-be white laminate countertop that no amount of Magic Eraser can seem to get clean and say goodbye to your appetite.

The rest of the house is similarly out of date: sunken living room separated by an iron railing, popcorn ceiling and a sliding glass door to the, so tiny it might as well not exist, backyard. It's a piece of shit, but it's home.

I don't stop complaining as I follow her the entire way down the hall, through the living room, and into the tiny dining area just off the kitchen. Unfortunately, my mom developed an immunity to my bitching and general shit baggery long ago and simply continues on, unfazed. We're held up a moment at the sliding glass door while my mom does her lift and pull trick to get it open, then she steps out into the yard. I let out a sigh and go along because what else do I have to do, really? She crosses to the rusty metal shed, unlocks the padlock on the door and leads us inside. The shed is packed full of everything from lawn equipment to tools to Christmas decorations. It's basically a garage minus the cars. Mom picks her way over fallen tools, half-used pails of paint, and wood scraps and stops beside two large plastic bins. "Your sketchbooks." She pats the bins and smiles, obviously pleased with herself. "They were too heavy to lift into the attic, so I stored them here."

I take a tentative step toward her. I haven't seen these books in forever. "You kept them?" I ask.

She nods. "Every single one. Took a look through a few of them, too. Interesting stuff."

"How so?"

"Look for yourself." She walks back to the shed door and pauses just long enough to pat my shoulder before heading back to the house. I stand there a while and stare at the dingy-gray bins that hold a visual history of my life, then turn around and step back out of the shed, locking the door behind me.

Thirty-Six

Are We Having Fun Yet?

Stella

This class has been a complete waste of time. I've been so distracted the professor could have been spouting nonsense about alien invasions, and I would have nodded along. Finally, Gibson finishes off the lecture by saying, "I've posted a sign-up sheet on the wall outside with the times I'll be available to meet with you this week. I strongly recommend you take this opportunity to go over your work with me before beginning your final books. Class dismissed." Students pour down the steps and out the door. A few pause to say goodbye to Professor Gibson, while one couple—two guys—hovers by the door talking. I get up slowly, not really feeling up to having this conversation, but knowing it has to be done. I've already procrastinated for three weeks, and I'm running out of time. Professor Gibson is focused on packing his laptop and charger into his briefcase and doesn't notice me when I approach.

"Excuse me, Professor," I say, startling him.

"Oh, Ms. Leone." He grips his chest and laughs. "You snuck up on me."

"Sorry."

He waves away my apology. "It's fine. I just get lost in my own head sometimes. How can I help you?"

My heart is pounding, which is so stupid. It's not like he's going to yell at me or fail me or something. Professor Gibson's a totally cool guy. Logically, I know this, but I'm still so frigging nervous. "I needed to talk to you about the project."

He sighs, like he's had this conversation a hundred times before and is over it. "That's what the sign-up sheet is for. You and your partner—"

"That's just it, sir," I interrupt. "My partner is withdrawing from school."

"Really," he says, drawing back in shock. "I don't remember receiving any messages about that."

Of course, you haven't because he didn't give a crap enough to officially withdraw. "He had a medical emergency and won't be back." My voice cracks on the last bit, and I have to stop and take a breath before continuing or risk crying… again. "I'm afraid I can't complete the novel without him, sir."

He seems to consider this a moment, then asks, "How much have you finished?"

"The story's written, and we've put together about half the layouts, but that's all."

"I see." He taps a finger against his lips thoughtfully. "Go ahead and turn in what you have, and I'll see about coming up with a short alternate assignment for you."

Thank god. I let out a sigh of relief. "Thank you, sir."

"But I'm going to need a medical excuse from him. Are you two still in contact?"

If you want to call it that. "Yes, sir."

"Good. Tell him to send it to me, and we'll get this all worked out, alright?"

"I will. Thank you."

He smiles and bids me goodbye.

That was honestly a lot easier than I expected. Some professors could be such hard-asses about shit like this.

I send a text to Jacob.

Me: I need you to send a medical excuse to Prof. Gibson, so he doesn't flunk me.

Jacob: Okay.

Me: Can you do it today?

Jacob: Yes.

And here we go again with the one-word answers. Great.

I step out into the courtyard. Winter's finally decided to make an appearance, the temperatures plummeting into the forties. I whip my hood up over my head and cross my arms. Yeah, I'm a wimp. I'm a born and bred Floridian, and I hate the frigging cold. Especially this wet cold that chills your bones. I sprint to the cafeteria doors and shut myself inside, relishing the warmth.

The cafeteria is essentially the college version of a mall food court. It consists of a bunch of fast-food stalls and a solitary crappy Chinese restaurant. Not a healthy morsel in sight. I'm not really hungry, so I grab a coke and take a seat at one of the smaller tables. I check my phone. Jacob hasn't written anything else. I don't know why I'm even checking. All I ever get from him these days are one-word answers and the occasional clipped sentence. Calling is actually worse because then I can hear in his voice how little he wants to talk to me, which only gets me more upset. But as always, I'm a glutton for punishment, so I text him again.

Me: How about I drive over for a visit this weekend?

Jacob: I wouldn't waste your gas money. I'm crappy company.

Me: I don't mind.

Jacob: Not this weekend, okay?

That's what he said last weekend and the one before. Charlie says I shouldn't take it personally, that he's just depressed or whatever, but that's easier said than done.

Me: *You keep telling me not to visit. You got some sexy girl over there you're trying to hide from me?*

Jacob: *Yep. Got girls banging down the door to hang out with the jobless, college dropout who can't leave the house without his mom.*

Me: *I really wish you'd stop that.*

Jacob: *What?*

Me: Putting yourself down.

Jacob: It's just a joke.

Me: No, it isn't.

I drop my head in my hands and groan. I wish I knew what to do. Everyone says to give him time, but I think it's only making things worse.

Something hits the table with a bang and my head pops up. "Hey, Chicka." Emma's grinning down at me like she just won the lottery. She's radiating energy—practically vibrating with it. I can't remember the last time, if ever, I've seen her so worked up.

"Hey." I cock my head to the side. "What's going on?"

"Guess who got cast as Velma in the fall production of Chicago?"

I jump to my feet. "Oh my god! Seriously?"

She squeals and hops up and down and her happiness must be contagious because I start hopping up and down with her. "That's so amazing! We've got to celebrate," I say.

"Can we go to Rubies? Please? Please? Please?"

Okay. Maybe a night out at Rubies wasn't the best idea. It seems that Charlie and Ryan got into some sort of spat and now she's gone bat shit crazy. She and Emma have spent the last two hours drinking up half the bar and dancing—or dry humping, if you prefer—with half the guys in the club. And here I am, the last bastion of sobriety, sitting on a bench, sipping my coke and checking my phone every three seconds to see if Jacob's texted.

Yes. I am that pathetic.

As it turns out, this club will serve every underage female that sets foot through that door—everyone except me, that is. Normally, I wouldn't let it bother me. I'd just go dance. But without any alcohol to shut off my brain, there's no point. I can't enjoy myself. We came in an Uber, and I've been seriously considering just taking one home. I'd feel bad leaving Emma's mini celebration though, and I'm honestly a little worried about Charlie. I don't know what happened between her and Ryan, but I don't remember her being this flirty with guys when she was single, let alone in a serious relationship.

My phone pings and my pitiful heart leaps at the thought that Jacob's texting me.

Except, it's not Jacob.

Ryan: *Hey Stella. Sorry to bug you, but have you seen Charlie? She's not answering her phone.*

She didn't tell him where she was going? That's not a good sign. I'm pretty sure she stuck her phone in her bra, but she's so wasted, I wouldn't be surprised if she didn't notice it buzzing. I don't type that, of course. Instead, I write—

Me: Yeah. She probably didn't hear your call. We're at the club. It's loud.

Ryan: What club?

Now, I think there's a section somewhere in the best girlfriend's handbook that says not to give out your friend's location to a guy—like ever. So, I reluctantly get up and step onto the raised floor to get Charlie. The moment my feet hit the dance floor, every sleazy-looking guy in the place seems to take it as an invitation to grope me. I'm slapping away hands left and right and would have totally kicked this one guy in the junk if Charlie hadn't wrapped a sweaty arm around my shoulders and began hip bumping me.

"Hey," I try to yell over the music, but Charlie's oblivious. I grab her around the chin and force her to look down at my phone with Ryan's message. She rolls her eyes, takes the phone out of my hand, and types something before handing it back to me.

Me: Fuck off!

Holy shit. I can't believe she did that. On my phone.
I quickly type out a lie.

Me: Sorry. That wasn't meant for you.

Charlie's back to dancing with some skeezy-looking guy who must have taken a bath in cologne for me to smell the putrid scent wafting off him among all these bodies. I push between them, ignoring the guy's protests and mouth, "What the fuck?" to Charlie. Her answer is to make a face like she ate something foul, and no way I'm letting that slide. I grab her arm and drag her off the dance floor. It's a testament to how drunk she is that she doesn't fight back.

"What the hell, Charlie?" I say when I get her to a quiet spot next to the restrooms.

She crosses her arms and presses her lips together. "What?"

"What's going on with you?"

She sags against the wall. "I asked him for some space, and he can't even give me that."

I knew they were having problems, but I didn't realize it was that bad. "You broke up with him?"

"No. Not exactly. I just told him I needed a break. He's always talking about all the crazy, exciting things he does. But does he do them with me? No. Because I'm a 'good girl' or some other bullshit," she says, making air quotes. "If I wanted to be with some uptight, boring guy, I wouldn't have chosen him. He's always treating me with kid gloves, and I hate it."

"Did you tell him that?"

She shrugs and lowers her gaze. "Not like that."

"Then talk to him."

"I don't want to—"

Emma sprints into the hallway, her face red and breathing heavily. "Hey," she says and leans over with her hands on her knees to catch her breath. "I don't mean to spoil your party, but we've got a slight problem here." She points out into the club, and son of a bitch, if Ryan and Malcolm aren't weaving through the crowd, eyes scanning the place.

"Asshole," Charlie says. She doesn't even pause to consider her next move before stomping out of the hallway, across the club, and over to her man, who she immediately starts reaming out.

"Oh, Malcolm, Malcolm, Malcolm," Emma says with a sigh, her body sagging like a rag doll. She follows Charlie's path to where the guys are standing, and I lean against the wall, watching the four of them. Ryan and Charlie are having a heated discussion, of course, though I can already see her posture softening.

It takes less than a minute for Emma to cave. Taking Malcolm's hand, she leads him out onto the dance floor. She's probably trying to give Charlie and Ryan privacy, though I doubt Malcolm's going to see it that way.

I'm so tired. This night's been a complete bust and I just want to go home. I turn on my phone to call an Uber and find a text from Jacob waiting for me. I'm briefly excited until I realize he's writing because of Ryan. Do they talk? Does he actually have conversations with him? With Malcolm?

Jacob: Is everything alright over there? Ryan is blowing up my phone asking where you all are.

Wow, look at that! Whole sentences. This is truly a momentous day.

Me: Yeah. He's here.

Jacob: K.

Me: At the club.

Jacob: K.

Me: We're dancing and drinking. I'm totally sloshed.

A lie, but jealousy worked once so—

Jacob: K. Have fun.

Asshole. I blow out a breath. Screw this shit. I close up messages and open the Uber app. I've got a bottle of vodka at home calling my name.

Thirty-Seven
Surprise!
Jacob

Stella: 2 down and only 2 more exams left to go.

Me: Great!

Stella: Last exam is at 11:00 on Friday. I'll head out right after.

Me: Okay.

Stella: I can't wait to see you!

Me: Me too.

Soft fingers brush against my stubbled cheek, waking me. I blink my sleepy eyes open and my heart leaps when I see Stella smiling down at me.

"Hey you lazy bum," she says. That voice. That beautiful fucking voice. I didn't realize how much I missed hearing it for real as opposed to over the phone. The sound of it spreads in a warm rush through my body.

Stella's here? Already? What time is it? I glance at the clock. It reads a quarter to five. Shit, I slept the whole day away. I meant to take a shower and shave and clean this nightmare of a room before she came, but at the moment I'm just really fucking happy to see her. All the words I want to say get stuck in my throat and my traitorous eyes are burning with tears that I refuse to let fall in front of her. All I can seem to do is sit up and wrap my arms around her and pull her against me. The swell of her breasts against my chest, her breath tickling my neck, the press of her fingertips against my back. It's all so familiar yet so foreign. It feels like I haven't touched her in months or years and not only a few weeks, and all I want in this world right now is to touch her and kiss her and fuck her until the rest of the world disappears, and it's just us.

Stella lets out a whoop as I flip her onto her back and position myself between her legs. Aware of what is most likely a nasty case of morning breath, I go straight for her neck, kissing and sucking and biting until I'm thwarted by the collar of her shirt. The urge to rip the damn thing off is fucking overwhelming, but I lift her instead, so I can drag it over her head and unsnap her bra. She's bare and beautiful, and I'm so turned on, it'll be a miracle if I don't blow my load the minute she touches my cock. I take her nipple into my mouth, sucking it hard and grinding my aching cock between her legs. She arches her back, offering herself up to me, and hell if I'm not going to take every bit of what she's giving. I continue to suck and tease her nipple while I take the other between my fingers, tugging and pinching and rolling it until she gasps, and her legs tighten around my waist. I release her nipple from my mouth with a pop and move to the other. Her hands are in my hair, gripping it tight enough to sting, but that edge of pain only amps me up. I reach between us and unbutton and unzip her jeans, then slip my hand under the fabric and into her panties. My two fingers delve between her legs to find her soaked. She moans and bucks her hips as I run my fingertips along her center, spreading her wetness up and around her clit then back to her entrance, where I press a finger inside of her and watch her eyes roll into the back of her head. I pump one finger, then two, my thumb slipping along her clit.

"Jacob." She speaks my name like a prayer, and she runs her hand up and down my cock through the fabric of my boxer briefs. She tugs the waistband, exposing the tip of my cock, and wraps her delicate fingers around my shaft. Just that touch has me bowed over her and panting into the crook of her neck. She strokes my length gently, teasingly, and she's fucking killing me. I reflexively jerk my hips. She tightens her grip, and runs a thumb over the tip, spreading the bead of pre-cum in circles around the head of my cock. I'm painfully hard and I need to be inside of her right fucking now. Pulling from her grasp, I kiss down between her breasts and over the planes of her stomach. Then, I hook my fingers around the waistband of her jeans and drag them down her legs and toss them aside, followed by her panties. Stella's completely naked below me and she's so fucking beautiful, it's like she's taken my heart in her fist and squeezed. I run my hands along the inside of her thighs, spreading her. Arousal glistens along her sex, and I'm torn between the urge to taste her or fuck her. I drag my tongue up her center, relishing her taste. She squirms and whimpers beneath me, while I circle her clit with my tongue while I slide a finger inside and out of her.

Too soon, Stella shoves my chest, pushing me back onto my shins.

She pulls my shirt up and over my head and tugs down on my underwear, freeing my cock. She gives me a sexy smile and says, "My turn." And before I can even really process what she's about to do, she has her hot lips wrapped around the head of my cock, circling it with her tongue.

"Fuck," I say. She smiles around my cock, eyes holding mine as she works her way down my shaft until I'm hitting the back of her throat. "Fuck," I say again because there are no words for how fucking amazing this feels. Stella pulls me even deeper, my cock sinking into her hot, wet throat. She swallows, and I gasp as her throat constricts around me, then again, as she begins moving up and down my shaft. Her hand slips between my legs to cup my balls, and it's all I can do not to come right here and now.

I thread my fingers through her hair and because I can't fucking control myself, I start rolling my hips, matching her movements. She stills and runs her hands up my chest, relinquishing control.

God, I fucking love this girl.

I begin pumping into her mouth, softly at first, then harder as she eggs me on, bobbing her head and moaning around my cock until I'm full-on fucking her mouth.

Unable to hold out even one second longer, I push her off of me and flip her onto her back. I position myself at her entrance and work my cock into her a little bit at a time, fighting the urge to simply pound into her. I want to make this last, never want it to end. She digs her nails into my ass and lifts her hips. "Do it," she demands, but I ignore her, filling her inch by inch, savoring the sensation of being slowly swallowed into her wet heat until I bottom out.

I press my body into hers and begin to move. Her skin is fucking glorious as it glides against mine. She's so tight. Her walls grip my cock like a vice, and I swear I can feel it in my toes. "Fuck." I groan and increase my speed while tilting my hips, so they drag against her clit with each thrust. She meets me thrust for thrust, her gasps turning into screams as she nears climax. The tightening in my balls and cock verges on the point of pain as I struggle not to come. I pound into her harder and harder. My tether on control is stretched almost to the breaking point. Finally, she cries out, her walls tightening around me as she comes. I release the last of my self-control and drive into her until I explode—climaxing so hard I fucking see stars.

We hold each other through the aftershocks. I pull out, roll over onto my side and drag her against me, her back to my chest. And for a little while, life doesn't suck quite as much.

Thirty-Eight
Should've Seen That Coming
Stella

"So, all he has to do is press this button," Jacob's mom, Gloria, taps a red digital button displayed on her phone and a message box where the time and date are listed. "It records the incident and notifies Ana and me so we can check in and make sure he's alright."

Gloria has spent the last hour showing me all the gadgets they've been using to monitor Jacob's seizures. First, she shows me the cameras hooked up to a live feed all over the house—except in Jacob's room and the bathrooms because Jacob said he'd move out if she tried to watch him pee—and now we're sitting at the dining room table as she goes through the phone app they'd been using to track his seizures. It's pretty cool actually, and I appreciate her sharing all of it with me because I'm hoping he'll be coming home soon, and I'll need to learn all of this.

Unfortunately, Jacob doesn't seem to see it that way. He just looks pissed, which I really don't understand. Is he embarrassed? He shouldn't feel that way around me, but given my experience with men and their ridiculous egos, it's not out of the realm of possibility. He hasn't added anything to the conversation, not a single word, only watches us with that broody expression on his face.

Finally, Gloria sets down the phone, and keeping up her phony cheerful persona, offers to cook us dinner. I agree while Jacob makes some guttural noise I'm assuming is a yes, and the woman makes a beeline for the kitchen. You know shit's gotten bad when your own mother doesn't want to be in the same room with you.

Jacob rubs the back of his neck and turns for the couch. "TV?" he asks, without looking at me. In the span of a few hours, our interactions have gone from mind-blowing sex to zero eye contact and one-word utterances or grunts.

Fabulous.

I follow him to the couch because what else am I going to do? I sit, squished up against his side, and lace our fingers together. He gives my hand a squeeze, which eases my concern a little, and begins scrolling through the channels, stopping on some home improvement show. We sit like that for a while, watching the show but not really watching it. The tension radiating off of him is palpable. I'm seriously considering taking him back to his bedroom for a quick blow job just to take the edge off when the front door swings open.

"Let's get this party started," my mom hollers, and I give a mental eye roll, as she strolls into Jacob's house, hips swinging and wine bottle raised in the air like something out of a shitty B-Movie.

Jacob gives me a knowing smirk. "I'd love to say she's here for you, but this seems to be a regular Friday night activity."

Our eyes meet and my mom's smile turns up a few more megawatts. "Hey, baby," she says and crosses to where Jacob and I are seated on the couch, and she gives me one of her dizzying "let's swing back and forth until Stella pukes" hugs.

"Hi, Mom."

Next, she hugs Jacob, but with him, she's more careful. Just a quick squeeze and she moves on. Normally, my mom would hug Jacob with as much gusto as me, but she's treating him differently now—like he's breakable—and I don't have to see Jacob's face to know it bothers him.

Shit, it bothers me.

Gloria steps out of the kitchen with a flourish and belts out, "There she is Ms. America," and even my tone-deaf mom cringes at how badly off-key she is. Gloria scoops up the wine and gives my mom a quick peck on the cheek. Gesturing to me with the bottle, Gloria says, "Look who decided to stop by."

Mom smiles. "Yep. Of course, she comes here first instead of seeing her poor dear mother." She lays a hand on her chest as though I've hurt her heart. She always was a drama queen.

"Whatever, Mom."

"Do you see how she treats me?" Mom says to Gloria as she follows her into the kitchen. Gloria just laughs. Yeah. She knows my mom's full of crap.

"You came straight here. Didn't stop at your mom's first?" he asks me, his voice barely above a whisper.

I turn my head to look at him, but he's focused on his hands clasped between his knees, so I'm basically answering the side of his face when I say, "Yeah."

He nods but doesn't comment further. There was a time when I could read Jacob like a book, but right now, looking at him, I haven't got a clue.

After a minute, our moms return with wine glasses the size of pineapples and filled to the rim. I wouldn't be surprised if they'd managed to empty the entire bottle into those two cups. My mom plops down beside me on the couch and ruffles my hair like I'm five.

"So, Stella," Gloria begins, taking a seat in the recliner across from us, "Anything new?"

I pause, unsure how to answer. I do have some things I wanted to talk over with Jacob, but not anything I'd like to get into in front of his mom or mine. "You know. Same old-same old," I reply, trying to keep things vague.

"Oh, did you tell Jacob about the job?" my mom asks, all happy exuberance until she sees the death rays I'm glaring at her.

"What job?" Jacob asks, followed by his mom's, "Yeah, what job?" right on cue like this is a poorly-written sitcom and not my life.

At least my mom has the decency to look properly chagrined. "Who wants chips?" she says, and bolts for the kitchen.

Wow! Thanks for the support, Mom.

"I... Um... It's really not a big deal. We can talk about it later."

His eyes narrow. Shit. He knows something's up. "What's the job, Stella?"

I glance at Gloria, silently begging her to leave. Luckily, she takes the hint and says, "Let me go check on Lucy," and follows my mom's route into the kitchen.

My heart thunders in my chest. I'm part excited, part terrified because I have no idea how he might react. I'd meant to gauge his interest before springing it on him, but that's no longer an option, so I just push ahead. Taking a deep breath, I look him straight in the eyes—trying to appear more confident than I feel. "So, I was talking to Malcolm," I begin. "He says hi, by the way."

Jacob nods and waits for me to continue. The warmth has completely drained from Jacob's eyes and a muscle pops in his jaw like he's clenching his teeth. Jesus, he's already pissed, and I haven't even said anything.

I wring my hands nervously. Suddenly, I'm thinking this was a terrible idea, but it's too late to stop, so I just spit it out all at once. "He has this uncle who's in advertising and they do a summer internship for graphic artists and he—we—thought you might be interested." Still no reaction. I drop my gaze, unable to stomach the cold look in his eyes for one more second. "He said you don't necessarily need to be a student to apply, and it's paid. Not a lot, but..." I trail off, sounding fucking pitiful.

"So, you and Malcolm were talking about me?" he asks, and hell if I can understand what's going on in his head.

"He came over with Charlie and Ryan and asked me if I thought you'd be interested. I told him I'd ask you, that's all."

"And how, exactly, am I supposed to do an internship right now, Stella?"

I bristle at his tone but take a breath and push it aside. He's going through a lot. I have to be patient and give him some time to come to terms with everything. "It's not until the summer. You would need to apply now, but it wouldn't start until late May."

"And this is back in Mason?"

"Yeah."

He sighs and rubs his eyes. "Stella, I appreciate what you're trying to do, but there's no way I can plan that far ahead. There's no way to know if my seizures will be better before then."

"Your mom said the doctor thinks the medication is starting to help."

"It's barely been a month since I started the meds. He can't possibly make that judgment yet."

"I get that, but the application period is now and if you can't do the internship when the time comes, then you don't accept."

"And it's that easy?"

"I didn't say it was easy—"

"How am I supposed to get to a job if I can't drive?"

"I'll drive you or you take the bus. My lease is over in May, so I thought we could get a place next to the bus line."

"Together?" he spats, as if the idea of us living together is completely ridiculous.

I shoot to my feet and stalk across the room to put some much-needed distance between us before I punch him in his perfect fucking face. When I'm as far as the walls will allow, I round on him. "You don't have to sound so disgusted by it. Excuse me for thinking my boyfriend might want to move in with me. I mean, what kind of asshole am I, right?"

He stands but doesn't make a move toward me, away from me, or anything else; just clutches his hands at his sides like he's trying to stop himself from hitting something. "That's not what I mean."

"Then explain it to me, Jacob. What exactly do you mean? Because all I am getting from you is distance. You're pushing me away when all I want is to be here for you."

"I don't need a fucking nursemaid, Stella."

"Is that what you think this is? Me pitying you?" I fling my arms out, frustration getting the better of me. "I fucking love you, you idiot. I. Love. You. And I miss you, and every day I go without seeing you is torture. I don't expect everything to be easy but at least we'd be doing it together."

He stuffs his hands into his pockets and turns his head as if looking out the window, but I know he's just avoiding looking at me. "I just think I need some time."

My breath catches in my throat. "Time to get better or time away from me?"

For a moment, he opens his mouth to speak, then presses his lips shut, and I watch as his whole body deflates as if in defeat, and I shatter.

Tears sting my eyes. "You never said it. I thought you were just scared. I thought..." Befuddled, I pause, and ask, "Was this all about sex?"

"What? No. Stella—"

Oh, god. Hot bile rises in my throat. I slap a hand over my mouth and race out the door and into the front yard, where I drop to my knees in the damp grass and double over. I clutch my midsection and breathe—in and out, in and out—trying not to heave my guts out into the dirt.

Jacob's voice calling my name barely registers over the roar of blood in my ears. Jacob's warm hand rubs up my spine, and I flail my arms. "Get away from me!"

He drops back and another set of hands, accompanied by the scent of red wine, rest on my back. My mom. I bury my face into her chest, humiliation clawing away at my insides. "Please take me home," I whisper.

I feel, rather than see, my mom's head bob, yes. She helps me to my feet, and god bless her, puts her body between Jacob and me as she walks me to her car.

I hear Jacob and his mom arguing behind me. He calls my name again, but I ignore it. It's all just noise, meaningless noise, and right now, all I want is silence.

Jacob: Hey. Can we talk?

Jacob: Please?

Jacob: I was an asshole. I'm sorry.

Jacob: Stella?

Jacob: Please answer me.

Jacob: Fine. I'm coming over.

There's a knock at my door and I instinctively know it's Jacob. He's been calling and texting me non-stop for the past few days. Of course, he feels the need to stop by on Christmas day because it wouldn't suck enough otherwise. My mom answers the door because she's cool like that, and I hear Jacob on the other side asking if he can see me.

Mom says, "I don't think that's a good idea, honey."

The deep timbre of his voice carries through the doorway and my heart gives a little skip of excitement before I stamp it down.

"I just want to apologize, please. I can't do that if she won't talk to me."

Then perhaps you should take a hint.

My mom sets a hand on her hip. "I don't think an apology is going to do it this time, Jacob. Everyone knows you're going through a lot, but that doesn't make it okay to use Stella as your emotional punching bag."

"I'm not—"

"You are," my mom cuts in.

This is ridiculous. I'm a grown damn woman. I can't leave my mom to fight my battles like this. "It's okay, Mom." I stand up and cross to the door.

"Are you sure?" she asks, still blocking the doorway with her body, like my own personal human shield. I love her for it, but I need to deal with this myself.

"Yeah."

She moves out of my way. I step out onto the porch and close the door behind me. I could have invited him inside. It's rainy and cold out here, and there's only about a two-foot space in the center of our tiny porch that the rain hasn't reached but being on the porch gives me a means of escape into the house if he won't leave.

Maybe it's cowardly, but a girl has to protect herself.

The minute I'm outside, Jacob begins spewing his apology while simultaneously making excuses for his behavior, which basically negates the entire apology. Not that I didn't expect as much, but it still irks.

"I was just upset about you and my mom making all these plans without even asking me my opinion and that internship." He shoves a hand through already disheveled hair. "I never meant that I wanted to break up. I just needed some time to—"

"To what, Jacob?" I interrupt, sick and tired of his bullshit. "To continue stringing me along, only coming around when you're horny or need someone to dump on. This back and forth, hot and cold act is giving me whiplash. I have no idea where I stand with you or what you want. You can't even say you love me."

"I do—"

"No," I cut him off, pissed off at myself for the way my voice breaks. "Don't you dare say it. Don't you dare say that to me because you think it will make me happy. It won't because I know you don't mean it. And if you don't love me now, after all the shit we've been through, you will never love me. I'm sorry you're going through all of this, and I want to be there for you, but I also have to protect myself. Goodbye, Jacob." I spin around, open the door and step into the house.

"Stella, wait—" he begins, and I shut the door in his face.

Thirty-Nine

Ghosted

Jacob

It's been two weeks. Two fucking weeks and she still won't take any of my calls or respond to my texts. It's driving me crazy.

I fucked up, badly. I know I did. It's my stupid fucking pride. I couldn't stand the idea of her pitying me or having me move in with her so she could take care of me like some goddamned charity case. I'm a grown-ass man. It's supposed to be me taking care of her, dammit.

Nobody gets it. They all feel bad for me, sure—for losing football and having to move back home. But the truth is, I couldn't give a flying fuck about any of that. It's the loss of my independence, of suddenly becoming a burden to anyone who cares about me, of being weak, that's eating me alive. And watching Stella and my mom talk about how to take care of my sorry ass, like I was a child, like I wasn't even in the fucking room.

Yeah. It pissed me off.

So, when she asked me if I needed time from her, I didn't refute it. I was too angry and embarrassed, my delicate pride too bruised to admit what was really bothering me, so I didn't say anything. Of course, she saw my silence as an admission. Anyone with half a brain would have seen it that way, but obviously, my brain was out to lunch because it took me way too long to catch up. I could have fixed it. All I had to do was tell her I loved her, give her the reassurance she needed, and I could have avoided all of this, but I didn't do that.

Because I am a man-sized chicken shit.

I'm so afraid of putting myself out there, and potentially getting hurt, that I destroyed the only good thing going on in my life right now.

I'm sitting on my bed, sketching her face for the billionth time and mentally chewing myself out when I hear a knock at the door.

What now?

"Yeah," I answer, because I'm an asshole like that.

"Can I come in?" Ana, of course. My mom's probably fed up with me by now and is sending in the big guns. She knows I can't refuse my sister anything.

I sigh, loudly. "Fine." I close my sketchbook and toss it aside. The last thing I need is her seeing how hung up I am over this whole thing with Stella.

The door squeaks open. Adriana sweeps into my room and plops down next to me on the bed like we're BFFs and everything is hunky-fucking-dory. "Hey, big bro," she says way too cheerfully.

I love my sister and would never want to hurt her, but the fake happy crap is going to get her kicked out of my room really quickly if she keeps it up. "Hi, sis," I reply, being a smart ass.

"Whatcha doin'?"

I groan and tip my head back against the wall. "What do you want, Ana?"

"Well, someone's in a shit mood. Not that I expected anything different." She picks at her skirt absentmindedly. "I wanted to check and see how you're holding up."

"Not great," I say, being honest.

Ana presses her lips together and makes a humming sound the way people do when they're only half-listening because they're really just waiting to say whatever they have on their minds. "Has Stella answered you at all?"

"Nope."

"You want me to talk to her?"

I drop my head and give my sister a hard look. "No."

Not fazed in the least, Adriana does her little humming thing again, though this time she manages to make it sound condescending as hell. "So, what are you going to do?"

I close my eyes and pinch the bridge of my nose. Knowing that she means well does absolutely nothing to lessen my irritation. For all that I try to speak calmly, my words come out clipped and forced. "If I knew what to do, Ana, I would be doing it."

"Would you?"

My eyes pop open and I glare at my sister, not even trying to hide my irritation anymore. "What the fuck is that supposed to mean?"

She shrugs, my irritation bouncing off of her like rubber off a wall. "It means have you given up because you really don't want her back or because you don't think you deserve to have her back?"

"I haven't given up," I say, basically ignoring the whole point of her question. She already knows the answer.

"Might as well have." She pulls her knees up to her chest, with her forearms resting on top. Her expression turns earnest, and I have to look away because I can handle all the sarcasm and condensation in the world, but actual feelings will knock me on my ass every time. "What are you afraid of?" she asks the back of my skull.

I shake my head, afraid that if I speak, the tiny thread of control I have over my emotions will break. Adriana places a hand on my cheek and gently turns me to face her.

"What are you afraid of?" she asks again, her voice firm but not harsh.

"That I'd be a burden. That she'll end up resenting me and stay with me out of obligation." I blow out a breath and let out that final hard truth I can hardly admit to myself. "That she won't respect me anymore." The words come out soft and small, but I know she heard me.

"So let me ask you something, then?" I don't say yay or nay, just wait for her to continue—not like I could stop her, anyway. "If your roles were reversed, if Stella suddenly developed an illness that required a little extra work on your part to help her through it, would you resent her for it?"

I flatten my expression into my best "fuck you" look. "That's different," I say.

"How so?"

I see the trap she's laying for me. I see it but leap right into it anyway because I am an idiot. "I'm supposed to take care of her."

Ana's brows scrunch up in confusion. "And she isn't supposed to take care of you?"

"No."

She leans back and searches my face like I'm a riddle she can't decipher. "Is this some stupid male pride thing?"

"Shut up, Ana."

"Wow. So, you're telling me you demolished what could have been the love of your life because you—what—don't think you're good enough for her anymore?"

I don't answer, couldn't answer if I wanted to. My throat's so sore and swollen, it hurts to breathe, much less speak. Instead, I bury my face in my hands and finally let the tears fall.

"Look at me." Ana takes my face in her hands and lifts my head, forcing me to meet her eyes. "She has loved you her entire life, Jacob. I saw it. Mom saw it. The only person who didn't see it was you. She loved you when you were a snot-nosed kid with a giant chip on his shoulder. When you were a cocky womanizer in high school. She didn't even stop loving you when you played pranks on her that would have had most girls running—this one included. And you think she'd stop now because it's inconvenient?"

Well shit, when she says it like that...

She releases my face but keeps her eyes locked on mine. "And as far as her losing respect for you, she couldn't care less about football or college. The only thing that would cause her to lose respect for you is when you act like a sorry sack of shit because things don't go your way."

"Jesus. Don't sugarcoat it, Ana. Tell me how you really feel."

"I will." She smirks.

I drag a shirt sleeve over my wet cheeks. "So, what do I do now?"

"I don't know that I'm the right person to answer that," she shrugs, "but I do have an idea I think you might be interested in."

I'm almost afraid to ask. "What's that?"

"If my scholarships come through for NU, which they should, I was planning on moving there in the fall. But... I talked to Mom, and she said she'd help us swing it for the summer so we could room together."

I open my mouth to say, "Hell the fuck no," but she interrupts me.

"Hear me out. We could find a two-bedroom for you, me, and if you can get her on board, Stella. You would have someone else around in case you needed help with stuff, so you weren't as dependent on Stella, and I'd feel safer with you being there. And of course, Stella is awesome, so there's that." She smiles. "What do you think?"

"You'd do that for me?" I ask, floored by her offer. Ana would never make me feel guilty for asking for her help, just like Stella, but having her there would ease the stress on Stella—if she takes me back.

And that's a big if.

Ana's expression turns unusually serious. "I remember what you did when we were kids. Maybe you thought I forgot because I was so small, but I remember every single time..." Her voice cracks. She pauses to take a breath and blinks back the shine in her eyes. "Every time you let him hurt you to protect me. I can't take back what he did, but I can help you get through this. Let me help you."

I pull her into a crushing hug. I've been so focused on what I've lost, I've forgotten the things I still have—an amazing sister being one of them. "You don't owe me anything," I say because she doesn't. That's what big brothers do.

She pulls back and shakes her head. "I owe you everything." She lays her head on my shoulder and we just sit like that for a while in comfortable silence.

"Did I ever tell you how I met Stella?" I ask.

She shakes her head.

"It's kind of ironic, really, when you consider everything we just talked about. It was my first day at that horrible elementary school, and I was starting halfway through the year. Everybody had already formed their little friend clicks, and I was way too shy to introduce myself to people anyway, so I just kept to myself. I'd noticed Stella. She was in my class, at the table beside mine. I remember thinking how sweet and innocent she looked—all big smiles and a sunny yellow dress. The exact opposite of me. Anyway, I was sitting alone at recess, drawing in the dirt and one of the fifth-grade boys—a kid so big you knew he had to have flunked—thought it would be funny to get in my face and talk shit. A teacher got wind of it and chased him away, but not before I'd told him to 'Fuck off.'"

Ana's head snaps up. "You really are incredibly stupid. You realize that?"

I chuckle. "Yeah, yeah. I guess that pissed him off pretty good because he grabbed one of his buddies and waited for me after school in the back lot. The two of them jumped me right there in front of half the school and not a single person stepped in to help. A couple of assholes even started to chant, you know, 'Fight. Fight.'" I pump my fist in the air to demonstrate. "Then out of nowhere comes this tiny girl—I mean she was so small she could have passed for first grade—and she swung her book bag at the big kid, clocked him right in his ugly face."

Ana laughs, and I can't help but laugh with her. "The kid she hit fell flat on his ass, and his friend booked it the hell out of there. I just stood there, fucking stunned, watching this sweet little girl stand over that boy with zero fear and ream his ass out. She even gave him a couple of kicks to the gut."

Ana is barreled over with laughter. "Oh my god, that sounds just like her," she says between wheezy breaths.

"The best part was that when someone finally got a teacher out there, Stella told her a sob story about how the boy had been picking on her and I'd come to her rescue. They bought it hook, line and sinker, of course."

"Of course." Ana chuckled.

"That was it for me. I was hooked. She couldn't have gotten rid of me if she tried. It wasn't because she was this little badass in disguise, though that was definitely part of it. It was that she stood up for me. I'd gotten my ass kicked left, right and sideways at my old school. Kids might have run for the teachers sometimes, but nobody ever tried to defend me, until her. Sometimes I wonder if I've just spent the past ten years trying to pay her back."

I give Ana's arm a squeeze, crawl to the edge of the bed, set my feet on the floor and stand. My legs ache from holding the same position for so long. I stretch and groan, then glance behind myself at Adriana who's shimmying across my bed in her little skirt and trying—unsuccessfully—to avoid flashing her panties. "I guess I have some phone calls to make."

"That so?" she replies, a wide smile spread across her face.

"Yep. Oh, and one more thing."

"What's that?"

"Where does mom keep the keys to the shed?"

Forty
Eat, Sleep, Class, Repeat
Stella

When I was a kid, my teacher showed us this image, from the Hubble telescope, of thousands of galaxies in what amounted to a tiny speck of the universe, and I remember feeling so insignificant when compared to the vastness of space. I'm reminded of that now as all around me everyone else continues on with their lives, as if the entire world hasn't ended because, for them, it hasn't. Because in the grand scheme of things, my broken heart is insignificant. It doesn't matter how much it hurts; the rest of the world goes on. I have to go on with it or get left behind.

So, I slog through my days, going through the motions: wake up, go to class, do homework, go to sleep. I even throw some meals in there for good measure, though admittedly, the half a Philly cheese steak sandwich, which was essentially my breakfast, lunch and dinner yesterday, hardly qualifies as a meal.

My friends are concerned, sure, but they have lives that have to keep going, regardless of my feelings.

Case in point, Charlie's twenty-first birthday. She's the first of the four of us girls to turn twenty-one and it's kind of a big deal—for her, at least—and I'm not ruining it with my depressing bullshit. I'll put on a happy face and pretend everything is fine, just like I've done for the past two months. Also, I will buy chocolate cake, which is the perfect addition to any party, whether it be birthday or pity. And since I've hardly eaten and lost a shit-ton of weight I didn't need to lose, I can stuff my face all I want without an ounce of guilt.

The bell jangles over my head as I enter the bakery, and I'm hit with the delicious scent of baked desserts and chocolate, making my mouth water. The head of a girl about my age pops up from behind the counter. She's cute with her hair pulled back into pigtails and flour, or maybe that's powdered sugar, dusting her face and all over her blue apron with the words "Debbie's Desserts" emblazoned across the front in fat cursive letters.

"Hi," the counter girl says. "What can I do for you?"

"I ordered a cake. Stella Leone."

She holds up a finger. "One minute." Then she pats her hands all over the apron to remove some of the sugar, which, of course, results in white handprints all over her stomach, thighs and even one on her ass. Poor girl looks like she's been groped by a powdered donut. "I'll go get it."

I nod and she heads into the back while I peruse the displays. The cakes are beautiful—handmade with pretty impressive fondant cake sculptures representing everything from a mermaid's tail splashing into the water to a three-tiered cake made to resemble a stack of gifts. I would have loved to get Charlie something that looked so cool if it hadn't cost a small fortune to purchase.

I bet Jacob could have made something special for her, I think, then get pissed at myself for the twinge of pain in my chest that accompanies any thoughts about Jacob. Which is pretty much every damn thought I have. I can't get away from it. Everything makes me think of him: the shitty patch job he did on my wall, the couch where we sat to watch movies, the park that I never even went to with him but still reminded me of his landscape sketches. It's enough to drive me nuts. Part of it's my fault, because I can't find it in me to block his texts. He sends one or two a day and the constant reminders are definitely not helping me move on. Sometimes he's wanting to talk; others he's telling me about his doctor appointments or even a movie he liked. The worst ones are where he apologizes and begs me for a second (Ha! More like fourth) chance.

It's kind of ironic that now he's the one vying for my attention, and I'm the one who barely acknowledges his existence. If the dumbass had tried this hard two months ago, none of this would have happened. Then again, it's all sort of meaningless if he doesn't love me. No amount of texts or phone calls could have changed that.

The girl returns shortly, holding my chocolate cake with pink polka dots that says *Happy 21st Birthday, Charlie*. I pay and head out to Ryan's place to help set up.

By the time I enter the little bungalow Ryan shares with two other guys from the team, preparations are in full swing. The living room isn't big, perhaps twenty by twenty feet, but they're making good use of the space. Furniture has been pushed up against the walls to make room for a dance floor, hot pink and white streamers hang from every conceivable surface, and a snack table is set up on the right wall, strategically blocking the forty-eight-inch-wide screen TV that is, Ryan's roommate, Dave's pride and joy. Hanging in the archway directly opposite the front door is a huge silver sign with "Happy Birthday!" written in black script, which will be the first thing everyone sees when they enter the house.

I cross the room and through the archway into the cute little kitchen with white cabinets, black appliances and no dishwasher—which is pretty-much blasphemy in my book—and set the cake on the only empty shelf in a fridge literally packed with beer. Bottles of wine and liquor, and a mountain of plastic cups, are set up on the countertop along with a few bottles of coke, orange juice and some other flavored juices specifically supplied to make drinks.

The door to the backyard opens and Ryan enters the kitchen, followed by Emma. "Uh, exactly how many people are you expecting?" I ask them.

Ryan gives me a sheepish grin. "I might have gone a little overboard with the drinks."

Rolling her eyes, Emma says, "Ya think?" Then to me, she asks, "You get the cake?"

"Yep. It's in the fridge."

"Cool." Emma opens the backdoor and waves me over. "Check out the backyard. It's epic."

I don't know that epic is the word I'd use to describe the set-up in Ryan's backyard.

Perhaps, "Ill-prepared," "poorly executed," or simply "debacle," would have been more accurate seeing as, not only did Ryan and his entourage neglect to tell people to bring swimsuits, they also set up three kiddie pools and a slip-n-slide in what is essentially a dirt lot. So now, we have a bunch of drunk people running around in their underwear and covered in mud.

Ryan is standing by the back door spraying people with a hose before they go into his place while Charlie has spent the whole night with Emma and me, watching the chaos from the comfort of our lawn chairs.

"All I gotta say." Emma pauses to take a sip of the hard lemonade she's been nursing all night. She shudders at the tart flavor, then continues. "I'm just glad this isn't my place, because these guys are definitely losing their security deposit."

"You think?" Charlie asks, her expression pained.

"Oh yeah," Emma says with a sardonic laugh. "That hardwood floor is toast."

Charlie groans.

"It's not your responsibility," I tell her. "You specifically told him you didn't want a party, and he did one, anyway. That's on him."

Charlie's brows furrow as she watches her boyfriend struggle to keep mud-covered partygoers out of his house. "And yet, I still feel guilty," she finally says with a sigh.

Emma examines her bottle of hard lemonade. "I don't understand how people can drink this shit." She takes another sip, shudders again, then chucks the whole thing at a nearby trash can, missing completely. "Damn. I really do suck."

Charlie and I chuckle because, yeah, Emma couldn't hit the side of a bus. "Listen." I grab Charlie's hand and give it a tug to get her attention. "Today would have been a bad day to go clubbing, anyway. Tomorrow's Friday; we'll go out then."

"And no men invited," Emma chimes in. Her gaze narrows on Malcolm who's chatting up a few girls on the other side of the yard, and she crosses her arms. "I can't get my freak on with Malcolm watching everything I do like some jilted boyfriend. It's weird."

"Agreed," says Charlie. "Speaking of boyfriends," she turns her attention to me. "Have you spoken to Jacob lately?"

"He's not my boyfriend," I say, trying to sound nonchalant and by the look of pity in my friends' eyes, failing miserably.

"Alright," Charlie says, drawing the word out as if placating a child, which I suppose is me in this situation. I should be pissed, but I don't have the energy to let it bother me. It takes all my effort just to pretend like I want to be here, instead of where I'd really rather be, which is home, in my bed, reading a book, so I can forget myself for a little while.

Charlie continues, "But have you spoken to him recently."

I sip my beer and feign disinterest. "Define, 'spoken.'"

Emma flings her arms into the air like I'm so fucking exacerbating, "Oh my god, Stella. You know what she means." She ticks off fingers and speaks way louder than necessary, seeing as I'm simply being obtuse, not deaf. "Spoken, written, texted, sent smoke signals, whatever form of communication you may have employed to exchange information with your *ex,* "emphasis on the ex, "boyfriend."

"He texts me," I reply.

"And?" Charlie asks.

"And that's it. He texts me. I don't reply so the whole exchange of information isn't really happening. I read his texts because I'm an idiot, and I stupidly hope that at some point, he'll say something to make all of this better, but he doesn't because, he too, is an idiot. So, I don't write him back. Nor do I answer his calls or emails. Is that good enough for you?"

Charlie blows out a breath, and using her "don't bite me" tone, reserved for rabid dogs and irate best friends, she says, "I was just checking because I didn't want you to be caught off guard."

Fabulous. What now? "Caught off guard about what?"

Charlie scrunches her nose. "He didn't tell you?"

"Obviously not, Charlie," I say, with way more venom than she deserves, but spit it out already.

"He's coming into town on Monday." She says the words lightning-quick then draws back, as if expecting a punch, which only pisses me off more. I mean, have I been on edge lately? Yes. But for god's sake, give a girl a little credit. I'm not going to punch her.

I turn to Emma who shrugs as if this is the first time she's hearing this too. "Who told you this?"

"Ryan," Charlie answers, still watching me like I'm Freddy fucking Kruger. "He said Jacob got an interview for that graphic design internship and was coming in on Monday."

I shoot out of my chair. "He applied for the internship?"

"Uh... yeah. I guess."

"Son of a bitch." I'm pacing back and forth in front of my friends. Emma and Charlie share a worried look, but I'm too upset to care. After throwing that big-ass tantrum, now he decides to go after the job, seriously? Is he trying to piss me off? "Why wouldn't he have told me?" I throw my hands into the air and turn to face the girls.

"Maybe he wants to surprise you," Emma supplies, unhelpfully.

"Or he doesn't want to get your hopes up in case it doesn't go through." Charlie wrings her hands and glances back and forth between Ryan and me. He's still by the door, spraying off muddy partygoers, so he hasn't noticed our little discussion here, but I'm getting the distinct feeling, looking at my friend, that he asked her not to tell me.

"Charlie?"

She must anticipate what I'm about to ask because she ducks her head and draws her shoulders up around her ears, reminding me of a turtle trying to escape into its shell. "Yeah."

"Did Ryan tell you not to say anything to me?"

If possible, her head dips even lower. "Maybe."

I make a noise, which may or may not have been a growl, and storm across the yard—or as close to storming as I can get without wiping out in the mud.

I stop in front of Ryan, fists planted on my hips. "Why did you tell Charlie not to say anything about Jacob coming?"

Ryan shoots a glare at Charlie over my shoulder.

"Uh-uh," I say, drawing his attention back to me. "Don't look at her. She didn't do anything wrong. I asked you a question."

Ryan looks like a crapped-out carnival animatronic. His head swivels back and forth, bugged-out eyes scanning the crowd for help. He can't seem to decide if he wants to speak or not because he keeps opening and shutting his mouth with little grunts of "Uh" and "Um," but doesn't actually say anything.

Am I being overly aggressive here? Perhaps.

Am I overreacting? Probably.

Do I give a shit? Absolutely not!

If you had asked me a year, or even a month, ago if I had the ability to intimidate anyone, I'd have laughed in your face. Yet, here I am scaring the shit out of a guy twice my size, and I've got to say, it feels pretty good. "Well..." I wait.

"He told me not to tell you?" Ryan says though it sounds more like a question than a statement.

"Why?"

He shoots another disgruntled look at Charlie.

"Hey," I shout. Ryan's gaze snaps back to me. "Why?" I ask again.

Ryan's shoulders slump in defeat. "He wanted to talk to you and was afraid you'd avoid him if you knew he was coming."

Yep. That about sums it up. "Thank you," I say, though even I can admit, I don't sound very thankful. I stomp into the kitchen, through the living room and out the front door, where I take out my phone and send Jacob my first text in two months.

Me: *What the fuck?*

He replies almost immediately.

Jacob: *Hi to you, too.*

Me: *Why didn't you tell me you were coming into town?*

Jacob: *Does it matter? I've been talking to dead air for two months. Didn't even know if you blocked me.*

Me: *BS!*

Jacob: *No, it isn't.*

Me: *So, you weren't planning on trying to talk to me?*

Jacob: *I was.*

Me: *Why?*

Jacob: *What do you mean, why? Because I fucking miss you and you're ignoring me.*

Me: *Because I can't talk to you.*

Jacob: *You can.*

Me: *No!*

Jacob: *Why not?*

Me: *Because you broke my fucking heart, you asshole.*

Forty-One
Places to Go. People to See.
Jacob

I THINK THIS TIE is trying to strangle me. I tug at the offending material with my index finger, trying to relieve the pressure on my throat.

Ana slaps my hand away. "Stop it. You'll mess it up, and we'll never get it right again."

"Wearing this tie isn't going to do me much good when I pass out from oxygen deprivation."

She giggles. "It should be a slow death, though. Plenty of time to finish your interview first."

"You're hysterical."

The receptionist gives Ana and me a hard look and we both shut up. I feel like such a douche. What kind of guy brings his kid sister to an interview? I squirm in my leather chair. I think I'm in over my head here. This place is way too nice. The waiting room isn't huge, but it's posh. The receptionist's desk is a wood-paneled monstrosity backing up to a gray stone wall that features the company's name, "D.S.O. Creative," written in black letters and lit from behind. Blown-up adverts cover every inch of available wall space. Real plants—yes, I checked—dot the interior and there's even one of those waterfall fountain things surreptitiously placed in the back corner of the room.

As if my nerves weren't shot enough, we've been waiting thirty minutes—okay, probably more like ten, but it feels like thirty—to see this guy who's interviewing me, and I'm getting all sweaty, which isn't exactly a good look for an interview. Maybe it would be better if I just went—

"Jacob Gonzales." I start at the sound of the male voice calling my name. When I look up, a middle-aged man in a sharp, gray suit is headed my way. He's pudgy around the middle, with brown hair and deep wrinkles around the eyes and mouth that suggest he's someone who smiles a lot. He's smiling now, his hand outstretched, as he approaches me. We shake, and I relax a bit.

"Frank Douglas. Good to meet you."

"It's good to meet you too, sir."

He chuckles. "There are no formalities here, son. Frank is just fine." He turns his smile on Ana and says, "And this is?"

"His chauffeur," Ana replies with a grin and shakes his hand.

"Also known as my sister, Adriana."

"Nice to meet you." Frank claps his hands and rubs them together like he's gearing up for a steak dinner. "Ready?"

I nod and follow him into the back. Adriana and I spoke about this earlier, that I needed to do this alone, but I can still sense the worry radiating off her as I move out of her line of sight. I'm not going to lie, I'm a little worried too, but it's been two weeks since I've had a seizure, and I'm going to have to start navigating things on my own at some point. Might as well start now.

Frank leads me into a conference room with an oval table that could easily fit twenty people. He takes a seat at one end, and I take the one next to his.

Frank's expression turns serious as he regards me, and now I'm getting all nervous again. I rub my sweaty palms along my pant legs and try to keep my breathing even.

There's a manila folder on the table, I'm guessing has to do with me. Frank clasps his hands again—that seems to be a thing with him—and rests them atop the folder. "Before we get started, Malcolm informed me of your situation, and I want to assure you we do not discriminate based on medical conditions. All we care about is whether or not you can do your work."

"Thank you, sir."

His lip quirks into a smirk. "Frank."

"Sorry." I let out a nervous laugh.

"Can't fault a guy for good manners. Anyway, is there anything I should know that might affect your work?"

I realize I'm tapping my leg and quickly set my hands on the table. "I don't think so. The medicine seems to be working. I haven't had a seizure in a couple of weeks and my doctor says I'm doing well. I probably won't be able to drive for a while, but I plan on getting a place by the bus line, so getting here shouldn't be a problem."

Frank smiles and double taps two fingers on the table. "Good, because I'm really impressed with your work."

I'm trying not to grin at him like an idiot, but I can't stop the tremor of excitement that runs through me at his words. "I was worried I didn't have enough software experience, but I'm a fast learner. I just haven't had much in the way of access."

Frank waves me off. "I could put you in an online course and have you up and running in a few days. Teaching someone to see," he wags a finger at me, "that's the difficult part. You obviously have a great understanding of anatomy and movement, and the typography pieces show your sense of design." He leans back in his chair, hands resting on his slightly rounded belly. "I take it you haven't gotten around to a basic design course yet?"

"No, si—I mean Frank." Shit. I'm tapping my foot again. How long have I been doing that? I stop and mimic Frank's calm demeanor by sagging back into my chair. He sees right through me, I'm sure. It's hard to hide it when your whole body's wound up like a jack-in-the-box. "I'd been planning to. I took the typography course first because it fit my schedule that semester. I thought I had time."

Nodding sagely, Frank says, "I'm assuming that's why you included the paintings."

The paintings? Why is he asking about those? Do people not normally include stuff like that? There were only three. It was mom and Ana who insisted I use some of them. Crap. Why did I listen to them?

"I-I thought they might give you an idea of my sense of color and design." I stammer. "Was that wrong?"

Frank draws back as if in shock, a crease forming between furrowed brows. "Not at all. If anything, those were what made your portfolio stick out. I'm asking because I wanted to know if you had more."

I could have kissed Emma for telling me where they were, but now that I'm here, with Stella in my sights, I'm hesitating.

Stella and Emma are sitting on a bench in the School of Art's courtyard, talking. Stella's hair glows like a fireball in the sunlight, framing her face like a crimson halo. Her smile was always my undoing, and it's no different now. Just seeing that smile, even from so far away, sends my heart into a sprint. As a kid, I would do anything to see that smile—to feel its warmth. Every cell in my body itches to run over there, take her in my arms and kiss her stupid. But that's no longer welcome, and it's my fault.

I miss her so much sometimes, I can't breathe. It's like she stole part of my soul, and I need it back. I need her back. If she would just give me a chance.

Ana is standing beside me, waiting patiently for me to grow some balls. "Has she gotten prettier, or is it just me?" I ask.

"I think it's just you, Bro." I can hear the smile in her voice. God, I wish I could be so calm. Instead, I've got heartburn so bad, it feels like I swallowed hot coals. "Go talk to her."

I nod but still don't move until Ana pushes me forward with a hand to my back.

I've only moved about ten feet when Stella sees me. Her smile slowly dies, the light in her eyes dims, and fuck if it isn't a kick in the gut that my presence does that to her. I'm supposed to make her smile. Always.

She says something to Emma, then crosses the courtyard to meet me. It's a hell of a lot better than her running away, which is what I was afraid she'd do. She clasps her hands nervously in front of herself and gives me a tiny smile that makes my stomach flip. "Hi," she says.

"Hi." My breath's coming out all ragged, and I can't remember a goddamned thing I'd planned to say. "How are you?"

She shrugs. "How did your interview go?"

"Good." I can't even hide the excitement in my voice. "The guy really liked my stuff and is cool about my..." I pause, not wanting to say it.

"Epilepsy," she supplies.

I rub the back of my neck, which is starting to sweat in this monkey suit. "I hate that word."

"It's only a word," she says in that calm way of hers that somehow always made me feel better. "Better to know what you're dealing with than not, right?" She drops her gaze and picks at her nails. Instinctively, I reach out and clasp my hands around hers, and a charge of electricity snakes up my spine. She lets out a sharp gasp, and it's like a fucking chorus of angels singing because that means she still loves me. I just need to convince her I love her back.

I rub circles on the back of one hand with my thumb. The gesture's supposed to be soothing, but the fact she's letting me do it at all has my heart racing. "Stella. I was a mess."

"I know." She turns her head as if to glance over her shoulder, but her gaze is unfocused.

I'm not sure what to make of that, so I just plow ahead, the speech I rehearsed in my head the entire drive from Orlando coming back to me. "I was so fucking depressed and me pushing you away was about me hating myself. I love you, Stella." Her eyes snap back to mine. "You were right, I was too chicken shit to say it, but I do love you. I've loved you my whole goddamned life and I promise, I'll spend every day proving it to you if you give me a second chance."

She doesn't smile or shout or do any of the things I might have expected. She just searches my face as though trying to read my thoughts. Finally, she says, "Fourth chance."

"What?"

She pulls her hands free from mine, and my heart plummets. "You threw me out of your hospital room—twice. Both times you apologized, and I forgave you. Then you basically ignored me for three weeks, and again I forgave you. Which makes this the fourth time. And maybe if you'd apologized then, said to me the things you are now, I might have forgiven you because I know the shit you've been going through."

"Stella I—"

"Please, let me finish." A single tear escapes to run down her cheek and I have to stifle the urge to wipe it away. She shuts her eyes, takes a breath and continues, "I love you so much it hurts. I can't eat, can't sleep. Sometimes it hurts so much I can hardly breathe." She clutches her chest, her expression pained. "And even if you're telling the truth when you say you love me, that does not make what you did alright. You may have hated yourself, but the one you hurt is me. The one you treated like shit was me. If I take you back now—again—how can I be sure it isn't going to keep happening? I'm sure your father apologized a hundred times to your mom, but in the end, it didn't mean anything because nothing ever changed."

I reel back as if struck. "I'm not my father," I say.

"No, you're not. You would never hurt me... physically."

I'm stunned silent. All the times my father beat the shit out of me and my mom, then just apologized like it somehow took away the pain, play on repeat in my head. I lean over, hands braced against my knees for support, as the memories pulverize me from the inside. Jesus Christ. She's right. It's like I took a page straight from the abuser's handbook.

She lays her hand on my back, the warmth of her skin seeping through my cotton shirt. "I'm sorry, Jacob, but I don't think an apology is enough this time."

She turns to leave, and I grab her wrist, halting her mid-stride. "You're right," I admit. "About everything." I straighten up, pull the black journal from my back pocket and hold it out to her. "But I did write you. I just never sent any of it to you." I press the journal into her hands. "Take it. That's everything I couldn't say." I turn my gaze to the sky and take a breath to calm myself so I can finish speaking. "Because I was afraid of what you might think of me if you saw how weak I was." I chuckle, but there's no mirth in it. "Pretty stupid, huh? I don't expect it to change anything, but at least it's the truth."

She nods and clasps the journal to her chest.

I lean in to kiss her on the cheek and take in her warm vanilla scent, which was fucking stupid because it only makes me more upset. I mutter a quick "goodbye," spin around and head back to where Ana is waiting to drive me home.

"Didn't go so great," she says when I settle into the passenger seat of her beat-up truck.

I ignore her question because she obviously already knows the answer and instead ask, "You think you might be up for another trip?"

"You sure about this?" Ana says as she leans over me to gaze out the passenger-side window at the nondescript house in the ordinary Miami suburb. It's surprisingly pretty. The stucco exterior painted beige with white trim, the lawn trimmed, bushes neatly manicured and a sign on the door that says, "Friends Welcome."

"Nope. But I'm going to do it, anyway. You want to come with me?"

She shakes her head. I expected as much. This is something I need to do, but there's no need to drag her down with me. I take a calming breath and climb out of the car. Though it's really a short distance, the walk across the neat little yard seems to take an eternity. With each step, my anxiety multiplies. My heart crashes against my ribcage and my hands tremble. Why the hell am I so scared? He can't hurt me anymore. I have nothing to be afraid of, but still, I can't shake the feeling that I'm a prisoner making his final walk to the executioner.

I've only just stepped onto the porch when the front door swings open and a boy, perhaps ten years old, with messy brown hair and onyx eyes pokes his head out. "Who are you?" he asks.

"Hi. I'm looking for Victor Marin. Does he live here?"

"Dad," the boy calls over his shoulder. "Some guy at the door for you."

Dad? Jesus, he had more kids. Why hadn't this ever occurred to me before? *Because he hated you and your sister and said you ruined his life.*

"Who is it?" replies a man's deep voice, the sound of which sends a shiver down my spine. I couldn't have imagined what my father's voice sounded like just seconds ago, it had been so long since I'd heard it, but the moment he spoke, I knew it was him.

The boy's looking up at me, brows raised, waiting for my response.

"Tell him it's your brother," I reply.

The boy's eyes widen and his jaw drops. He doesn't say anything else, only stares.

"I'm Jacob." I thrust out my hand to shake, but he doesn't take it. I lower it back to my side, the silence becoming increasingly awkward with each passing second he spends gawking at me. "What's your name?"

The boy's gaze roams over my face, and he cocks his head, eyes squinting as though he's trying to figure me out. "Anthony," he says, finally.

I'm about to ask him if he has any siblings, but before I can get the words out, he's shoved out of the doorway and replaced by a wretched old man with my father's face. He's thin, wiry, but not frail. A dirty wife-beater tank (fitting) and gym shorts sag from his boney frame, as though he recently lost a lot of weight and hadn't gotten around to buying new clothes. What little hair remains clinging to the sides and back of his scalp is almost pure gray and his skin is leathery with deep wrinkles that speak of hard living. All in all, he looks like shit. I probably shouldn't feel good about that.

"Who are you?" my old man asks.

"Can't even recognize your own son, huh pop?"

His eyes widen briefly, and then my father does the absolute last thing I would have expected: he smiles. He gives me a huge white smile, like I'm an old buddy and not his estranged son. "Jacob. How are you?" he says.

I'm stunned. I can't even begin to comprehend what's happening. Is he delusional? He has to be because no sane person would act like this. Does he not remember why we left, or is he trying to play it off? I rub my eyes. The entire way here, I'd thought about what I wanted to say to him. I would lay into him about how he hurt me and Mama and Ana. I'd tell him about my epilepsy, and how I've lost everything I've worked for because of him. I'd let it all out: my frustration, my anger, my hate. I'd purge myself of all this pain and then maybe I could move on. But standing here now, looking at him, the only thing I really want to say is, "Do you hit him too?"

My old man's eyes narrow and his face takes on that nasty sneer I'm all too familiar with. "I don't need to listen to this shit," he spats. He tries to pull the door closed, but I slam my hand against the wood, stopping it short.

"Do you have a wife? More kids? How many kids do you have now, Pop?"

A middle-aged woman with kind eyes, with another little boy, this one around six, propped up on her hip, steps into view. "Victor, is everything alright?"

My father whirls on her. "Get back inside," he shouts, and the look of terror in the woman's eyes is all I need to see.

I back away a few steps, spin around and head to the car. My father is calling after me to "Get the fuck back over here," and the like, but I ignore it.

"What happened?" Ana asks, as I slip into the passenger seat. "Was that a kid?"

"Yes."

She smacks her hand on the steering wheel. "Jesus, Jacob. What are we going to do?"

The front door slams shut. I glance over my shoulder to make sure he's actually gone back inside and isn't coming after me, then I turn my full attention on Ana. "We're going to do what we should have done fifteen years ago."

Her lips tighten as comprehension sinks in. She hesitates only a moment before her eyes alight with determination, and I know she's with me. "Let's do it."

It's been a week since I turned my father in to the authorities. All these years, it never occurred to me he would start another family to abuse. I guess, in the back of my mind, I thought he did what he did because he hated us and once we were gone, he moved on. Turns out, for all the blame he threw around, he was just a mean asshole who liked to beat on women and kids. Although the statute of limitations had run out for Ana and me, we were able to convince the police to do a welfare check on his current family. The officer handling our case said the mom and boys all showed signs of long-term abuse. I'm trying not to blame myself for not turning him in earlier, but that kind of guilt is hard to shake. We didn't tell our mom. She already bears enough of her own guilt for our sakes. We can carry this for hers.

I finally listened to my doctor and started seeing a therapist. It's not so bad. He's a pretty cool guy, actually. I've also been spending more and more time in my bedroom painting and thinking, mostly about Stella. I miss her so fucking bad. Even before we started dating, she was a huge part of my life, and without her everything is empty. I try not to think about whether she's read the journal or not and what that might mean. I'm not sure it even matters at this point. If I'd talked to her the way I did in that journal to begin with, things would have gone a lot differently. Nothing I can do about that now.

I'm applying a blue wash over the top of my sketch. The faint red lines peek out from beneath the array of colors. I'll leave them like that for now and wait until the paper's completely dry before tracing over them in ink. I've used up all the large sheets of watercolor paper, and my mother's willingness to pay for them, so I'm working on small pieces now, using mostly paper torn from sketchbooks. They're not as grand as the bigger pieces I was making, and the paper is prone to pilling, but I'm enjoying the freedom of not worrying about wasting expensive watercolor paper if I screw up.

I'm extra grateful for the cheap paper when my door flings open and Ana barges into my room whisper-screaming my name. "Jacob. Jacob."

Startled, I swipe a line of blue straight down the center of the sheet and sigh. "What?" I ask, trying not to sound as annoyed as I feel.

She has my phone clasped between her hands, her palm covering the receiver. "It's the design guy," she says, jamming the phone into my chest. I fumble with it for a second, losing my grip on the brush in the process, but manage not to drop the phone on the hard tile. Ana's making little squealing sounds, hopping in place and tapping her fingers together in a silent clap.

I can't help but smile at her enthusiasm. Nice to know I've got someone rooting for me. I raise the phone to my ear and answer, "Hello."

Frank's cheerful voice replies, "Jacob. Hello. I'm glad I got ahold of you. I wanted to tell you, personally, that you've been accepted into the internship program. Congratulations."

"I got it," I scream, probably blowing the poor man's ears out, but he only laughs.

"Yes, sir."

It takes a shit-ton of control for me not to start jumping up and down with my sister. Instead, I reply with a breathy, "Thank you so much."

"Everyone was really impressed with your work."

"Thank you," I say again, though I could probably say it a hundred times and it still not seem like enough. I'm grinning like a lunatic, but I don't care. I've finally gotten a break. I can't wait to tell Malcolm.

"While we're on the subject of your work, I've got a bit of a proposition for you."

Curiosity peaked, I pause my mini celebration and reply, "I'm listening."

Forty-Two
Always and Forever
Stella

I WISH I COULD say I was excited to be going out, but that would be a lie. After reading Jacob's journal, which was scary honest and raw, my mind is stretched too thin to contemplate anything else. I've read it so many times, I have the entire thing practically memorized.

I don't know why I didn't tell you I loved you. I've thought it a hundred times. Maybe because then it would be easier to let you off the hook. So, you didn't feel obligated to take on the burden that I've become.

I shut you out because I'm afraid to admit how I feel. Ana says it's male pride bullshit. She's not wrong, but it's more than that. I'm afraid that once you see the real me, or at least what's left, you won't want me anymore.

The doctor says I'm improving, and that I should be well enough to go back to Mason this summer. Now, I just have to hope you'll take me back. Please, Stella, take me back. I'm fucking lost without you.

"Earth to Stella," Emma says.

I spin around to face my friend. "What?"

"Are you almost ready?" she asks, her tone suggesting this isn't the first time she's tried to get my attention.

"Yeah. Sure," I say and turn back to face the full-length mirror hanging on the door in Emma's room.

Charlie's sitting at Emma's desk painting her nails an obnoxious shade of hot pink, while Emma's on her bed, trying to choose a lipstick color from the five trillion shades she's dumped onto the comforter. I twist in front of the full-length mirror, checking out how my once slinky black dress now hangs off of me. I really have lost a lot of weight.

"Tell me again why we're going to a rock concert wearing cocktail dresses."

"It's a benefit, not a concert." Emma moves to stand behind me, looking into the mirror over my shoulder. She wraps me up in a hug and smiles at our reflection. "It'll be fun. And it's for Breast Cancer, so we're supporting a good cause."

"I thought you said Multiple Sclerosis," I shoot back.

For a moment, Emma's eyes take on a faraway look, then she waves a hand in the air dismissively. "Something like that. Anyway, Kat's band is the entertainment. That's all I know. They're just doing covers, but it's a good-paying gig, and she's really excited about it. So, we're going to go support her and eat all the free food." She tips her head and smiles. "Okay?"

"Yes, ma'am," I reply, with a two-fingered salute.

"See, now she's getting it," Emma says to Charlie, who just giggles, and with a pat on my back, she heads back to her lipstick pile.

The doorbell rings, and Emma and Charlie spring into action, scrambling to put on their shoes and stuff their purses with whatever ridiculous shit they've deemed a necessity for the event. "I'll get it," I say. Slipping my feet into my ballerina flats, I pad across the living room and open the front door.

Malcolm sweeps in. "Ladies, ladies, ladies." He does a little spin, obviously trying to show off his weirdly shiny gray suit. Ryan rolls his eyes at his friend's behavior and follows him inside the apartment. For all Malcolm's pomp, if I had to choose between the two, I'd say I much prefer Ryan's sleek all-black suit to Malcolm's flashier one.

Emma steps out in her long red dress with a slit up the leg and cleavage-loving neckline, looking like she just walked off a red carpet somewhere, and Malcolm's eyes almost pop right out of his head.

"Close your mouth, bro," Ryan whispers to his friend, though at a volume plenty loud enough for us all to hear. Then, of course, Ryan does the exact same thing when Charlie enters the living room in her sexy silver dress. It's gorgeous, like molten metal flowing over her curves and stopping at her knees, but it's the way the open back dips to just above her butt, that turns the dress from simply sexy to smoking hot. It's all part of Charlie's push to get Ryan past seeing her as a sweet, good girl. By the deer in headlights expression on his face, I'd say it's working.

"What are you wearing?" Ryan asks.

"A dress," she replies, ever the smart ass.

"Uh... Yeah... Uh, that's... Wow. You look good," he says, rubbing the back of his neck. Then, catching his mistake, Ryan's eyes widen, and he quickly tacks on, "I mean great. Um... Super great."

Shakespeare, he is not.

Charlie seems happy enough, though. She gives him a sly little smile and struts past him to the door. A dazed Ryan turns and follows her out like a puppy on a leash. Malcolm's biting his fist, trying to hold back his laughter, and Emma's face is so red, she looks like a tomato ready to burst. I'd probably be laughing too if I wasn't stuck in this funk. I do manage to muster a smile, even if it isn't very convincing.

Malcolm lets out a breath, his chest heaving like he'd been holding it a while. "Ahhh, those two." He rubs the moisture from his eyes.

Emma giggles. "They are such a train wreck."

Still holding back laughter, Malcolm nods his agreement. "Come on," he says. "We'd better get going or we'll miss the show." As he's ushering us out the door, Malcolm pauses to shake his head at me as if to say, "Are these people nuts or what?"

Why yes. Yes, they are.

By the time we've made it downtown, everyone's eager to get out of Ryan's shitty Explorer and stretch. The venue is in a busy area, so Ryan does a quick stop and drop, practically kicking us out of the car and hauling off before people start honking. It's Saturday night and the streets are bustling with people going to and from clubs and restaurants. Sweet and savory scents permeate the air, making my mouth water. I am definitely going to have to avail myself of some pastries before we leave. The sounds of unintelligible chatter, thumping bass, and wailing guitars, streaming from the multitude of venues, clash and overlap and merge into a turbulent hum, I can feel in my feet.

I'm beginning to catch a little buzz of excitement, which, considering my usual state of constant melancholy, is a welcome change. I follow the others into a sleek white stucco building with a sign reading Mickelson Gallery, and turning to Emma, who seems to be the de facto leader of this little exhibition, ask, "Are you sure we're in the right place?"

"Yep."

"But there's no music," I say. In fact, it's one of the few open businesses that isn't playing music.

Emma whirls to stand in front of me. Her hands grip me by the shoulders, and she lets out a heavy breath. "You know we love you. Right?"

Oh shit. What did they do? "Yes," I say, giving her the side eye.

"And we want you to be happy?" she continues.

I nod, too dumbstruck to form words, and glance at Malcolm and Charlie, hoping they'll be a little less cryptic, but it's obvious I'm getting nothing from those two. They both have their eyes rolled skyward to avoid my gaze. Charlie is literally twiddling her thumbs and Malcolm is pretending to whistle, though no sound is coming out because he obviously sucks at it. Emma she spins around and saunters inside, while Charlie, hands pressed to my back, ushers me through the door.

"What the f—" My words catch in my throat. On the wall dividing the entrance from the open gallery is an ink drawing of a little girl jumping in a puddle, the water splashing around her in bursts of color. Touches of color show on her lips and eyes and bits of skin and while the use of color is stunning, it's the joy depicted on the girl's face that draws me in.

And the fact that she looks a lot like me.

I check the label: Stomping in Puddles, age 8, by Jacob Gonzales. Oh my god, she is me.

My heart does a flying leap in my chest and seems to get stuck in my throat because suddenly, I can't speak.

Jacob painted this for me?

I turn and look at my friends, who are all wearing the same smug expressions on their faces. Emma holds her hand out to me. "Come on. There's more."

I take her hand because what else am I going to do? She leads me around the image and into a large open room with canvasses lining the wall and free-standing partitions, exhibiting what appear to be small sketches, dotting the space. The gallery is packed with people, making it hard to navigate. I try to search the faces for Jacob, but I don't see him anywhere. Is he here? He has to be, right? My chest tightens at the thought.

Emma pauses in front of another painting—of a small girl leaning over a much bigger boy and yelling. A laugh bursts out of me at the title: Tiny Badass.

"What is this?" Emma asks, head cocked as she inspects the image.

"The day we met."

She smiles warmly at me. "Now, that's a story I'd like to hear… later."

"Later," I agree, and we continue to follow the wall. Every single image is like looking into the past. Like the time I decided I was going to be a gymnast and thought it was a fabulous idea to do a backflip off a low-hanging branch in Jacob's yard. In the painting, I'm hanging upside down on the branch about to flip off, and Jacob's standing underneath, ready to catch me. Poor guy got booted in the face for that bit of chivalry. In another, I just released the rope swing and am flying spread eagle over the little freshwater spring we spent all our summers freezing our asses off in. He also painted my unsuccessful foray into playing guitar. In this one, I'm smiling and strumming along while everyone around me cringes. It's obvious from my fancy gown, that the next painting is from our senior prom. In it, I have my arms around my date's neck and we're slow dancing, but I'm looking over his shoulder and out of the canvas. And though, I'm wearing a tiny smile, my eyes are sad. I wanted so badly for Jacob to ask me, but of course, he didn't, so I went with someone else and hated every minute of it.

I've lost Emma and the others at some point, but I don't care. I'm too enthralled by the history playing up on these walls to even notice their absence. I finally make my way to the dividers and see that they are in fact covered with sketches—some of them young and childish, others refined, all of them of me.

"Hi."

I'm so caught up gazing at the drawings, the sound of his voice makes me jump. Spinning around, I find Jacob, looking like a lady's wet dream in a black suit and crisp white shirt. He's sporting a neat beard and his hair a little longer than I remember—and semi-tamed at best—yet he's the most beautiful thing I've ever seen. He gives me a wary smile that sets my heart beating double-time.

"Why?" I ask, the question spilling from me before I've even had a chance to consider it.

Jacob shrugs. "I had a lot of free time on my hands." He takes a step toward me. His presence is weighted, magnetic. The closer he comes, the more I'm drawn to him. I'm fighting the urge to move closer and to move away—even I don't know what to make of my conflicted feelings. "Truth is," he continues, "my mom found all of my old sketchbooks and when I looked through them…" He lets out a huffed laugh and shakes his head. "It was all of you, much more than I remembered and it was so obvious, even if I didn't realize it at the time, that I loved you. I've always loved you, Stells." He looks down at his clasped hands. "I royally screwed up. I was in all this pain and… I think I was trying to reject you before you'd reject me." He scrubs a hand through his hair leaving it sticking up this way and that. "Obviously, I'm a complete dumb ass. You kind of knew this already."

I can't help but smile at that. "Yeah," I breathe.

Another step and we're so close, Jacob's warm pepperminty breath caresses my forehead. His rough fingertips graze mine, then brush up my arms, setting my skin alight. Cupping my face, he runs his thumbs along my cheekbones. I squeeze my eyes shut and lean into his touch.

"Living without you feels like dying." His throat bobs with a hard swallow. "Please. Give me another chance. I promise I will never take you for granted again," he says, his lips almost, but not quite, touching mine. A single tear trickles down my cheek and he sweeps it away with the pad of his thumb. "Say yes," he pleads.

I run my hands up his hard chest and around his nape. "Yes," I say and press my lips to his. His hands splay across my back melding my body to his. I moan and his tongue slips between my lips and the first stroke of his tongue against mine sends shock waves through my center. I melt into him, our kiss deepening, and everything else falls away. It's only me and Jacob and a world that makes sense again. We pull apart, our breaths labored. "I love you," I say.

He smiles, a genuine smile this time. "I love you." He leans back in to kiss me.

The sound of a throat clearing breaks the moment. We turn toward the culprit and find Adriana grinning like a doofus.

"Sorry," she says, though she looks anything but sorry. "It's really great to see you, Stella." She pats my arm. "And I'm super happy you two made up but..." She wiggles her nose. "It's just... People are beginning to stare." We both take stock of the room and sure enough, everyone is watching us.

My face heats up in embarrassment, and I start to pull away, but Jacob holds me tight.

"Fuck 'em," he says and lays another kiss on me.

Four Months Later...
Jacob

"Welcome, welcome, welcome." Ana waves guests into our little two-bedroom apartment with enough pomp for a charity gala at the Ritz. I'm not going to get on her about it though; let her have her fun. If there's one thing I've learned from the craziness of the past six months is to appreciate what I have. And what I have right now is an overpriced, piece of shit apartment on the bus line, a pretty cool new job, and Stella.

Life is fucking great!

Oh, and my sister, Ana's living here too, which is cool. She and Stella like to gang up on me from time to time, and I give them hell about it, but the truth is, I kind of love it. My seizures have also improved a lot—another thing to be thankful for because that isn't always the case for everybody.

And so, to celebrate, my beautiful girlfriend and my sister are throwing a housewarming party with all of our friends and pretty much the entire football team. Which means the place is so packed that people have spilled out into the entryway and into the parking lot.

Yep. The neighbors are going to love us.

"Hey there," says a honey-warm voice behind me. A smile stretches across my face, and I turn around to see my girl looking so beautiful it hurts my eyes, smiling at me. She wraps her arms around my waist, and I plant a kiss on her lips.

"Having fun?" I ask.

She just smiles and nods.

Someone's turned on the TV and whatever they're watching is creating a sort of strobing effect in the living room. "Hey," Stella shouts. She picks up an empty two-liter, chucks it at the two guys sitting in front of the screen and nails one of them in the side of the head.

"Ow." The guy turns around, rubbing his head, eyes searching the crowd for whoever hit him. I can't help but laugh. The strobing doesn't really seem to bother me too much, but Stells is still a little overprotective. It just means she loves me.

"Turn off the TV," she tells the guy. His face is all screwed up in anger and he opens his mouth like he's about to give her shit but stops short when I raise my brows at him. Nobody messes with my girl.

Grumbling, he turns off the TV.

"Oh my god, you guys," Emma shouts barreling into the two of us. By her rosy cheeks and glassy eyes, I'd say she's well and truly shit-faced. She grabs Stella and me each by a shoulder and shakes us—well more shakes herself because she's a mess. "Will you please, for the love of God and baby Jesus and whoever else I'm forgetting, tell Malcolm to stop glaring at my date like he's going to kill the poor guy? He's gonna run him off."

I peer past Emma to where Malcolm is sitting on the arm of our couch, and sure enough, he's glaring at some skinny blond guy sitting by himself in the armchair. Poor guy's wringing his hands and shifting around nervously. He looks about a half-second away from pissing himself. "I've got it," I say, and make my way over to the guys. Malcolm's so intent on Emma's date, he doesn't even notice me until I clap him on the back. "Hey, Bro. Come on. I've got something to show you."

Malcolm gives me a bland look that says he knows exactly what I'm doing, but he gets up anyway to follow, though not before throwing another death glare at Emma's poor date.

"Bro, you've got to stop this shit. You're only pissing her off."

He sighs. "I don't get it. I mean look at that guy. Could she have chosen a bigger dork?"

I have to admit, Malcolm has a point. The guy is tall and skinny, his blond hair in serious need of a trim, and he's wearing wire-framed glasses—pretty much the quintessential nerd. "Maybe she's into nerdy guys."

He shakes his head. "She's just trying to get under my skin."

I love Malcolm like a brother, truly I do, but some days I really want to slap the crap out of him. "No. She's not. She's said a hundred times that she wants a guy who will take her seriously and, in her eyes, you only want to get her into the sack."

"And that guy doesn't?" He gestures to Emma's date who's grinning up at her like a little puppy dog that's found its owner.

"I don't know. Obviously, she sees something she likes. Regardless, the way you're acting is pissing her off."

"Alright, most knowledgeable and sage master," he says, voice thick with sarcasm. Folding his arms across his chest, Malcolm continues, "Please impart your wisdom upon me. What that fuck do I do?"

"Why are you asking me? I crashed and burned about a dozen times with Stella before things stuck. Go ask Ryan. He got Charlie easily enough."

Malcolm throws his head back and laughs—a full-on belly laugh. And I'm glancing around myself like, did I miss something here? "That boy has royally screwed up that relationship. She's got him so wound up, he can't tell if he's coming or going. I'd have better luck getting advice from a tree stump."

Well, that was oddly descriptive.

"Talk to Stella then," I say, then catching myself quickly add, "or better yet, Kat."

"Who's Kat?"

I drag a hand down my face. "Emma's sister," I say and wait for recognition to dawn. It doesn't. "Look, bro. You can't expect her to think you really care about her if, after two years, you don't even know she has a sister?"

"She never mentioned a sister."

"Did you ask?"

Malcolm doesn't answer at first. He just stares at me, his expression sort of shell-shocked. "No."

"Well, there you go."

Malcolm snaps his fingers. "Wait, was she the one who went after Dean with a bat?"

"That's her."

"Sounds like my kind of girl." He bobs his head and grins.

I'm shaking my head at my dumbass friend when I hear, "There you are, my sexy man." Stella steps around from behind me and wraps her arms around my neck. She gives me the tiniest of smiles and it sets my heart alight. I lean in and give her a kiss, not really giving a shit that Malcolm's still standing here or that we're in the middle of a party at my place. All I care about is Stella. Her soft lips crushed beneath mine, our tongues stroking and teasing, her warm and soft body pressed against mine. By the time we pull apart, we're both panting, and I'm fully prepared to take her into the bedroom and forget this party.

"You two are disgusting," Malcolm says. He pats me on the back and smirks in a way that says that he's happy for us then moves away.

"He doing all right?" Stella asks, her head tipped back to look at me.

"Yeah. I think he's more bothered by the fact that she's turned him down than anything. That doesn't happen often."

She wrinkles her nose. "I bet it doesn't. If you ask me, I think he just hasn't found the right girl yet."

I brush the bridge of her nose with mine and squeeze her a little tighter. "I guess not everyone is so lucky as to fall in love with their best friend."

Her smile is so warm, it sets off tiny fireworks in my chest. "I love you," she says, the words so soft and breathy, they're barely audible.

"I love you too." I kiss her forehead. "And I promise," I brush a kiss across one eyelid, "to spend the rest of our lives," then the other eyelid, "proving to you just how much." Finally, I press my lips to hers, the kiss lasting only a moment before she pulls away, giving me a wicked grin.

"I can think of a few ways you can prove it to me right now." She bites the corner of her plump lower lip and watches me from beneath her lashes.

"Really?" I ask, my face lit up in a stupid grin that I couldn't hide even if I wanted to.

She nods, and taking my hand in hers, begins walking me down the hall toward our bedroom, her hips swaying seductively. When she glances behind and sees me watching, she smiles.

It's beaming and beautiful and everything I've ever wanted.

I sure hope I don't screw it up.

Thank you so much for reading *Never Moving On*! If you enjoyed it, please take a moment to leave a review on Amazon, Goodreads or the seller of your choice.

Hankering for more stories about our friends at *Never U*?

Keep reading for sneak peeks of:
Never Backing Off, the second book in the *Never U* series, and **Never Letting Go**, book three in the *Never U* series.
Available now on Amazon.com and Kindle Unlimited.

Also, scan the QR code below and read Ryan and Charlie's story, **Love is a Scary S.O.B**, FREE when you sign up for my newsletter.

Forty-Three
Sneak Peek of Never Backing Off
There's No Place Like Home

Emma

STANDING, HALF-SOAKED IN A shower so small it might as well be a coffin, scrubbing vomit from my mom's hair wasn't exactly how I'd pictured my morning. Hell, it wasn't exactly how I'd pictured my life. But it is what it is. No use bitching about the things we can't change, right? Well, actually, I do bitch about it, excessively, but it's my mom, so I just have to suck it up and do what needs to be done.

Of course, all of this would be a lot easier if my sister, Kat, would get off her ass and help, but that's something for another bitch session.

I drag my mom out of the shower and onto the towel I'd already set out on the floor. To say I have this down to a science would be an understatement. I fold the towel around her like a burrito and use it to drag my mom into her bedroom. My phone alarm chirps, telling me I have thirty minutes before my first class. I let my mom's shoulders slump to the floor, pull my phone from my back pocket and hit speed dial.

Kat answers on the first ring. "Hey," she says, the word drawn out and gravelly.

"Jesus, Kat, are you still in bed? It's almost two."

"Your point being?"

"That unless you're a fucking vampire, you should be up by now."

"Bitch, I work nights."

"Oh please. Ninety percent of your sets are over by midnight and getting high with your bandmates until the ass crack of dawn does not constitute working."

"It's called 'the creative process.' You should try it sometime."

"It's called 'you're full of crap.'"

She sighs. "Whatever." There's some shuffling on the other end of the line, which I'm hoping means she's getting out of bed. "If you only called me to bitch, I'm going to hang up. It's way too early for this shit." I could remind her it is, in fact, not early at all, but there really isn't any point.

"I need you to come over to Mom's and finish things up for me. There's puke all over the floor, Mom's still sopping wet from the shower, and if I don't leave now, I'm going to be late for class."

Kat lets out a long groan. "Dammit, Em. We've talked about this. You've got to stop coming to her rescue all the time. She's never gonna learn—"

"She's our mom," I remind her for the trillionth time.

"And a grown woman. If you keep enabling her—"

I growl, actually growl at her. This is what she's turned me into—a frigging dog. "I don't have time for this. Are you coming or not?"

"No."

"Thanks a lot, sis. You're the best," I say, my enthusiastic reply like something out of a cheesy sitcom.

"What? You already got her cleaned up. Just throw a blanket over her and go to class. Naked on the floor is still a step up from passed out in a pool of her own vomit."

"Wow, your altruistic virtue is truly mind-blowing."

"Quit your bitching and go to class. You're only wasting time talking to me," she says and hangs up.

Just because I do as she says doesn't mean I think she's right, only that I have no other choice.

Not that rushing did a single damn thing for me. I swear, whatever demon/corrupt government official is in charge of stoplights has a vendetta against me, because nobody's luck is *that* bad. Then again, perhaps the gods of crappy daughters are punishing me for leaving my mom lying like a piece of trash on the floor of her trailer. A fitting punishment if there ever was one.

By the time I make it to the Nasser University campus, I am already five minutes late and literally running across the quad. This sucks, not only because I am severely out of shape, but because my ridiculously large boobs are bouncing around like two basketballs on a trampoline. Hugging my chest while hauling a heavy backpack and a full venti mocha—don't judge me. It's been a rough morning—is no easy task. By the time I've stepped into the Liberal Arts building, I'm huffing like an eighty-year-old smoker and dripping sweat. I pity the poor person forced to sit next to me in class.

Thank God I know my way to the Psych 101 lecture hall from walking Charlie there last semester, or I might have lost my shit completely. Being late on the first day of class is akin to being late for the first day of work—everything you do from that moment on will be viewed through the lens of that one infraction. I shouldn't care what the stupid psychology professor thinks. I'm a theater major, for Christ's sake. Unfortunately, not caring really isn't in my vocabulary. Kat, on the other hand, makes not giving a shit into an art form—only one of the many things I envy about her.

Caught up in my internal monologue, I'm not paying attention when I round the corner and crash face-first into a blue backpack. My coffee goes flying, but not before the scalding hot liquid spills down the front of my used-to-be-white tee, leaving a murky brown stain and burning boobs in its wake. The offending cup hits the floor, further spewing my precious lifeblood all over my feet, the wall, the thickly muscled legs of the person standing in front of me—oh, damn. Dragging my attention from the catastrophe that is my morning cup-o-sunshine, I run my gaze up a man's lean body, broad shoulders, and almost too-full lips, coming to rest on the most beautiful eyes I've ever seen. They're gray. Not blue-gray or hazel-gray, but a pure, almost silver color that practically glows against his dark auburn hair and trimmed beard. That color must have some strange hypnotic properties because any prior knowledge of language and speech has been completely tossed out of my brain and is now swimming happily in my coffee puddle on the floor. I'm so struck by those crazy peepers, it takes me a while to notice that he's talking to me, even longer to comprehend the words. And with every second that passes, his expression becomes more and more panicked.

The poor guy's forehead is a scrunched-up mess, and his brows are drawn so close they've practically merged. He's hovering over me, arms outstretched, like he wants to touch me, but knows he shouldn't, and I've still only managed to catch the tail end of his question. "... burned you?"

My addled brain hasn't quite reset yet, so the only word I come up with is, "What?"

"The coffee," he says, hand hovering precariously close to my boob. "Are you okay? Did it burn you?"

Now, if you had asked me three seconds ago, I would have said that it burned the living crap out of me, but at the moment, I honestly don't feel a thing. "I... I think I'm alright," I squeak out, my voice sounding like a sloshed Minnie Mouse.

His shoulders visibly relax and a smile warms his expression.

"Everybody, get back," says an old man dressed in a navy custodian's uniform. He tosses a *wet floor* sign on the ground beside my feet and the gorgeous guy—whose name I still haven't gotten—curls a hand gently around my bicep and steers me out of the way.

The brush of his warm, slightly rough palm against my skin sends a bolt of electricity straight to my belly, and once again my brain has decided to go on hiatus. Ugh. Get it together, Emma. "Uh... I'm... class."

I'm class? What the fuck? Sentences, Emma, sentences. "Um… I mean, I… uh… have class." Oh, yeah. That's way better. He probably thinks I'm here for a follow-up on my lobotomy.

Whether he's noticed my idiotic behavior is hard to say. He does, however, seem to suddenly realize that he's still gripping my arm because he jerks his hand away, expression chagrined, like a kid caught stealing a candy bar. Stuffing the offending hand into the pocket of his basketball shorts, he says, "Me too. I'm super late, but it's my first time here, and I can't find the classroom." He swivels his head from side to side as if glancing around but doesn't seem to be actually looking at anything.

Hold up.

Brain on.

I can help with this.

"What's your class?" I ask, relieved to have constructed an actual coherent sentence.

"Psychology 101."

And jackpot.

My girly parts are totally throwing a party right now. Finally regaining some of my composure, I am ready to get my flirt on. "Me too." I flash my patented don't-you-wish-you-could-tap-this smile. "It's right there." I point at the lecture hall door. "Come on."

I grit my teeth as the doors screech open, then shut with an echoing thunk behind us. The entire room of two-hundred-plus people turns at once to glare at us. I immediately break out in a sweat and I'm sure by the warmth suffusing my skin that my face is bright red. Thank God this lecture hall has a set of doors in the back of the room, so we don't have to walk past the professor because I might have simply passed out.

The guy—I really need to learn his name already—presses a hand to the small of my back and leads me to a nearby set of seats. Once the attention has shifted back to the professor again, he reaches into his backpack and pulls out a white shirt, handing it to me. "Here. Dry yourself."

"I'm not going to ruin your shirt," I whisper, pressing it back into his hands.

He shrugs and scrubs the shirt up and down his coffee-splattered legs, then, smirking, holds it back out to me. "It's already ruined."

I'm sure my smile has graduated from don't-you-wish-you-could-tap-this to oh-my-god-you're-nuts-and-I-love-it. I take the proffered shirt and rub it along my neck and chest, fully aware of the way his eyes follow my every move. Next, I move on to my legs, and I have to admit, though I'm still sticky, it's so much better to be dry. I hand over the now-ruined shirt. "Thank you."

"Dante." He thrusts out a hand.

"Emma," I say, feeling a bit shy—which is seriously weird because I don't do shy—and take his hand. There's a gravity between us, a current that buzzes along our points of contact and sets my heart fluttering. I can tell by the way his breath hitches, he feels it too.

I quickly pull out my laptop and open up the syllabus which, thanks to my anal-retentive nature, I chose to download last night. The professor, whose name, according to the syllabus, is Dr. Gregory Mitchell, is a middle-aged man with a receding hairline and a beard bushy enough to house small animals. I'm so focused on the man sitting beside me, I've pretty much tuned Mitchell out as he drones on about class requirements, when Dante turns to me and asks, "You want to be partners?"

Partners? I give him a questioning look. *Maybe ask a girl for a date first—*

"For the projects," he says, index finger pointing to a section of the syllabus that reads, "Partner Projects."

"Oh... Uh, sure," I finally reply. Is it possible to spontaneously combust from embarrassment? Because my face is so red hot right now, it's verging on nuclear meltdown.

Never Backing Off, the second book in the Never U series, is available now on Amazon.com and Kindle Unlimited.

Keep reading for a sneak peek of of book 3: Never Letting Go.

Forty-Four
Sneak Peek of Never Letting Go
Sorry, Not Sorry

Kat

IT'S OFFICIAL. MY SISTER is a witch or an alien or the product of some top-secret program that teaches mind control. It's got to be one of those things, right? Because those are the only plausible explanations I can come up with for how my sister constantly gets me to do shit I don't want to do.

Case in point: my mom's sentencing. That's right, sentencing, not trial. There was no reason to have a trial because the woman was found to have a blood alcohol level almost three times the legal limit when she wrapped her car around a tree and ended up in the hospital. She's lucky she didn't kill anybody. And I'm supposed to stand here and plead with the judge to get her into a court-ordered rehab facility like she deserves another chance?

She's had eight years' worth of chances, and it's all amounted to exactly zero. But Emma, ever the optimist, can't stop herself from trying. I stopped trying a while ago.

Does that make me a crappy daughter?

Maybe.

Okay, probably.

But trust me when I say, that woman was a much crappier mom.

The courtroom looks straight out of Law & Order. We've got the judge in his poofy black robe sitting on his pulpit looking all... judgy, with the lawyers, wearing their tailored suits and regulation douchebag haircuts, situated across from him at their tables. The prosecutor's been standing for the past I-don't-know-how-long rambling to the judge about all my mom's priors. She's got quite the rap sheet. I'm almost impressed. The public defender constantly shifts around in his seat like a little kid who needs to pee. I wonder if that's because he knows this case is fucked or because he simply doesn't want to be here.

Finally, the prosecutor finishes his monologue and my mom's lawyer stands. "Mrs. Chase's daughters have prepared a statement, Your Honor."

"Proceed," says the old judge, and I have to stifle my giggle at his ridiculously pompous attitude.

Emma and I step up to the podium, but I don't speak. This is her show. I'm just eye candy.

Well, in truth, Emma's the eye candy. Even with her long blonde hair pulled into a tight bun and her silky green blouse buttoned so high it's probably cutting off the blood to her brain, there's no hiding it. How do you hide double Ds? I may be slightly envious of her perfect heart-shaped face and delicate features, but I am so glad I don't have her boobs. I like my C cups just fine, thank you very much. People say we look like twins but that's only because they're blinded by all the blonde hair, which is why I dyed mine pink. I'm also a good five inches shorter, my eyes are a much darker blue and my lips are so full you'd think I got collagen injections—I didn't.

"Your Honor," Emma begins. "My sister, Katherine, and I—"

Ugh. I hate it when she uses my whole name.

"We've come to you to ask for your help. When our father died of cancer eight years ago, it broke our mom, and she's never really recovered. We've tried to do our best to help her, but what she needs we can't provide. That's why we're asking you, for our sakes, to sentence our mother to a mandated rehab facility."

My mom shoots out of her chair. "What the fu—" The lawyer slams a hand over her mouth before she can finish that statement, but I'm pretty sure we all got the gist. The lawyer apologizes to the judge while our mom glares daggers at the two of us, her hands balled into fists at her side. Splotchy patches of red bloom across her cheeks.

It's possible Emma and I told her we were here to ask the judge for a lesser sentence. Oops. Guess that's what she gets for being a stubborn lush.

The judge slams his gavel on the wooden block. "Enough."

Damn. Now, I really feel like I'm on Law & Order.

"Mrs. Chase," the judge says, forcing our mom to pause her death glare to focus on him. "I'm going to give you two choices, and I suggest you make the smart one." The judge laces his fingers together and rests them on his desk. "You can go through a three-month detox in rehab or a three-month detox in prison. Which would you prefer?"

"Your Honor I—" Mom begins.

The judge raises a hand, stalling her argument. "I've heard enough. Let's be clear, Mrs. Chase. Given your priors for possession and prostitution, I was leaning toward a jail sentence. The only reason I am giving you this choice is because of your daughters. Now, I will ask you again, which do you choose?"

Mom's grinding her teeth so hard; she's probably tasting enamel right now. "Rehab, Your Honor," she says.

Good choice.

He gives a curt nod. "Belinda Chase, having pleaded guilty to driving while under the influence, I sentence you to three months mandatory rehabilitation in a state-approved facility with probation pending upon your completion of the program."

Holy shit. She did it. I glance at Emma, who's wearing a smile so big it's practically taken over her face. She grips my hand and squeezes, and my heart sinks at seeing her so happy because that only means the devastation will be that much worse when it all goes to hell.

You know those people who narrowly escape death and develop a new lease on life? Yeah. I'm not one of them. I mean, how am I supposed to feel? I'm just chilling in my living room on a rainy Saturday afternoon, shredding Black Sabbath's *War Pigs* on my guitar and trying to drown out the sound of my sister and her boyfriend going at it in the next room. Someone really needs to talk to that girl about volume control, or better yet, gag her. I'm supposed to be heading off for band rehearsal in a few minutes and am seriously considering calling it off because, the way the rain is coming down out there, my piece of crap car is likely to hydroplane off the edge of a cliff. I'm just hitting the first notes of the bridge when the earth rattles, and I hear what can only be described as a bomb going off in my bedroom.

Note the words: my bedroom.

Not the hallway or the kitchen or the parking lot, but my bedroom.

Startled, I drop my guitar, cringing at the dissonant echo of the body hitting the floor. "Fuck," I shout, but don't stop to pick it up. Instead, I'm hauling ass for my bedroom. That's right, like the heroine destined to get sliced and diced in every horror movie ever made, I, in my infinite wisdom, run toward the sound.

When I hit the open doorway, I stop cold.

There is a tree in my bedroom, and not simply in my bedroom but spearing a fucking hole dead center in the middle of my bed. If that isn't some kind of ominous warning, I don't know what is. Well, it's not an entire tree—thank the gods—but rather a giant limb that's broken through the ceiling, leaving a gaping hole where water now pours through like a waterfall. The rest of the tree must be resting on the roof because the entire back half of my room, from the ceiling fan, now hanging by its electrical cords to the busted windowpane, bows under its weight. Shards of glass litter the floor, bed, and furniture blanketing the room in a blue-gray shimmer.

"Holy shit."

I jump at the sound of Emma's voice and spin around to find my sister and her boyfriend, Dante, standing behind me. They managed to get their private bits mostly covered—thank the gods—and are both gaping at the hole that used to be my room with their hands thrown over their mouths and wearing matching expressions of shock and disbelief. I might have laughed if it wasn't the destruction of everything I owned they were staring at.

It's Dante who regains his senses first. "We need to get out of here. Now." He shoots back into their room and quickly returns with a pair of jean shorts which he tosses at my sister and a shirt for himself. Then he's rushing us down the hallway and into the living room. Shorts only partially zipped, Emma throws open the front door and the two of them haul ass outside. They stomp down the stairs like two rabid elephants, but I pause to snatch up my guitar before racing down the stairs, and into the rain, after them.

By the time I reach Dante's car, I'm half soaked and shivering. I'm vaguely aware of Emma talking to our apartment manager on the phone as I sit in the back seat and hug my guitar to my chest. What am I going to do now?

Three hours, two firetrucks and one police car later, Emma, Dante and I enter the shitty motel room looking like something out of a zombie movie. I don't even care about the dirty walls, kelly green carpet or the canvas-like comforters covered in a fat tropical leaf design. I'm so exhausted; I just want to lay my head down and sleep. Adrenaline crash is no joke.

"Ah, vacationing at its finest," I say, dripping sarcasm. I flop down onto the nearest bed and cringe when it screeches like a pissed-off donkey. "You'd think the complex could have sprung for something even moderately less shitty," I say, wrinkling my nose at the reek of mildew wafting off the sheets.

"I think we're lucky they sprang for this," Dante says. "I'm not sure of the legalities of it all, but I don't think they're required to pay for it."

"Well, that's bullshit," I say.

"Indeed," Dante replies absently, his gray eyes trained on what I'm assuming is the bathroom door on the other end of the room. I have to smile. The man is a world-class geek, and I say that with all the love in my heart. What other twenty-year-old uses the word, "indeed?" He treats my sister like a queen though, so I'm not complaining. Usually, I'd say I'm not into redheads—Dante's hair's more of a dark auburn to be exact—but I have to admit, the man is hot. He's tall and broad shouldered, muscular but lean, and he has the perfectly proportioned features of a Greek god, just like his stupid—gorgeous—stupid brother, Malcolm.

Crossing the room, Dante stops in front of the bathroom door and nudges it open. Then, feet still planted in the shag rug, he reaches an arm across the threshold, flips the light switch and leaps back as though expecting a hoard of roaches to attack him the moment the light comes on.

And this one is meant to be our protector.

We're doomed.

Emma sits on the bed facing me, elbows propped on her knees. "The manager seemed to think he could have someone out tomorrow to remove the tree and patch things up."

I roll my eyes. There is nothing worse in my book than optimism. Seriously, sometimes I want to tell people to take their sunshine and rainbow bullshit and shove it up their asses. "Yeah. Sure. Or maybe I'll go climb a tree and wait to get struck by lightning. I think my chances might be better."

"Hey, don't get pissy with me. Okay? I'm just trying to help."

"Says the person who has someplace to go and is actually choosing to stay in this dump for the night."

"We're not staying at Malcolm's," Dante says, sitting beside my sister.

"Uh, technically, it's your apartment too, and you said he was over his crush on Emma, so what's the problem?" I reply.

"*He* said he was over it." Dante pulls Emma up onto his lap and wraps his arms around her. "And whether or not he's over her is irrelevant. It would be too uncomfortable."

Emma leans against him all sweetly. God, they make me want to barf. "Every time we hug or kiss, it would be like we were rubbing our relationship in his face," she says.

They certainly don't tone it down for my benefit. "I don't think you give the guy enough credit, but whatever. I'm not going to say I don't appreciate the company." I close my eyes and try to relax. I'm exhausted but strangely wound up at the same time. Too bad my nightstand, where I had my stash, is buried under a big ass tree right now. I could really use the help relaxing. Speaking of relaxing, I wonder if my vibrator survived.

"*You* could stay with Malcolm," Dante says, breaking me from my thoughts.

I laugh because, surely, he jests.

Dante doesn't seem to get the joke because he continues, "Look, even if the manager gets things patched up tomorrow, it'll be a while before your room is habitable again and your bed is most likely ruined."

I scoff. "Still an upgrade from this piece of shit."

A silhouette with cascading blonde hair blocks the overhead light. "Come on, Kat. Be serious," Emma says.

I drag myself up to sit and eye my sister and her adorable ginger-haired boyfriend. "I'm sorry. I must have heard you incorrectly. You want me to go beg your brother, who despises me with every fiber of his being—"

"You've got to admit, his reasons are pretty valid," Dante unhelpfully supplies.

Emma nods in agreement.

I blow out a breath. So, I called him a stalker and told a couple jersey chasers he had herpes. And okay, maybe the rumor about him having herpes went a teeny-tiny bit viral online. How was I to know Mr. I'm-so-sexy quarterback would be so sensitive? Dude needs to learn how to take a joke. "Yeah. Well, the sentiment goes both ways there, bucko."

Dante rolls his eyes. "Whatever. Look, Mal's a good guy. You tell him you need a place to stay for a few days, and I'm sure he'll be happy to help."

***Never Letting Go,* the third book in the *Never U* series, is available now on Amazon.com and Kindle Unlimited.**

Also By C. R. Lee

<u>Never U Series</u>
Love is a Scary S.O.B. (prequel)
Never Moving On
Never Backing Off
Never Letting Go

Wanna Hang?

Scan the QR code below to visit my website, where you can learn about my new releases, connect with me on social media and sign up for my newsletter.

Acknowledgments

I would like to take a moment to thank my marvelous beta readers: Sherry Fowler-Schafer, Chrissy Farmer, Emilee Ann Lamica, Kat Vander, Kelly Vazquez and Morgane Gey. You are all rock stars! This book would probably be a hot piece of trash without you.

Another great big thanks to my amazing proofreader Charity Chimni, without whom this entire book would be riddled with typos and a messed up timeline.

And thank you to my ARC Team superstars and especially my ARC/Street Team Leader, Jenny Steve-James, for all your support and hard work in getting the word out about this book!

Last but not least, a special thanks to my husband and amazing cover artist. I would never have had the courage to do this without his support and encouragement. You're a badass, baby! I love you!

About Author

C. R. Lee is a writer of romance filled with angst, humor and a whole lot of steam. She prides herself on creating troubled, yet compelling characters, then putting them through hell for your entertainment.

You're welcome.

But no matter how cruel she may be, rest assured, all of her books are guaranteed to have a HEA.

C. R. Lee currently lives in North Carolina with her husband, two children, two dogs, a cat, and a leopard gecko. When she's not writing, she enjoys reading and drinking copious amounts of coffee—preferably at the same time.

Never Moving On is her first published novel.

Printed in Great Britain
by Amazon